Son of an Earl

by

Bronwen Chisholm

and

Λ Lady

Cover art by Sieck Photography.

Editorial assistance provided by Jessica Cale at Historical Editorials.

SON OF AN EARL

ISBN: 9798778638211

DEDICATION

This has to be for my husband. For years, I have said I could not or would not write a series and he would respond with "you could and you should." As usual, it took me longer than it probably should have, but here it is. Love you!

.

CONTENTS

ACKNOWLEDGMENTS

I cannot begin without acknowledging Jane Austen and the amazing characters she created. As I have said in the past, her works have touched and inspired so many over the years and I humbly offer my attempts in the hopes they bring some joy.

Thank you to my beta readers, MK Baxley and Connie Hays. This story would be lacking in many ways without the unique insights each of you have brought to it. And to my editor, Jessica Cale. Without you, there would be so many anachronisms and Americanisms.

Thank you again to Heather Sieck of Sieck Photography. Somehow, you find the picture behind my ramblings and then make it better.

To my readers around the world, I thank you again for your patience with me this past year as my family went through the transition of getting my youngest out of high school and into university. I should be more consistent in my writing, posting, and responses to emails (until the next upheaval).

And finally, to my family. Though my kids are spread about now, they still have to listen to my Regency ramblings, and I am certain they feel sorry for their father who still has to live with me. Thank you for your support and patience. Love you.

PROLOGUE
LONDON
2 DECEMBER 1811

"Aunt Esther, I want to visit my cousins!"

Elizabeth Darcy saw her husband grimace when the screech assaulted their ears as they entered the Matlock townhouse. She looked to him with her brow raised, but he only shrugged.

"They are *not* your cousins, Anne." From her tone, the patience Lady Matlock was known for had finally reached its end.

"Papa said that is what I should call them. I want to see Sam and Tabby."

Elizabeth's eyes grew wide, and she stood perfectly still. Fitzwilliam reached out to her, but she shook her head before ignoring propriety and listening to the ladies' conversation.

"I have *no* idea where those girls are." There was a brief pause. When Lady Matlock finally spoke again, her voice was lower and calmer. "Your mother kept you from society far too long, pinning her expectations on Darcy when no one believed he would offer for you. Anne, you must establish proper connections in order to find a suitable husband and take your place as Mistress of Rosings."

Seeing the footman waiting for them, Elizabeth stepped forwards and nodded for him to announce them. Her husband tugged at his cuffs and straightened his waistcoat as he did when he was about to face something unpleasant, but he smiled before escorting Elizabeth into the drawing room. It was not surprising to find the ladies alone.

"Ah, Darcy and Elizabeth." Aunt Esther rose and embraced them both. "Your uncle and cousins await you in the study, Darcy."

The look of relief which flooded Fitzwilliam's countenance brightened Elizabeth's smile. When he met her gaze with a guilty expression, she offered her cheek for a kiss and sent him on his way while she took a seat between the ladies and accepted a cup of tea from their aunt.

"I understand what is expected of me," Anne de Bourgh said in a haughty tone reminiscent of her mother's, "and I have every intention of doing as you ask. I only request that I be able to see my cousins. We were young girls when last Papa and I visited them. After he passed, Mamma would not allow me to speak or even write to them."

"I am surprised she allowed you to meet them at all," Lady Matlock muttered before biting into a tart.

"Do you speak of Samantha and Tabitha Evans?" Elizabeth asked, causing her ladyship to choke on the pastry.

"Yes! You know them?" Miss de Bourgh grasped Elizabeth's hand.

"I attended school with them for a brief time."

"You were at Reading Abbey?" The young lady appeared surprised. "Mamma said you were uneducated and—"

Lady Matlock interrupted, "We do not need to hear more of what Lady Catherine had to say about Elizabeth."

"I visited the abbey once," Miss de Bourgh said without acknowledging her aunt.

Elizabeth nodded. "I remember."

"You were there then?"

"My eldest sister, Jane, and I were there the autumn of 1798. The Evans sisters still correspond with Jane once or twice a year."

"Then you know their directions!" Miss de Bourgh fairly bounced in her seat.

"I do not, but my sister will be arriving tomorrow with her fiancé and his sister, who also attended Reading Abbey. I am certain Jane will know them."

Lady Matlock frowned. "It would be inappropriate for you to meet with them."

Miss de Bourgh sat taller and took a deep breath, but her ladyship continued before she could be interrupted.

"However, I believe a correspondence would not draw attention."

"They are not in London, if I remember correctly," Elizabeth offered to calm the younger of the ladies and reassure the older.

"Very well," Miss de Bourgh replied. "You will bring your sister to tea tomorrow."

"She will have just arrived," Elizabeth reminded her. "I am certain you will meet Wednesday evening as we are all to attend the theatre."

"Have Miss Bennet write the directions out. I will not have you speaking of the Evans sisters while we are in public." Lady Matlock set her cup aside. "Anne, you appear a little peaked. Perhaps you should lie down until dinner."

Miss de Bourgh arose directly and turned for the door until Lady Matlock cleared her throat. The lady stopped and curtseyed. "It was nice to see you today, Mrs. Darcy. I look forward to meeting your sister."

"It was nice to see you as well, Miss de Bourgh," Elizabeth replied.

The lady looked to her aunt, who nodded, before turning and leaving the room. The moment the door closed, Lady Matlock fell against the back of her seat.

"That girl will be the death of me."

Elizabeth struggled to suppress her laughter. "I am certain it is strange and new to her. Though she has improved."

Her ladyship looked at her with her brow raised expectantly.

"She spoke to me and called me Mrs. Darcy." Upon first meeting Anne de Bourgh, Elizabeth had been ignored until Fitzwilliam made it clear he would not tolerate disrespect to his wife. After which, his cousin spoke to Elizabeth only when necessary and *sometimes* refrained from repeating her mother's opinions of their marriage.

"Because you have information she desires." Lady Matlock sat forwards. "You *do* know the relationship between Anne and the Evans sisters, do you not?"

"I was seven when I attended the Abbey, but I remember some of the comments made about them. It is a shame such lovely young ladies must suffer for the sins of their father. They were quite fond of Sir Lewis de Bourgh, whom they called Uncle Lewis. He appeared to dote upon them when he visited."

"Sir Lewis was a gentle man. I imagine Anne would have been quite different had he lived longer." Lady Matlock sighed then gave herself a little shake. "Shall we notify the gentlemen they are able to leave the study?"

"They are afraid of Miss de Bourgh?" Elizabeth asked, incredulous that a spoiled girl could send them into hiding.

"They dislike the uproar. My Demi could send them running when she was in a bad humour." She patted Elizabeth's hand. "Wait until you have a daughter. Darcy will adore her, but the moment she becomes discontented or demanding, he will disappear from sight."

Elizabeth's cheeks warmed. It was not the first time Lady Matlock had mentioned children, and she found herself thinking of motherhood frequently. She wondered if she would more resemble Mrs. Bennet or Aunt Gardiner and hoped it was the latter. Unconsciously laying a hand upon her stomach, she followed her hostess from the room.

The ladies made their way to Lord Matlock's study and, after a quick knock, her ladyship entered with Elizabeth close behind.

"We have come to announce you may leave this room. Anne is resting until dinner."

"Has she seen reason?" Lord Matlock asked as the gentlemen rose and approached the ladies.

Lady Matlock glanced at Elizabeth. "We have come to a compromise."

Her husband stopped, obviously waiting for more information.

"I am familiar with Miss de Bourgh's cousins, sir," Elizabeth offered. "My sister corresponds with the Evans sisters."

"Miss Bennet will provide their directions to Anne, and I have agreed that they may correspond." Lady Matlock took her husband's arm and led the group back to the drawing room, requesting the footman stationed there send for fresh tea when they entered.

"Do you believe this wise, Mother?" Ashton asked as they took their seats.

"Personal correspondence is not widely known to others." Lady Matlock straightened the lace on her sleeve. "The Evans sisters have not been spoken of for some time."

"But with Anne's return, will not the rumours be revisited?" her eldest son pressed.

"There will always be rumours, Ashton." Lord Matlock sighed. "I am certain someone will create a more interesting and newer scandal once the *ton* returns in full."

"May it not be Anne," Ashton muttered.

"Which is why we must press for an engagement as quickly as feasible." His father stared at him.

"I will *not* marry Anne!" The viscount stood and paced the room.

"Have you another young lady whom you will be courting this season?" The earl sat forwards, his hands upon his knees.

"No, sir, but that does not preclude the possibility I will meet a young lady better suited to me."

"Very well." Lord Matlock sat back in his seat once more. "By Easter you will have had sufficient time to survey the available ladies and determine if there are any who 'suit' you, as you say. If no such lady has been found, you will propose to your cousin."

Elizabeth had never seen Ashton in such a state. His jaw hung agape, his eyes raced about the room, and she was uncertain if he still drew breath. Finally, his gaze fell upon his brother and he found his voice.

"What of Philip? He is in need of a fortune to marry. Surely he is the better candidate to wed Anne. I have no need of another estate."

"I have spoken to your brother and agreed not to press him at this time."

"Why?" Ashton demanded.

Philip cleared his throat. "I have been given time to explore a possible match."

"Who?" His brother appeared wounded that he had not been consulted on the matter.

"Have you been blind?" Lady Matlock spoke up. "Your brother and Miss Bingley danced twice at the Netherfield ball and were often in conversation."

"We were all frequently in conversation; we were there for days." Ashton folded his arms. "You would approve of such a courtship?" he asked his father.

"Your brother is the younger son."

"And if I do not have a son, he would be next in line

for the earldom.”

“Then I suggest you marry and have one.”

Ashton stormed from the room without a backward glance.

“Henry,” Lady Matlock softly scolded.

Her husband reached out to her and squeezed her hand. “This is nothing which has not been said before.”

“But much has changed recently.” Her gaze fell upon Elizabeth sitting beside Fitzwilliam.

“I fail to see how my marriage affects my cousin.” Fitzwilliam slipped Elizabeth’s hand about his arm.

“He has been witness to your happiness, Darcy. Forgive me, Elizabeth, but you are not the wife we anticipated for our nephew.” Her ladyship had the decency to blush. “In our circle, there are expectations.”

“Expectations be damned,” Fitzwilliam muttered. “Has Ashton met a lady in the past who did not meet the *ton’s* ridiculous expectations?” he asked, looking at his cousin.

Philip’s gaze fell upon his father, but he did not speak.

“Years ago. The lady has since married elsewhere.” Lord Matlock pinched the bridge of his nose. “He was not ready to marry, and I do not believe he pines for her.”

Philip rolled his eyes. “Ashton has always hidden his emotions behind humour, Father. If he were pining, you would not discover it easily.”

“Then he does think of her?” Lady Matlock leant towards her younger son.

“I do not know,” Philip replied with a slight shrug. “As I said, he conceals his feelings, even from me. In some ways, he is better at it than Darcy.”

“I beg your pardon,” Darcy huffed.

“Your emotions are written in your eyes, dear, if anyone took the time to look.” Elizabeth patted her husband’s hand. “Ashton is capable of acting a role, something which you detest.”

“A trait I taught him,” the earl said with a sigh. “It is necessary in politics. Much like cards, you do not want your opponent to know what you hold in your hand."

"You taught him too well, Henry," his wife gently admonished. "He has perfected it to the point where he is able to hide from us as well."

The earl rose and looked to his younger son. "Where will he be?"

Philip gave it a moment's thought before glancing out the window. "Perhaps the billiard room since it has begun to rain."

****

Ashton struck the cue ball with more force than aim, sending it careening down the table before bouncing off the distant side and somehow striking nothing. He cursed and rounded the table to do it again.

"If you are going to break the cue in a fit of pique as you did when you were first learning, I would prefer you use an older one."

Setting the stick aside, Ashton turned towards the door and met his father's gaze with a calm expression. "Have you another demand to place upon me?" he asked in a bored tone.

The earl closed the door and took a seat. "Ashton, I pray you would forgive my bluntness earlier. As your father, I want only to see you settled and happy."

The viscount raised a brow. "This is a change, Father. To what do I owe this newfound interest in my happiness?"

"I have always wished for my children to be happy. Philip and Demi tell me what they desire, but you remain silent."

"As the eldest son, I was raised on what is expected of me. I was not aware my desires had a place in it." Taking up the cue once more, he chalked it and lined up his next shot.

"That is unfair." The earl sat straighter in his seat and

uncrossed his legs. "There are expectations upon you as my heir, but they do not exclude enjoyment and, yes, happiness. Your mother and I—"

"Spare me the tale of how you and Mother love one another. I see your affection now, but I also know it was not always so. Do not forget, I am your *eldest* child." He struck the ball, sending it ricocheting about the table. "I remember Mother weeping when you would return to London without her. I heard the rumours of your liaisons. It is not a life I wish to force upon another."

His father's countenance reddened. "That was *many* years ago. I was young and full of myself, and, I might add, following my father's directions." He rose and pulled the cue from his son's hands. "*My* father told me to marry, and I married. *He* would not take your desires into consideration."

"Then I am certain you have made him proud."

Ashton turned on his heel and left the room but paused a few steps into the hallway. He considered returning and speaking openly to his father and was about to do so, when he heard the earl curse and the crack as the cue splintered. Realizing he was unprepared for another confrontation, he retreated to his rooms to determine his response and think on what might have been.

PART ONE
1806

CHAPTER ONE
LONDON
8 APRIL

Despite the fact that Ashton Fitzwilliam, Viscount Grayson, was rapidly approaching his twenty-fifth birthday, his father, the Earl of Matlock, seemed to believe the man was still in leading strings. He had yet to attend a society event without his esteemed father at his side. For the life of him, Ashton could not determine what had the man so fearful that his heir could flounder in such a manner as to cause the complete destruction of the political power the Matlock earls had accrued in the past hundred years. Even now, at opposite ends of a ballroom, he could feel the man's gaze upon him, but he refused to acknowledge it.

Sipping the punch, weak in flavour and potency, he surveyed the gathering and determined it well matched. An impoverished knight attempting to foist his daughter on a wealthy gentleman here, a desperate lady preening like a peacock in an attempt to hide the fact she was quickly approaching spinsterhood there. The faces changed but the stories remained the same. He finished the vile drink and handed the glass to a passing footman.

Perhaps his cousin, Fitzwilliam Darcy, had the right of it. Darcy despised society and its expectations. He avoided events such as this like the plague. Of course, the man had also lost his father during the winter, which Ashton did not envy. Reluctantly, he turned towards his own sire and nodded when the man tipped his head in the direction of a gaggle of ladies.

A tremour ran through the group as he approached; postures were adjusted and simpering smiles affixed. Checking off those ladies he was decidedly against encouraging, he bowed and asked Lady Gertrude, daughter of his father's closest friend and recently engaged, for her next dance.

"I fear my dance card is full, Lord Grayson," she replied with a smirk. "May I introduce Miss Carrington? She has recently arrived in London from Virginia. Our mothers were presented the same season."

The lady curtseyed but kept her eyes lowered. Her complexion held a healthy glow missing from the near sickly paleness of the *ton,* and her black hair shone in the candlelight. The lavender silk gown draping her frame hinted at a pleasing figure but revealed no more than absolutely necessary.

"Miss Carrington," Ashton said with a bow. "May I have the pleasure of your company for the next two dances?"

"You may," she replied, her voice so soft he nearly missed it.

Her eyes remained glued to the floor, and the current dance was not yet ended. Several of the ladies looked to Ashton expectantly, but he had dismissed the prospect of dancing with them earlier. He could wander away, but there was truly no one present with whom he wished to speak.

"How fares your mother, Lady Gertrude?" he asked, hoping she would fill the time with meaningless small talk.

"She is well, but I thought I had seen you greet her earlier." The lady's eyes shone with mirth.

"Oh yes, you are correct." Ashton frowned at the woman who had been his sister's playmate and always found a way to annoy him. She could clearly see through him and was determined not to come to his aid, so he turned to her friend. "You are from Virginia, Miss Carrington?"

"Yes, sir," she responded in that damnable quiet voice.

Ashton fought the urge to lean forwards to hear her better for fear she think it an attempt to look down her décolletage. "And how do you find London?"

"Crowded."

Her simple answers suddenly amused him, and he chuckled. "Yes, I suppose it is. I understand Virginia is quite rural."

The lady nodded.

Ashton narrowed his gaze as he noted Lady Gertrude's amusement. This Miss Carrington appeared determined not to speak. She was a worse conversationalist than Darcy before the years of instruction his cousins had provided. The viscount was about to admit defeat and seek another distraction, when the lady lifted her head and met his gaze. Grey eyes, the colour of a winter sky before it snows, stared at him from behind a thick fan of ebony eyelashes. Ashton felt as though he were drowning but without any desire to struggle.

"Miss Carrington," Lady Gertrude said with a laugh, "I believe you have affected a small miracle. No one has ever silenced Lord Grayson before."

A becoming blush crossed the lady's countenance, and her gaze fell to the floor once more effectively breaking her spell.

"Forgive me," Ashton managed to say before bowing to the ladies and walking away as casually as he could muster. The moment he was out of sight of the group, he ducked into an alcove and took a deep breath. Never had he been affected in such a manner.

"Ashton?" his father said from the edge of his sanctuary. "Are you well, son?"

"Yes." The viscount straightened his waistcoat and stepped out to stand beside the earl. "I needed a moment to catch my breath."

His father studied him suspiciously. "You sound like Darcy. I noted you appeared pale when you left the ladies." He chuckled. "Did they refuse your request to dance?"

"Lady Gertrude's card is full, but I secured her friend's hand for the next two dances."

"Her friend?"

"Yes, a Miss Carrington from Virginia."

The earl's smile slipped into a frown. "American." He sniffed. "Freddy mentioned something of the sort. Daughter of his wife's friend." He sniffed again. "I suppose one set will not be an issue." His eyes wandered over the room. "You have not danced with Sir Patrick's daughter this evening."

"Nor will I." Ashton followed his father's gaze to where the insipid lady stood with her parents. "I nearly fell asleep during our dance at Almack's. You would not want me to embarrass you."

His father's frown deepened. "What of Miss Haverton? You have danced with her more than once before."

"I have secured a dance with her later." He turned to face his father fully. "Is there a reason you wish me to dance this evening?"

"I do not wish to see you standing about like your cousin. Since Philip left for the continent, you have not been as gregarious."

"I thought I was becoming a sheep's head, sir. At Demi's engagement ball, just two months past, you accused me of being overtalkative."

"So, it is to be extremes with you? There is no middle ground?"

Ashton noted the earl's colour had risen and saw his mother quickly approaching. "If you will excuse me, sir, I believe the next set is forming." He dipped his head as Lady Matlock arrived and turned abruptly back the way he had previously traversed.

By the time he reached the place he had left the ladies, only those he had dismissed remained. The previous dance had ended, increasing the numbers surrounding him. His indignation grew as he surveyed the crowd for the lady who was to be awaiting his return. Finally, he found her on the distant side of the ballroom, standing with Lady Gertrude's parents. Taking the quickest route available to him, Ashton stopped before the small group just as the first notes of the dance were played.

"I believe this is our dance, Miss Carrington." He bowed to her companions, hoping they had not recognized the pique in his voice. Their smiles, perhaps a bit strained, did not show him any ill will.

The lady placed her hand upon his arm, barely touching him so that he might have thought her a spirit and not flesh and blood. Indeed, those haunting eyes felt unworldly when they briefly searched his features before returning to the floor as before. Since the dance had begun, they joined at the bottom of the set, a place Ashton rarely held, and awaited their turn.

"Are you enjoying the ball?" he asked with a bit of a challenge in his tone.

"Yes."

Silently cursing himself, Ashton searched for a question which would demand more than a single word answer. "When did you arrive in England, Miss Carrington?"

"Last autumn."

"Did your family accompany you?"

"My father."

"Has he enjoyed his time here?"

The movement had finally reached them, and they stepped together as she replied, "He was called back to Virginia."

Ashton frowned. "You are to remain in England, then?" he asked when they next approached each other.

The lady simply nodded as the steps of the dance drew her attention.

Though he made a few more attempts, Ashton failed to procure any lengthier response.

The dance ended, and he escorted the frustrating woman back to her companions. His hopes of a quick retreat were dashed when Frederick Howard, Earl of Carlisle, asked after his sister. Certain his parents had already provided the information, Ashton responded following Miss Carrington's example, with simple, short answers.

"Gertie and Demi nearly ended their friendship over who would marry first," Lady Carlisle said with an amused wink at Miss Carrington. "They have been friends since childhood, much like me and your mother, Adsila."

Ashton stared at the young woman as a pleasant blush covered her countenance yet again. The name was foreign and beautiful, much like the lady herself.

"They came to an agreement?" Miss Carrington asked, her voice just loud enough to be heard over the music and a fraction stronger than Ashton had yet heard from the lady.

Her ladyship nodded. "Demi will marry here in London and will arrive in Cumbria following her wedding trip to attend Gertie's wedding. It was the most convenient option for all."

"Will you attend the weddings?" Ashton asked.

"Of course she will," Lord Carlisle said with a laugh and a wink at the lady. "Miss Carrington is to make her home in England now. We hope to see her following Gertie and Lady Demetria to the altar ere long."

Ashton noted the blush which travelled down her neck

and warmed her chest. "Virginia has lost its charm?" he asked, hoping to distract her.

"Never!" she replied as her head lifted and she stared at him directly. For a brief moment, lightning flashed in her stormy eyes. All too soon, she looked away and was once more the meek ghost. "It is my father's wish," she whispered.

Taken aback, Ashton was unable to reply before Miss Carrington's next partner claimed her hand. He was watching them walk away when his father's friend laid a hand upon his shoulder.

"Mr. Croome will be a good match, I believe. His family could use her dowry, and his position will not be injured by marrying an American." Before Ashton could respond, the earl continued. "Have you danced with Lady Gwendolyn? I am certain it would please your father."

Ashton thanked His Lordship for his advice and claimed the wallflower's hand for the next dance. Only required to answer with brief affirmations to the lady's mindless rambles, he was able to watch the newcomer as she danced with her current partner. By the final note, he was fairly certain there was a great deal to Miss Carrington that she and her chaperons were concealing, and by the time he entered his father's coach for the short ride home, he was determined to uncover every detail.

CHAPTER TWO
LONDON
9 APRIL

Ashton returned to the breakfast room about the time he suspected his sister would be rising but found the meal had been cleared. Stepping into the hall, he beckoned to a footman.

"Has my sister already eaten?"

The man peered at him quizzically. "Begging your pardon, sir, but Lady Demetria always takes her breakfast in her chambers."

"Of course," he said while internally scolding himself. His sister did as their mother, yielding the breakfast table to their father, who had a fondness for reviewing his plans for the day, including a detailed, if one-sided, discussion of any bills coming before the House of Lords.

He wandered the halls, uncertain of his sister's daily schedule or plans, until he heard her running scales on the pianoforte. Her eyes widened as he entered the music room, and she stopped playing when he took a seat.

"Have you a message for me?" Demi asked.

"No." Ashton shook his head. "I did not see you last

evening and wondered if you and Bedlington enjoyed the theatrical performance."

Her eyes narrowed and she tipped her head. "You wished to ask me if I enjoyed my evening?"

"Yes," he said with a laugh. "Can a brother not speak to his sister about her activities?"

"Certainly, he can." She rose from the bench and joined him on the settee. "However, *you* rarely do so, and then only when there is something specific you wish to know."

"Demi, you are far too suspicious." He picked a bit of lint from his sleeve. "What was it you went to see?"

"Lord, I don't know," she said with a flutter of her hand. "Some comedy or such. It did not hold my attention, and I doubt it will play long."

Demi's sudden smile made Ashton's skin crawl, making him think of her pet cat just before she toyed with a mouse.

"And you, brother? Did you enjoy the ball last evening?"

He frowned. "It was much the same as any other ball— a bit more insipid than some, but just as boring overall."

"You met no one new?" she asked in an offhanded manner which felt quite calculated.

"I saw Lady Gertrude. Her betrothed was not there, but she had a friend with her, a young lady from Virginia."

"You met Miss Carrington?" Her expression was suddenly unreadable.

"I danced with her as your friend was unavailable."

"How did you find her?"

Ashton shrugged. "Her features are striking, but she rarely spoke, and then when she did, it was in a near whisper. I believe Lord Carlisle was pushing her towards Mr. Croome. It may be suitable as I am certain he would speak enough for both of them."

Demi shivered. "That man is exceedingly dull, yet he believes himself an expert on nearly any subject. Only a deaf mute would suit him."

Ashton chuckled. "I must agree with you. In fact, I nearly pitied Miss Carrington when he led her to the floor."

"I am certain she will find a way to dissuade Lord Carlisle from the match. Gertie will help her if necessary."

"And what are your thoughts on the young lady?" Ashton asked casually.

His sister studied him once more before speaking. "It appears she might be quite different among women, or perhaps in a smaller, more familial group. She stated her opinions most decidedly when we had tea last week."

"I was surprised her father accompanied her to England but returned rather quickly. It appears she is to make her home here, though she prefers her native land."

Demi crossed her arms and squinted at him. "Are you searching for gossip?"

"No!" Ashton huffed. "It was simply odd to me." He rose from his seat. "I will leave you to your practicing."

He was about to open the door, when his sister said, "From what Gertie says, there were limited marriage prospects for her at home, so her mother asked Lady Carlisle to sponsor her."

Ashton turned about and bowed to his sister. "Have you plans for this afternoon? I thought, should you require an escort, I might attend you. It has been ages since we spent a day together."

"We have never spent a day together unless Mamma insisted upon it." Her lips pursed as she studied him. "Very well, I must visit a few shops and would appreciate an extra pair of hands to carry my purchases."

"You were not going to have a footman attend you?" Ashton said with a smirk. "Very well. What else? Shall we take tea at Gunter's?"

His sister had made her way back to the instrument. "Perhaps," she said as she regained her seat. "Or, if you do not overly annoy me, we might visit Gertie and her new friend."

"As you wish," Ashton said with a slight tip of his head. Once in the hall, he allowed a smile to spread across his lips.

****

"Demi!" Lady Gertrude cried as she embraced her friend. "I am so pleased you were able to join us. I wish we had been able to accompany you to the theatre last evening; I am certain it held ever so much more entertainment than the ball."

"Oh, I suppose, but I found it a bit tripe."

"Tripe? Shakespeare?" Lady Gertrude affected a laugh. "Demi, you are so droll."

"Well, I have never had a head for such things. Herbert loves the theatre and so, to the theatre we shall go." She turned her attention to the others. "Did you enjoy the ball, Miss Carrington? My brother tells me you danced with Mr. Croome."

"And with Lord Grayson," Lady Gertrude added.

Demi tipped her head to the side as she studied her brother. "Yes, he mentioned it."

"Miss Carrington took pity upon me when Lady Gertrude refused me."

"My card was full, Lord Grayson, as you waited too long to request a set."

"I shall remember to approach you earlier in the future." Ashton dipped his head in her direction. "Did you enjoy the ball, Miss Carrington?" he repeated his sister's question.

"It was everything I expected from a London ball," she replied.

Ashton was pleased she spoke in a louder, though still soft, voice. "I am uncertain if that is a compliment or critique." Before she could respond, he asked, "How did it compare to such events in Virginia?"

He was pleased to see a hint of the lightning he had spotted in her eyes the night before as she responded.

"I am certain balls vary only slightly from one location to another. It is the company which sets them apart."

"And you would prefer Virginia?" he pressed.

"You put words in my mouth, *my lord.*"

Ashton had never heard his honorific hold such umbrage. "I dare not," he replied.

"I am certain Miss Carrington prefers Virginia, but she is content to make due with us, given the circumstances." Lady Gertrude smiled at her friend, though Ashton noted her eyes widened a bit after a moment.

Miss Carrington took a deep breath before painting a similar smile upon her lips. "Of course, do all of us not prefer that to which we were born?" she asked in that frustrating whispery voice.

"Have you been north?" Ashton asked in an attempt to further the conversation.

"My father dislikes winter in Cumbria, of which you are aware, Lord Grayson." His hostess eyed him suspiciously.

"Forgive me, I had forgotten." He settled back with his cup of tea and allowed the ladies to carry the conversation for a time, hoping he had not raised any suspicions in Lady Gertrude.

Miss Carrington followed his example, and the two friends turned to their favourite topic of late: their weddings. The hands on the mantle clock appeared to slow nearly to a halt as Ashton remembered why he rarely spent time with his sister.

"Oh, dear," Demi cried, startling him from his stupor. "Mamma is expecting us. Forgive me, Gertie, but we must go. I lost all track of time." She turned on her brother. "Ashton, you should have told me we were going to be late."

"I was so enjoying the company, I too forgot." He smiled at their hostess. "Lady Gertrude, it has been a pleasure as always." He bowed to her before turning his attention to her friend. "Miss Carrington, I look forward to seeing you again." He repeated the gesture before offering his arm to his sister and escorting her to their carriage.

Once they were settled in the squabs and Demi had finished waving to her friend, he asked, "Mother is expecting us?"

"No, but I feared either you or Miss Carrington would drop your cups or snore, so I thought it best we leave."

A laugh burst from his lips before he could suppress it. "I thank you for saving us from any embarrassment."

"Did you find what you were seeking?" Demi asked, one brow arched in challenge.

"What I sought?" He looked out the window. "I have no idea to what you refer."

"Miss Carrington is a bit of an odd duck. She is lovely, certainly, and I thought for a moment we might have a rousing discussion, but then she simply stopped."

"After her friend gave her a quelling glance," Ashton muttered.

"Did she?" Demi tapped a finger against her cheek. "I wonder what Gertie is trying to conceal."

"She is your friend; does she not tell you all her secrets?"

Demi laughed freely. "Ashton, do you truly believe that ladies share everything with their friends?" Her eyes widened as he frowned. "You do! Well, I suppose sisters might, but friends can easily become enemies, and you do not want to hand your enemy a loaded gun."

"You do not trust Lady Gertrude?" He could not express his surprise at this revelation.

"Do you fully trust any of your friends? Beyond Philip and Fitzwilliam, of course." Her expression challenged him once more.

"I suppose not, but I had believed ladies held deep confidences."

Demi laughed once more. "Oh, my poor brother. You

are quite naïve when it comes to ladies, I fear. You really should listen to Mamma. She is far better at diplomacy than Papa. I suspect *she* has seen to the success of more of his projects than him alone."

The carriage pulled to a stop, and a footman opened the door. Ashton stepped down before handing his sister out. As they approached the front door, he nudged her side. "I found our afternoon quite interesting, Demi. You have surprised me. I thank you for sharing your opinions and observations with me."

She gave him a genuine smile. "I too enjoyed it. Shall we go walking tomorrow, during the fashionable time? Perhaps we will encounter Gertie and her friend."

Ashton laughed and agreed. "Will Bedlington not become jealous?" he asked as they entered the house.

"Oh, he is in meetings most of the day. I will see him tomorrow evening when he comes to dinner." She handed her outerwear to the footman before turning towards the drawing room.

Ashton frowned, having not previously paid attention to his future brother's habits. "I would think a man in love would want to spend every available moment at your side."

"A man in love?" Demi's expression returned to what it had been in the carriage. "Ashton." She laid a hand upon his arm. "We do not marry for love. Bedlington is handsome, and he shares many of Papa's stances. He is a good man who does not over imbibe or gamble, and he is serious about his work. He will provide well for me and our children."

"Do you not want more, Demi?"

"What more is there?" She patted his arm. "I am certain that, one day, we will love each other as Mamma and Papa do. I simply must make myself as indispensable to him as Mamma is to Papa." She winked. "Luckily, I have learned at her side."

She released him and continued down the hallway, only turning back when she realised he was no longer with her.

"Are you coming? I thought I would tell Mamma about our day."

Ashton shook his head. "No, I think not. I would ask, if you please, that you do not share my . . . curiosity regarding Miss Carrington with her."

"Of course." Demi frowned as she tipped her head, then returned to his side and placed a kiss upon his cheek. "Thank you for today, Ashton."

He watched her until she disappeared into the drawing room, then called for his horse. He suddenly felt the need to be away from the house.

CHAPTER THREE
LONDON
8 MAY

Ashton waited impatiently while his valet retied his cravat and reminded himself not to tug upon it within the man's sight again. His parents had set aside this evening for the only gathering not related to his sister's nuptials: a dinner in honour of his birthday. Normally, he would be pleased to spend an evening with friends and family where he was the centre of attention, but instead he felt somewhat anxious.

True to her word, Demi had set aside time from her mother's wedding demands to join Ashton in promenades and teas where they coincidentally encountered certain ladies. These casual meetings allowed him opportunities to speak privately with Miss Carrington while Lady Gertrude and Demi discussed their weddings. The friends' constant need to outdo one another highly amused their companions. The frustration came in that, other than humorous comments regarding the brides, he had yet to learn anything personal about the lady who intrigued him. Ashton was still unable to shake the feeling she hid something from him and all of London society.

Of course, he was not a vicious man, unlike some who lived for a crumb of gossip they could use to ruin some poor unsuspecting newcomer just for amusement. Ashton simply felt compelled to know everything there was to know about this exotic beauty who had entered their midst. Perhaps, should he discover there was nothing so sinister regarding Miss Adsila Carrington of Virginia, he might be able to expel her from his thoughts and, more importantly, his dreams.

Ashton was not a fool. He knew his father would be unsupportive should he begin an official courtship with the lady. She was an unknown and, worse, an American. Mr. Carrington had been born and raised in Virginia, coming to England only to attend university, where he met his wife. Lucky greenhorn! So far from home he need not seek parental permission before securing the lady which suited his fancy.

The valet frowned as he looked the viscount over but reluctantly nodded his approval.

"Am I presentable now, Carter?" Ashton asked with a smirk.

"The best I can do at present," the man replied, drawing a laugh from his master.

"I promise not to fidget and ruin your work." He clapped the man on the shoulder before striding from the room. If he remained another moment, Carter might remember a more intricate knot.

His anxiety notched upwards as he entered the drawing room to find a gathering of many of the young ladies he had already eliminated from his list of potential wives. The urge to frown was nearly overwhelming, but that would not please his father. Keeping his features as neutral as possible, he approached his mother and kissed her cheek.

"Forgive my delay, Mother. My man was determined to strangle me."

Lady Matlock smiled at her son. "He turned you out

well this evening. Come, greet our company."

He thought he had hidden his grimace, but his mother squeezed his arm before raising her brow as her smile intensified. When he returned the expression, hoping he did not appear pained, she relaxed and pulled him towards the preening wallflowers littering the room. After fifteen minutes of inane conversation with ladies he had no intention of pursuing, the butler entered to announce Lord Carlisle and his party. The forced smile upon his lips disappeared as Miss Carrington followed His Lordship's family on the arm of Mr. Croome. The lady's gaze was fixed upon the floor and he was unable to see her expression, but he suspected she was as thrilled as he was with her companion.

"Viscount Grayson," Lord Carlisle trumpeted after greeting his hosts. "A happy birthday to you." The man stepped nearer and spoke in a faux whisper. "Good timing, lad. I was becoming bored with all the matrimonial talk."

"Couldn't agree more, Freddy," Lord Matlock bellowed as he clapped his friend on the shoulder. "And you have arrived in time for dinner." He dipped his head towards the door, where the butler had just returned to make the announcement. "Ashton, please escort Miss Haverton," he commanded as he returned to his wife's side.

Reaffixing his smile, he bowed to the lady and offered his arm. Her bubbly, mindless chatting began as they joined the procession, paused only when necessary, and finally ended as the ladies left the gentlemen following the meal. Ashton had only to smile and nod where appropriate. It reminded him why he and his brother had recommended the lady as Darcy's dinner companion: very little was required of Miss Haverton's escort.

The door closed behind the ladies, and port was poured for one and all. Ashton accepted his welcomingly and savoured the first sip, allowing all the dinner conversations to drain away.

"Five and twenty!" Lord Carlisle crowed. "Ah, to be

five and twenty again, eh, Henry?"

"The youth know not what they possess," Lord Matlock replied as he raised his glass in salute to his friend.

"Were you and Lady Matlock married by then?"

Ashton's father shook his head. "Engaged." He sipped his wine. "We married the following year."

"That's right. You beat me to the altar by two years. Your father was breathing down your neck, was he not?" His lordship sat back in his chair and chuckled. "Feared Anthony might be needed if you didn't have the requisite heir." He sobered a bit and shook his head. "Shame there. He was a good man."

"My father thought Anthony was a bit of a cake, and he could be, but he was a good soldier."

"Aye, that he was. A true hero." Lord Carlisle lifted his glass and everyone drank to Ashton's late uncle. "Now, what are your plans for this one?" He sloshed his glass in Ashton's direction. All the gentlemen chuckled at the viscount's surprised countenance.

Ashton forced a smile before saying, "I believed I was the guest of honour this evening, not the fatted calf." He elbowed the man nearest him, but his smile faded when he realized it was Mr. Croome.

"We must all submit to the parson's mousetrap sooner or later. I have received a few pushes myself of late," the man said with a nod towards Lord Carlisle.

"Yes," Ashton replied, turning away from the others. "I noted your arrival with Miss Carrington."

"Lovely lady, is she not?" Mr. Croome puffed on his cigar. "Rarely speaks, but her dowry is handsome for an American. She is accustomed to being a distance from society, which suits me."

"Your estate is near Wales, is it not?"

"Cornwall."

"Ah." Ashton narrowed his eyes. "But you are frequently in London."

"Aye, but my wife need not be." The man chuckled.

Lord Matlock cleared his throat, drawing Ashton's attention. He smiled at his son, much like his wife had done earlier. Playing the obedient child, the viscount affixed a smile to his lips.

"Excuse me, Croome, I believe my father wishes to speak to me. " He dipped his head before striding away from the cod's head. Miss Carrington was the sort of beauty you paraded about, not settled on a dusty shelf out of sight.

"Ashton," Lord Matlock began before his son could speak. "When we return to the drawing room, I expect you to pay equal attention to all the ladies. You have been delinquent in your addresses to Sir Patrick's daughter as well as a few others."

A quick glance assured him the knight was out of hearing before he replied, "Father, I pray you would stop encouraging that lady. We discussed this before; unless you wish me to sleep my life away from boredom, I will *not* be considering Miss Harris."

Lord Carlisle appeared amused by Ashton's statement. "You need not be in frequent company with the lady, Grayson. Do as many others of the *ton*—"

"You will forgive me, my lord, but I dislike many practices of the *ton* regarding marriage and mistresses."

"No one is saying you need take a mistress, Ashton." His father's meaty hand fell upon his shoulder. "Nor am I saying you need marry Miss Harris."

"But your father would be appreciative if you would allow her father to see you speak to the lady so he can bargain upon a bit of influence," Lord Carlisle inserted.

Ashton suppressed the urge to frown and nodded once to acknowledge his understanding before redirecting the conversation. "I will agree to your terms, sir, if I might be allowed a few moments of conversation with other ladies this evening."

His father frowned. "Which ladies?"

"Lord Carlisle, your ward is an intriguing creature." He

noted his father's brow furrow. "A bit of a mystery, to be honest."

"Nothing of interest there for you, Grayson." Lord Carlisle shook his head as he met his friend's gaze. "The young lady is not of the *ton*. We will see her well settled with a man who will not abuse her. It will please her parents to know she has a proper husband and home."

This declaration stole all thought from Ashton. It sounded as though the young lady was *damaged* in some manner. Could she have been ruined and her father sent her to England where no one knew of it? His mind raced over the multitude of possibilities. Perhaps she was a simpleton, but their prior conversations did not show signs of that being the case.

"We are in agreeance, Ashton?"

The viscount realized the conversation had moved on without him. His options were to agree without knowledge of what was said, a foolhardy action, or confess he had not been listening to his sire.

"Forgive me, Father, I was woolgathering. To what did you wish me to agree?"

Lord Matlock gave a soft huff but held back a reprimand. "Circulate amongst the ladies, speaking to all, but you need not linger overlong where there is no interest."

Ashton tipped his head forwards to acquiesce to his father's request. "Very well. Is it time to rejoin the ladies?"

"Get it over with, eh?" Lord Carlisle asked as he clapped Ashton on the back. "Good attitude."

Lord Matlock frowned at his friend but led the men back to the drawing room.

"We had begun to wonder if you would be joining us," Lady Matlock scolded when they entered.

"Forgive me, my dear. We lost track of the time." The earl kissed his wife's hand, sending a blush across her cheeks.

Ashton made his way towards Miss Harris and the

small group about her. He glanced at his father in time to see his pleased smile. After suffering through a monotone, overly long conversation of which he could not remember a word, he moved on to a group of giggling ladies experiencing their first season. This group he also deserted as soon as was polite. Slowly, he worked his way about the room, thanking everyone for joining them to celebrate his birthday, flattering those who would appreciate the attention but not read more into his words, and listening distractedly as they spoke. Finally, he found himself approaching Miss Carrington. She sat on a distant chair, a handkerchief held to her nose, surrounded by Mr. Croome and a few other young men.

"Gentlemen," Ashton said as he breached the group. "And Miss Carrington." He inserted a hint of surprise into his voice. "What are you thinking, gentlemen? Allow the lady some air." He held out his hand. "Might I escort you about the room, Miss Carrington? Away from the foul smell of cigar smoke?"

He was uncertain, but he thought he glimpsed a look of relief in those stormy eyes as she quickly accepted his offer with a soft, "You will pardon me," to the gentlemen.

Within a few steps, the slight hint of green receded from her complexion and she lowered her handkerchief.

"I am pleased I could be of assistance," Ashton said.

"Are you scolding me for not yet thanking you, Lord Grayson?" The lightning flashed through her grey clouds.

"No, madam, I would not think of it." His lips twitched.

"Then you are laughing at me."

"Never." He allowed the smile to move across his lips. "I simply believe the colour green might complement you, but as a fashion piece, not upon your countenance."

His companion fell silent, but her handkerchief once more raised to her lips. From the corner of his eye, Ashton could see her shoulders begin to tremble. When she next spoke, her voice held a hint of humour.

"With tobacco being such a large crop in Virginia, one might expect me to have a stronger stomach for the smell of it."

"I am certain, had it been one gentleman, you might have. The fact that the buffoons surrounded you with the smell must be the overwhelming factor." He guided her about the edge of the room, sidestepping his father, and found her a seat by his sister. "Ah, the ladies' *parfum* might be more appealing."

Miss Carrington thanked him and joined the cluster. Ashton bowed before turning to his father, whose smile held a hint of anger.

"What are you thinking, singling out *that* girl?"

"A gentleman would never allow a lady to become ill due to the odours of the men about her. Croome and those oafs wreaked of smoke, and they had her surrounded. She was positively green."

Lord Matlock huffed but agreed his son had done the correct thing. Ashton surveyed the room while his father instructed him on whom to speak with next. Miss Carrington was looking his direction with a small lift to her lips, but Croome was glaring at him intensely. Ashton smiled and tipped his head towards the gentleman before accepting his father's direction.

CHAPTER FOUR
LONDON
9 MAY

"What were you about last night?" Demi asked as they strolled through Hyde Park.

Ashton's hand pressed against his chest. "Me? I was simply following Father's directions and being pleasant to all our guests."

"Mm-hmm." Demi waved to a couple some feet away. "What a lovely bonnet, Miss Sherrington."

The lady smiled, batting her eyes at Ashton, who nodded but did not speak. They continued a short distance.

"Gertie teased poor Miss Carrington regarding your chivalry."

"I would have done the same for any young lady there." He watched his sister from the corner of his eye. "How did Miss Carrington respond?"

"She said you would have done the same for anyone in her situation."

Ashton smiled. "And she was correct." They walked a few more steps before he asked, "Was anything else said?"

Demi frowned but quickly recovered before nodding to another passing couple. "Not then, but previously. That chatterbox you escorted to dinner was being most disrespectful regarding your lady."

"She is *not* my lady. Father and Lord Carlisle made that clear last evening."

His sister's brow cocked upwards.

"I merely asked a few questions regarding Miss Carrington. They took it upon themselves to squash any expectations they presumed I had."

A smile spread across Demi's features. "Gertie!" She released her brother's arm and rushed the few steps to grasp her friend's hands. "And Miss Carrington. I am so pleased to see you both today."

Ashton joined them and greeted the ladies. "I am pleased to see you fully recovered from your discomfort, Miss Carrington."

Her eyes remained glued to the ground, and she mumbled a reply he was unable to hear. Demi linked arms with Lady Gertrude, but Her Ladyship resisted the tug to begin walking. Instead, she stepped closer to her father's ward.

"We were just taking some fresh air but must return home shortly. Mamma insists on another fitting as we will be leaving London the day after your wedding."

The siblings exchanged a questioning glance before Demi responded. "There is ever so much to do. You must be looking forward to being home to personally oversee some of the details. Miss Carrington, are you anxious to see Naworth Castle?"

The lady looked to Lady Gertrude before returning her gaze to the ground and speaking once more in that whispery voice. "We are travelling to Castle Howard, but I am anticipating being away from the city."

"Castle Howard?" Demi looked to her friend.

"Oh, did Mamma not tell Lady Matlock?" She blushed. "She decided I should be married from Yorkshire instead of Cumbria."

"Of course. It is, after all, slightly nearer to London. It will be lovely."

Ashton was uncertain, but believed his sister might have been grinding her teeth as this last was said with a clenched jaw. He was about to offer to escort the ladies home, when Lady Gertrude said her goodbyes and set an exceptionally fast pace out of the park.

"That was odd," he said, turning to find his sister growing purple with rage.

"How *dare* she?" Demi hissed through gritted teeth.

"Forgive me, did I miss something? Lord Carlisle does have two country seats."

"But Castle Howard is an additional two days' journey from the Lake District," Demi said with a huff. "Lord Bedlington and I will have to end *our* wedding journey early in order to attend *her* wedding."

His sister turned about, walking towards home at an unbecoming gait and without sparing a glance for any of the passers-by. More than one young lady began to address Demi but was utterly ignored. Hoping to smooth over any unintentional cuts, Ashton smiled, nodded, and greeted any they passed while attempting to maintain a normal distance from his sister and presenting a relaxed and unconcerned air. It was exhausting, but, with the pace set by his sister, they were soon climbing the stairs to their townhouse.

"Mother!" Demi cried as the door closed behind them. "Do you know what the Carlisles have done?"

A maid chased Demi down the hall, attempting to claim her outerwear while his sister made her determined way to Lady Matlock's favourite drawing room. Ashton casually removed his hat and gloves and handed them to the footman. His sister's voice could no longer be heard.

"Has Mother company?" he asked the butler.

The man's countenance reddened. "Lady Carlisle, sir."

"I see." Ashton smirked. "I will be in the library."

"Yes, sir."

****

"This is *your* fault!" Demi cried as she stormed into the library half an hour later. "Lord Carlisle has decided they must remove from town in order to separate Miss Carrington from *your* continued interest, but he must not be so far from London as Cumbria."

Ashton raised his eyes from the book in his lap and studied his sister. If Demi's heightened colour was any clue, his sister was livid, and he was her target.

"If I remember correctly, Lord Carlisle was anticipating being at Naworth Castle a month prior to the wedding. This earlier exit from town would not interfere with them then continuing northward on the appointed date."

"However," his sister said with a nasty glare, "Lady Carlisle determined they could expect a greater number of guests in Yorkshire." She dropped into a chair in an unladylike fashion. "Mamma had been regaling her with the number of guests anticipated at my nuptials, and it was greater than the number Gertie expected in Cumbria."

"Then it was due to Mother the plans were changed." Ashton picked up the book to continue reading.

"Only because Lord Carlisle had already announced they would be travelling to Howard Castle." She huffed as she crossed her arms. "I never should have indulged your curiosity."

He looked at her, but Demi was too busy pouting to notice. "Was something said regarding our meetings?" he finally asked.

"Mamma was quite upset with me for encouraging you."

Ashton set his book on the table and rose from his seat.

"Where are you going?" Demi demanded.

"To speak with mother."

He left the room, closing the door on her protestations. He was halfway down the stairs when she cried from the top, "Do *not* make this worse."

Ignoring her, Ashton continued until he stood outside his mother's study. There was a pause following his knock, and he wondered if she might be elsewhere, but then the door opened, and Lady Matlock stood before him. Neither spoke while she searched his countenance, then stepped aside for him to enter.

"Are you in love with her?" she asked as he was about to take a seat.

"Love? I barely know her."

"Well, thank heaven for that." She returned to her desk and studied him once more. "I do not know much, but I will tell it to you. Perhaps then you will be able to clear her from your mind."

Ashton nodded, trying not to fidget or tap his fingers impatiently. His mother knew how to torture by taking her time in revealing what one wanted to know. He was pleased when she spoke directly.

"Miss Carrington's mother wrote to Lady Carlisle last spring, asking if she would sponsor her daughter in London. Apparently, there was a young man in Virginia who was showing her unwanted attentions." She eyed her son with pursed lips.

Ashton shifted in his seat but said nothing.

"When Miss Carrington arrived, Lady Carlisle found her highly impertinent and outspoken. I cannot say I am surprised." Lady Matlock moved some papers about her desk. "The lady's mother was much the same. I believe no one was shocked when she agreed to marry Mr. Carrington and set sail for America."

"Miss Carrington was outspoken?" he asked, not really hearing anything said after this.

"Yes."

"The woman who barely speaks above a whisper and refuses to look anyone in the eye for any length of time?"

"Yes."

Ashton rose and paced the small area between the furnishings. He shook his head. "I knew something felt wrong regarding her, but I would not have thought it to be that she was hiding her true nature."

"Oh, Ashton." Lady Matlock rose and laid a hand upon his cheek. "You are remarkably naïve regarding ladies. We all of us hide our true nature until we have secured a gentleman."

"I am certain that is true, Mamma, but I had not thought it possible for a lady to present a picture so opposite to her natural inclination." He thought for a moment. "Though I have seen her in unguarded moments when her eyes flashed dangerously and she spoke in a firmer tone." He smiled at the memory.

His mother grasped his chin and stared into his eyes. "You are certain you are not in love?"

Ashton laughed and pulled away from her. "A mere fascination, I believe. I am sorry to have forced her from town, but I cannot see how Lord Carlisle could suggest that insufferable Croome as a suitor."

"Croome is in need of funds and will not be affected by her heritage." Lady Matlock returned to her seat.

"I realize she is half American, but I would hope the *ton* would at least give her a chance. There have been other American ladies who have participated in London society to great acclaim."

His mother waved a hand dismissively. "But they were not part savage."

"Savage?" Ashton regained his seat. "I do not understand you, Mother."

With a sigh, she set a letter aside and met his gaze directly. "Miss Carrington's father was a bit darker than she, or perhaps he was merely tanned as it was the summer months when I met him. The darker complexion with his strongly angled features caused rumours to circulate that he was part Indian. I believe his mother or grandmother.

Why, did you not wonder about Miss Carrington's name? Lady Carlisle said Adsila means blossom in—what was it?––Cherokee, I believe."

"But her eyes—"

"Her mother's eyes were a pale blue."

Ashton sat silently, considering all he had heard. Miss Carrington had indeed been concealing much from the *ton*.

"Have you any other questions?" his mother asked.

"No, I think not."

She nodded. "Then we will consider this episode concluded." She returned her attention to the letters on her desk.

Ashton rose and was about to leave the room when another question entered his mind, though not regarding Miss Carrington. "Why is Father insistent upon my finding a bride this season?"

Lady Matlock raised her head and laughed. "He cares not if you marry this year. There is a bill he wishes to pass, and he is hoping you will assist him by speaking to the daughters of the men he is attempting to sway."

"Well, why did he not simply tell me that?"

"Most likely he believes he has." She frowned. "Do you not listen to his mumblings during breakfast?"

"How do you know he mumbles at breakfast? You do not join us."

"That is the reason I do not join you. If there is something he requires of me, he must tell me, not expect me to understand him through a mouthful of eggs."

Ashton laughed, returning to the desk and dropping a kiss upon her cheek. "I will be certain to pay closer attention or request clarification in the future."

His mother nodded as she returned her attention to her correspondence once more. "That would be wise, my dear."

Ashton was nearly at the door when she said, "He will be pleased to hear this situation has been concluded."

He turned back to find her watching him closely.

Realizing she sought reassurance, he nodded before leaving the room.

He hesitated in the hall, not certain where he wished to go. If Demi remained in the library, he had no interest in returning there. Normally, he might take a ride, but the skies had darkened following their return from the park, and it could even now be raining. With a huff, he climbed the stairs to his rooms. If only Philip were here, or Darcy, he could talk out the thoughts rushing about his mind. Upon entering his room, he took a seat at the secretaire and withdrew a piece of paper. If he could not speak to his brother, he would simply write to him instead.

CHAPTER FIVE
LONDON
28 MAY

Ashton leant against the wall out of the way of the footmen bearing trays and out of sight from his father. It had been an exhausting week, and he was rather pleased his sister was finally married.

Demi sat on one side of the room, surrounded by single young ladies envying her new status, while her husband stood against the opposite wall, discussing politics with Lord Matlock and several other cronies. Having no desire to raise the expectations of the first group and no interest in the conversation of the second, Ashton had discovered a little-used part of the room where he could evade notice for a few minutes.

"Do you often skulk about the edges of society events?"

The voice startled him as it seemed to come from behind. Ashton turned to discover Miss Carrington sitting in the window seat. "Forgive me, madam, I did not see you there."

Her colour rose. "No, I suspected you had not. I was

skulking as well." Her lips tugged upwards on one side.

Suddenly, Ashton realized he was able to hear the lady without straining. Her voice was not soft and whispery but full and melodic. He wondered if she sang.

The lady frowned. "I had thought we might enjoy a brief conversation as we will not be meeting again for a month or more, but you have fallen silent."

"Forgive me." Ashton bowed. "It appears one of us always is when we meet."

Her cheeks became ruddy. "Yes, I suppose you are correct. I blame the ridiculous rules of society. What is your excuse?"

"Surprise," Ashton replied with a laugh. He glanced about before stepping closer. "Would you like to take a walk? The garden is in full bloom."

Miss Carrington tipped her head to the side as she considered his offer before rising and taking his arm. "That would be lovely, Lord Grayson."

They moved discreetly to the nearest door, then out into the garden. Several other guests had already done the same as the number of bodies within had caused the temperature to rise. Ashton led Miss Carrington away from the larger groups, where they could converse without being heard.

"So, I am finally to know you better, Miss Carrington?" Ashton asked when he had her alone.

"As I said, it is doubtful we will meet again before Lady Gertrude's nuptials, and never afterwards."

"Never? Why do you believe that?"

She inhaled slowly. "The roses smell heavenly." She stepped closer to a bush, bending to admire an orange bloom.

Ashton reached into his pocket, removed his folding pen-knife, and opened the larger fruit blade. "May I?" He motioned to the flower. When she nodded, he cut the stem and handed her the bloom.

They began walking again while he replaced his knife,

and she held the blossom to her nose.

"You did not answer my question."

"I did not realize it was necessary. Lord Carlisle has decreed that I am not to encourage you, so we will journey to Yorkshire tomorrow. You will arrive there in time for Lady Gertrude's wedding, then depart."

"And you?"

"Me." She looked about the garden before sniffing the rose once more. "I will marry Mr. Croome when I am told to do so, then journey to his home."

Ashton felt his anger rise. "You speak as though you have no say in the matter."

She looked at him with an odd expression and clouded eyes. "I do not. My parents sent me here to marry, and Lord Carlisle has found a man willing to have me."

"How can you speak of yourself in this manner? You are not property to be traded."

The lady's eyes flashed, and her lips twitched. "Am I not? A woman's possessions pass from her father to her husband. There are few men who actually appreciate their wife having a say outside her realm in his home. As long as he is well fed, the household accounts are balanced, and he is presented an heir, what more does he expect from his wife?"

Ashton laughed. "Do you normally give your opinion so decidedly?"

"In instances when it is not incumbent on me to present the façade Lady Carlisle has created, I prefer to speak my mind." She gave him an impertinent smile and turned down the next pathway.

He followed, of course, unwilling to allow any unnecessary distance to come between them. Ashton stopped beside her as she stared at a bush with reddish orange flowers. Her fingers caressed the blooms.

"Forgive me for being a terrible guide. I cannot name a plant beyond the common ones everyone knows."

"This is a flame azalea," Miss Carrington told him. "It

is native to the Appalachian Mountains, where my great-grandmother's people live."

"The Cherokee?" Ashton asked without thought.

Miss Carrington's colour deepened. "I did not realize you were aware—"

"It explains the difference between your healthy complexion and the pasty members of the *ton*. I noted it the first evening we met."

She continued walking down the path, and he followed again, fearful he had erred in mentioning her heritage, but curious nonetheless.

"Have you spent time with her people?" he asked.

She nodded. "I did. It was due to attentions from a Cherokee brave that I find myself in England."

"Did you love him?"

Miss Carrington stopped and looked at him. Her eyes were unreadable. "No. Onacona was a boy I played with as a child. Several years passed, and when I returned, we were both grown. He wished to court me, but my parents were against it. I knew him only as a playmate."

"Did you wish to know him better?" Ashton surprised himself with the question but held his breath waiting for her response.

She frowned. "I had not even considered it. The Cherokee have been moved farther and farther from their native land. It is not a life to which I was raised or am accustomed."

"Then why did it force your parents to send you away?"

The path they were on looped back. They were quickly approaching the other guests, but Ashton had no desire to return to the wedding breakfast so soon. Slipping his hand about the lady's arm, he turned her down another path leading away from the house.

Miss Carrington looked up at him with a smirk upon her lips. "We are not yet returning?"

"You have not answered my question."

Her gaze returned to the path. "You are impertinent as well."

A smile stole across Ashton's lips. He was quite enjoying the genuine Miss Carrington.

The rose was raised to her nose once more. "Onacona followed us back to Virginia. I suppose many of our neighbours were aware of our Cherokee blood, but his presence made them uncomfortable. I was sent away so he would leave. My parents hoped life would return to normal."

"And has it?"

She sighed. "I am uncertain. I have received few letters during my time here."

Ashton nodded. "My brother is fighting on the continent, and I rarely hear from him as well. Knowing your family is so far away and possibly in some form of danger can be difficult."

Miss Carrington stopped and looked at him. "You really do understand."

"Of course. How could I not? Or anyone, for that matter?"

"Mr. Croome has no interest in my family," she said as she began walking once more.

This did not surprise Ashton, who already had a low opinion of the man. He realized they were again approaching the house, but this time he understood they had been gone longer than was wise. As if in response to his thoughts, his mother and Lady Carlisle entered the garden as the couple approached the doors.

"Ah, here you are, Adsila." Lady Carlisle frowned at Ashton. "Lord and Lady Bedlington are preparing to leave."

"Lord Grayson was showing me the flame azalea."

"It was a gift from Lady Carlisle," Lady Matlock said, turning to her friend.

The woman's countenance reddened as Miss Carrington replied, "It must be a cutting from the one my mother sent her."

"I do not remember one in your garden." Ashton's mother studied her friend.

The lady linked arms with her ward. "Oh, it was so lovely, but it looked out of place in my beds. I knew you would appreciate it."

"I am pleased you thought of me. You know how I adore exotic blooms."

Ashton watched the ladies carefully. His mother appeared gracious, but her eyes flashed as they had when he and Philip were about to receive a tongue-lashing.

"We should not linger, or we will miss the bride and groom's departure." Lady Carlisle led Miss Carrington back into the house.

"They would not dare leave without my seeing them off." Lady Matlock grasped Ashton's arm and pulled him along, stepping around the ladies once in the hall. "Hurry now," she called over her shoulder.

Ashton bit his lip to contain his amusement. He nearly whispered "Like mother, like daughter," but knew his mother would *not* enjoy his ribbing.

PART TWO
1812

CHAPTER SIX
CHEAPSIDE
JANUARY 1812

Adsila stepped out of the carriage and lifted her head to examine the stone façade on the townhouse. It was not as fine as the Carlisles' home where she had stayed the last time she was in London, but it appeared well maintained. Her gaze shifted to the street, and she smiled to see four children dancing about a well-dressed woman. Gracechurch Street was not a fashionable neighbourhood, but it appeared to be friendly.

The lady dipped her head in greeting as she, the children, and a maid passed. Her smile was so genuine, it drew one from Adsila. She watched them a moment longer before climbing the steps and ringing the bell while her maid awaited directions regarding the trunks.

A plump, haggard-looking woman answered, a smile suddenly lighting her features. "Be ye Miss Carrington?" she asked in a strong brogue before Adsila could present her card.

"Aye," she replied. "You must be Mrs. Gallagher. Has my brother been driving you mad with his indecision?"

She stepped into the hall and removed her bonnet.

"I am pleased ye've arrived," the housekeeper replied judiciously as she accepted Adsila's outerwear after directing the carriage to the mews entrance. "Mr. Carrington is in his study, if ye'll follow me. I'll bring ye tea and biscuits in a jiffy."

"Thank you." Adsila followed the lady down the corridor. The hall narrowed as it approached the rear of the house, and there was no natural light.

Mrs. Gallagher knocked on the last door on the right, and Adsila heard her brother call for them to enter. The housekeeper opened the door and light spilled out, revealing dust motes filling the hall. Adsila stepped inside, and the door closed behind her.

"What is it, Mrs. Gallagher?" Thomas asked without looking up.

"Mrs. Gallagher is fetching us tea. Whatever has you so absorbed?"

He rose from his seat at the sound of her voice and rounded the desk. Before she finished speaking, she was lifted into the air and spun in a circle.

"Adsi! I am so pleased you arrived today. I was not expecting you until tomorrow." He set her down and kissed her cheek.

"It did not take as long as expected to close the house, and the roads were good, so we were not delayed by weather."

Her brother rushed to move a stack of books from the nearest chair. "Sit, sit," he said with a jerk of his chin. He dropped the books on the next clear flat surface, a rare find in the small crowded room, then returned to his seat.

"Thomas, where will Mrs. Gallagher set the tea things?" she asked as she picked up the items he had just discarded and moved them to a distant corner. She straightened and looked about. "You have been here a fortnight, and this room appears as though you have just unpacked."

A blush covered his cheeks. "Look what I have found," he said, pointing to the book lying open on his desk.

Adsila stood beside his chair but did not see anything overly unusual about the book. "What is it?" she finally asked.

"A treatise written by Alexander Codrington. Could it be one of our ancestors?"

Her excitement could not meet his, so she returned to her chair, frowning at the obviously dusty seat. "Lord, I don't know. Is he from Gloucestershire? If so, it could be."

After a quick look about the room revealed nothing to cover the cushion, she reminded herself she was already dusty from the road and sat just as the housekeeper returned with a maid. Seeing the open spot on the table, Mrs. Gallagher smiled at Adsila.

"Here ye are, dearies." She set the tray down. "Shall I pour?"

"No, thank you." Adsila rose again and looked over the dishes. "I hope you have not been spoiling my brother with lemon biscuits all this time? His dinner jackets will have to be let out," she declared before winking at the housekeeper.

Thomas—a tall, thin man—laughed. "A problem I've never had, as you well know." He patted his flat stomach.

"I am certain Papa ate as you did when he was your age, but now Mamma slaps his hand if he reaches for seconds."

"Will there be anything else, miss?" The housekeeper had shed a bit of her initial distressed appearance and smiled brightly.

"What is the cook preparing for dinner this evening?" Adsila asked, knowing her brother would have allowed the servants to make these decisions in her absence.

"A simple stew, if it be acceptable."

She nodded. "I will meet with you in the morning so we can bring some order to the chaos which normally surrounds my brother."

"Very well, miss." The housekeeper shooed the maid out of the room before following her.

"You make me sound indolent," he murmured as he accepted his tea.

"On the contrary, dearest. You are quite industrious; you simply leave a mess wherever you go."

Adsila fixed her own cup and plate and returned to her seat. "Have you left the house since you've been here? Other than exploring the nearest book store." She dipped her head towards the book on his desk.

"I met a welcoming couple," he replied after taking a sip of tea. "The Gardiners. He is in trade. You might have seen his warehouses when you entered the area. They have four children, two boys and two girls, who are lively and intelligent." Thomas took a bite of biscuit but continued talking. "They were walking in the park the other day, and I caught a stray ball before it hit an older matron walking nearby. Mrs. Gardiner said she would be pleased to meet you and introduce you to the neighbourhood."

"I believe I may have already seen her. There was a lady walking with four children and a maid when I arrived." A hint of caution entered her voice. "She appeared friendly."

"She is. I believe you will like this part of London far better than Mayfair."

His smile was warm and understanding. He knew of her aversion to the *ton*. They finished their tea while discussing what he had done in her absence and made plans for the next week. The next four months would pass quickly, and then they would be on a ship finally headed home.

Home. The last letter she had received from her mother had reassured her that people had chosen to forget about the Carringtons' connection to the Cherokee once more. Onacona had returned to the tribe and married, so she no longer needed to fear him returning to cause another uproar. Yes, it was time to go home and leave England and her impossible dreams behind.

****

Three days passed before Adsila allowed Mrs. Gallagher to hang the knocker. She had never seen so much dust in her life and began to wonder how long the house had sat vacant before they took the lease. From the moment she awoke until her head fell upon her pillow, she had directed, organized, and cleaned along with the staff. It seemed as though the dust multiplied in some areas—particularly those darker passages at the middle and back of the house.

This morning she sat by the window in the dining room, enjoying a cup of tea while watching the neighbourhood awaken. Thomas entered with his newspaper already opened.

"One day you will trip over something," she scolded lovingly. Her dear distracted brother. Thomas had been her saviour, and she would never forget it.

"Only if you rearrange the furniture again," he replied with a lopsided grin.

Adsila rose from her seat and joined him at the table after ringing for Mrs. Gallagher. The matron entered with her maid in tow as always. Sinead, the housekeeper's granddaughter, was in training to one day—many years from now—take the woman's place. At this young age, she was familiar with the expectations for scullery and laundry maids as well as a maid of all work, and she now spent most of her time in the kitchen assisting the cook.

Plates were settled before the siblings along with a fresh pot of tea. After assuring nothing more was needed, the servants returned to the kitchen, leaving the brother and sister to enjoy their breakfast.

"What shall we do today?" Thomas asked without tearing his eyes from the paper. "The weather has been pleasant for the last day or two; shall we walk about the park? Or would you rather visit the shops?"

Adsila would never admit it, but she wished the cleaning would have taken a few more days. She was still a bit leery of rejoining London society, even if it was not the same society she had known five years earlier.

"Adsi?"

She raised her gaze from her plate and smiled at her brother's worried expression. "What would you prefer? This is your first time in the capital."

He shook his head. "I have been here over a fortnight already and have checked several things off my list. Today it is your decision."

"A walk in the park would be nice," she replied.

"Perhaps we will see the Gardiners and I can introduce you."

She smiled but did not respond.

****

Thomas had been correct, the weather was pleasant. Surprisingly, the people of the neighbourhood appeared the same. While walking the path which circled a small lake or large pond, depending upon your preference, they passed several individuals. There was a governess with her pupils, a couple followed by their chaperon, and two or three families. All had smiled, nodded, or commented upon the lovely day.

The Carringtons had just reached the gates leading to Gracechurch Street when the four children Adsila had seen on the day of her arrival appeared, this time tugging upon the hands of an older couple.

"Mr. and Mrs. Gardiner," Thomas called as he squeezed his sister's arm. "What fortunate timing. My sister and I have just completed a circuit of the park."

"Mr. Carrington," Mr. Gardiner greeted with a large grin. "Does this mean we will not have the advantage of your excellent reflexes today?"

"Not at all," he looked to Adsila. "We would be pleased to walk a bit longer."

She smiled and nodded.

"My sister, Adsila Carrington. This is Mr. and Mrs. Gardiner, who I told you about."

"It is nice to meet you," Adsila said with a brief curtsey.

"We are pleased to make your acquaintance, as well." Mrs. Gardiner slipped her hand from the lad at her side. "Since you have already walked, shall we have a seat in the sun while the gentlemen entertain the children?"

"That would be lovely," Adsila replied, following the matron to a nearby bench.

"Adsila is a lovely and unusual name," Mrs. Gardiner said as she watched Mr. Gardiner and Thomas lead the children towards the pond. "Please do not allow them to get wet, Edward." She turned back and smiled. "Last summer my eldest, Michael, pushed his brother into the pond." She rolled her eyes. "We do not want a repeat in winter."

"I believe I saw your children walking to the park the day I arrived in town, but you were not the lady with them."

"Oh, you must have seen my niece, Elizabeth. She visited the children this week to celebrate Abby's birthday."

"She lives nearby?"

"She is recently married, and her husband has a home in Mayfair."

"He is not in trade?" Adsila asked without thinking, surprised a member of the *ton* would visit Cheapside.

Mrs. Gardiner laughed. "No, he is a gentleman, Mr. Darcy of Pemberley in Derbyshire. My niece is a gentleman's daughter, though our brother rarely brings his family to town."

"Mr. Darcy?" Adsila vaguely remembered hearing the name when she had taken part in the season all those years ago. "I do not believe I have made his acquaintance."

"I daresay you have not. He, like our brother, has little patience for the intrigues of the *ton*." She laughed once more. "The poor man has been trying to take his wife on a wedding trip for nearly a month but keeps being delayed by family matters. You have friends in Mayfair?"

Adsila hesitated. "My mother's friend sponsored me when I first arrived in England some years ago."

"Well, then," Mrs. Gardiner said as she watched her family. "I am surprised you remain unwed. You are quite a beauty."

"But I am also American." She could hear the hint of bitterness in her voice and hoped it went unnoticed by Mrs. Gardiner.

The matron shrugged. "I suppose that might affect some in the *ton,* but Lizzy and her husband do not hold with such prejudices. They are more concerned with a person's character."

"It is good to hear, if somewhat shocking."

The youngest children were running towards them. Mrs. Gardiner stood, so Adsila followed.

"Mamma, Mamma!" the girl cried. "Eugene dropped a rock in the pond and woke up the frog."

"Tattler," the boy mumbled as he reached them.

"Papa said he will not get dessert tonight," the girl continued as she grinned at her older brother.

"Was it purposefully done?" Mrs. Gardiner asked her son.

The girl nodded enthusiastically. "Uh huh. He saw the frog and tried to hit it."

"I asked your brother, Abigail." The matron presented a stern countenance, and the small girl bowed her head, all her vivacity muted.

The boy dug a toe into the dirt and refused to meet his mother's gaze. "I saw the frog before dropping the stone, Mamma."

"Did you intend to injure it?"

Eugene's head snapped up. "No, ma'am. I read that

frogs hibernate in the winter and awaken slowly. I wanted to see if it would even notice the stone."

The gentlemen had rejoined them with the older children. None spoke as they witnessed the confession.

"And you have your answer," Mrs. Gardiner looked away from the group for a moment. "Was the creature injured?" she asked as her gaze once more fell upon the youngest son.

"No, ma'am. He swam a short distance and settled back into the mud."

"And you are certain he was uninjured?" Mrs. Gardiner asked with an eye on her husband.

Both the man and his son nodded, the boy with a bit more vigour.

"Then it was a poorly thought out experiment, would you not agree, Mr. Gardiner?"

"That is one way of looking at it," her husband replied with a soft smile.

"And will you undertake such rash actions in the future?" she asked her son.

"No, Mamma." The boy's eyes were large as saucers as he shook his head.

"Good." Mrs. Gardiner turned her attention to the youngest girl. "Now, Miss Abby, we will discuss *your* actions."

The girl's lip began to quiver.

"None of that." Mr. Gardiner said in a soft yet firm voice.

"Was it your responsibility to tell me of your brother's actions?" Mrs. Gardiner's calm voice had a soothing affect.

"No, ma'am." Abigail was so much quieter than when she had tattled on her brother.

"I believe I sensed a hint of pleasure in your voice when you spoke of it."

The girl nodded, and a single tear rolled down her cheek.

Mrs. Gardiner sat upon the bench and motioned the

child closer. Abigail scuffed the dirt as she reluctantly approached.

"Your father had already pronounced a punishment for your brother, had he not?"

Abigail nodded, her eyes focused on her mother's skirts.

"And your father always tells me when there is an altercation requiring attention, does he not?"

This nod was slower, and another tear slid down her cheek.

"So then it was not your responsibility to embarrass your brother as you did, was it?"

The little girl's voice was barely a whisper. "No, ma'am."

Adsila felt for the child but was impressed with the manner the Gardiners used to reprimand their children.

"To help you remember the lesson you have learned today, you will share your brother's punishment for his reckless behaviour."

Abigail's head snapped upward but quickly lowered again as she nodded. "Yes, Mamma."

Mrs. Gardiner placed a kiss upon each child's forehead and motioned them to lead the way home. Once all four children were a few feet ahead, Mr. Gardiner held out his arm for his wife.

"For a moment, I thought you would laugh, my dear."

"For a moment, I nearly did," she replied as she accepted his arm. "Mr. and Miss Carrington, it would be our pleasure to have you join us for dinner tomorrow evening, if you are available. My niece and her husband will be joining us, as well as her sister and her fiancé."

"Oh, we would not want to intrude upon a family dinner," Adsila replied.

"Nonsense," Mr. Gardiner cried. "Lizzy and Jane will love to meet you. They are a bit overwhelmed at the moment as they are being introduced to the *ton*, and they will welcome any distraction they can find."

"My sister can sympathize, I am certain," Thomas responded as he nudged Adsila. "We have no plans of which I am aware."

Adsila acknowledged they did not have plans, and Mrs. Gardiner declared she would not accept no for an answer. Warm conversation flowed amongst them until, upon reaching their stoop, Adsila found herself happily anticipating the following evening.

CHAPTER SEVEN
CHEAPSIDE
23 JANUARY

The Gardiners' home was as warm and inviting as the couple themselves. Adsila and Thomas entered the sitting room to find two gentlemen speaking to their host.

"Ah, our new neighbours have arrived," Mr. Gardiner said as the housekeeper announced the Carringtons. "Darcy, Bingley, this is Mr. Thomas Carrington and his sister, Miss Adella Carrington."

"My sister is Miss Adsila Carrington, Mr. Gardiner." Thomas bowed to the group.

"Forgive me, Miss Carrington. I suppose I should stick with last names." Their host smiled jovially, but his cheeks had pinked when corrected.

"All is well, Mr. Gardiner. It is a common occurrence." Adsila smiled good naturedly as she curtseyed.

"This is my new nephew, Mr. Fitzwilliam Darcy of Pemberley in Derbyshire, and my soon to be nephew, Mr. Charles Bingley. My nieces, Mrs. Darcy and Miss Jane Bennet are upstairs with Mrs. Gardiner putting the children to bed."

Mr. Darcy bowed. "It is a pleasure to meet you both. The Gardiners have spoken well of you."

Mr. Bingley nodded as he rose from his bow. Their host motioned for all to sit. Once everyone was comfortable, Mr. Darcy looked to his host, but Mr. Gardiner presented an odd grin in return, and Mr. Bingley refused to meet his gaze. With a sigh, the gentleman shook his head before speaking.

"I understand you are from America."

"Yes," Thomas replied with a smile. "Virginia."

Mr. Darcy nodded. "Have you been in England long?"

"My sister arrived in the autumn of '05 and participated in the season. I came over the following summer to attend university." He smiled at her. "Adsi kept house for me."

She returned the smile. "I made certain he remembered to tie his cravat and that his shoes matched before he left the house."

Mr. Gardiner laughed. "Ah, a bit inattentive? I believe it is a prerequisite for a scholar."

"I believe Mr. Bennet, my wife's father, might enjoy Mr. Carrington's company."

"That he would, Darcy," Mr. Gardiner said as he slapped his hand on the armrest. "If you ever wish some time away from town, you must visit my brother. He will enjoy the company as his eldest daughters have left him alone with the sillier members of the family."

"Miss Carrington," Mr. Bingley began once Mr. Gardiner had ceased laughing. "Please forgive my saying so, but I am surprised you came away from a season in London unwed."

Adsila could feel her cheeks warm. "My sponsor had arranged a connection, but once Thomas arrived, I no longer felt the need to enter into what would have been a most disastrous situation."

"My sister is being kind. The man was a wiseacre. The moment I met him, I insisted Adsi join me in Oxford." Thomas's countenance reddened with the indignation he had felt those years prior. "The fact that Lord——"

"Thomas, it is in the past and no longer matters. It is my understanding the gentleman married. I bear no ill will towards him or the poor lady he chose." She stopped short of granting any absolution to Lord and Lady Carlisle and was pleased when she heard their hostess approaching.

"Ah, they have arrived." Mrs. Gardiner entered the room followed by a blonde woman and the young lady Adsila had seen the day she had returned to London. "Lizzy, Jane, this is Mr. Thomas Carrington and his sister, Miss Adsila Carrington. Is that not the loveliest name? Mr. and Miss Carrington, these are my nieces, Mrs. Elizabeth Darcy and Miss Jane Bennet."

"I have seen you," Mrs. Darcy said as she rose from her curtsey.

"Yes," Adsila replied. "I had just arrived in London when I saw you and your cousins walking towards the park."

"That is it precisely." Mrs. Darcy smiled. "Are you enjoying the city?"

"My sister has yet to venture farther than the park." Thomas pursed his lips. Whether it was displeasure or suppressed amusement, Adsila could not tell, though she suspected the latter.

"I saw all I needed to see of London when I was here in the past."

"Oh no," Mrs. Darcy replied with a shake of her head. "London is always changing. Have you not visited the shops, at least? Prior to my marriage, I loved to wander through them when I stayed with my aunt and uncle. I imagined making grand purchases, designed entire rooms around a single chair, and tried to picture what sort of person would lay down money for the ugliest items."

"Now she simply buys what she likes." Mr. Darcy raised his wife's hand to his lips, and the two fell silent as they shared a personal communication with their eyes.

"Now, Mr. Darcy, you will lead these fine people to

believe I am spoiled," she finally said.

"Perhaps not yet, but if Darcy has his way, I am certain you will be," Mr. Gardiner responded, causing his niece to blush and spurring everyone's amusement.

Before more could be said, the housekeeper entered to announce dinner, and they all made their way to the dining room. Though Mr. Darcy escorted Mrs. Gardiner, Mrs. Darcy slipped her arm through Adsila's, and they left the remaining gentlemen to follow with her sister.

"What does Adsilla mean?" Elizabeth asked. "Did I say it correctly?"

"Nearly. It is Ahd-SEE-lah. It means blossom in Cherokee." She held her breath while she waited for the lady's response. In all the time she had been in England, Mrs. Darcy was the only person to ask about her name. The Carlisles already knew the origin and meaning and had a habit of changing the subject if anyone else approached the topic.

"How appropriate! You are as lovely as a fresh spring blossom. Is Cherokee not one of the Indian tribes?"

Her companion's eyes widened, but the genuine interest which shone there allowed Adsila to exhale in relief as she nodded.

"Fitzwilliam," Mrs. Darcy called to her husband when they gathered about the dining table. "Miss Carrington's name is Cherokee."

"That accounts for its beauty," he replied before smiling at Adsila. "You must forgive my wife's exuberance. She is an avid reader and, if I understand it correctly, there was a time she had a grand fascination with the Indians in America."

They took their seats, and Miss Bennet began to explain. "When we were quite young, Lizzy lost her favourite doll when she ran off to scold a boy for abusing a tree." She smiled at Mr. Darcy, who returned the gesture. "In an effort to make her feel better, we began creating stories of the doll's travels."

"The books we read determined her destinations," Mrs. Darcy said. "I found a book in my father's library about wars with Indians in the western territories, but Jane would not allow me to send Cathy there."

"She had already travelled to India the year prior," the eldest sister said in a most rational voice. "All that time at sea would have ruined her complexion."

The sisters laughed, and the others joined them. Adsila felt joy bubble within her. In all the time she had been in England, the ladies she had met had been pale in complexion and personality. Mrs. Gardiner and her nieces were vibrant and glowing in comparison. A spark of hope warmed her as she began to believe she might actually make a friend here.

****

Adsila sat beside Mrs. Darcy when they returned to the drawing room so they could continue a conversation regarding the *ton* which had begun during dinner.

"It has been a few years," she said, "so things may have changed since I was introduced to London society."

"And you were entering the marriage mart," Mrs. Darcy replied with a sigh. "I confess I would be less concerned if that were my story. Instead, I have married the most eligible bachelor in England."

"Of which you are exceedingly pleased," Miss Bennet scolded her sister. "You make it sound as though marrying Darcy is a chore or a curse when everyone who knows you can see you are happier than you have ever been."

A blush covered the lady's cheeks. "I never said my marriage displeased me. I am simply anxious about entering a society which will, for the most part, believe I am undeserving of my current position."

"But you have powerful allies, Lizzy." Mrs. Gardiner passed cups of tea to her nieces and Adsila.

"Darcy will not allow anyone to mistreat you," Miss

Bennet said as she accepted her refreshment. "And Lady Matlock alone is a force."

"Lady Matlock?" Adsila asked before she could bite her tongue.

"Yes, have you met her?" Mrs. Darcy's smile brightened. "She is Fitzwilliam's aunt."

"Your aunt now," their hostess gently reminded her niece.

"Yes, but I cannot bring myself to call her Aunt Esther, even though she insists."

"She will not allow anyone to speak ill of you." Miss Bennet shivered. "She is a force to be reckoned with. I hope to never fall out of grace with her."

Mrs. Darcy's laugh was light and unaffected. "Oh Jane, as if you could. I am the one who speaks without thinking. There are times I feel as though I am sixteen once more and watching Aunt Gardiner for clues as to what to say or do."

"Or what not to say," Mrs. Gardiner said as a crooked smile tugged at her lips.

"Precisely." Mrs. Darcy shook her head. "Though I do feel for Miss de Bourgh." She turned to Adsila. "She is Lady Matlock's niece, who is finally taking her place in society at five and twenty."

"She has not been introduced before now?"

"No, her mother expected her to marry Fitzwilliam and enter society in my position."

"And Lady Matlock is supporting you?" Adsila asked in surprise.

Mrs. Darcy pursed her lips before speaking but was unsuccessful in suppressing her grin. "Lady Matlock and the earl's sister are not on the best of terms. I believe she is revelling in Lady Catherine's displeasure."

"Is she still pressuring her son to marry Miss de Bourgh?" their hostess asked.

Adsila held her breath, waiting for Mrs. Darcy's response, but the men chose that moment to join the ladies. Conversation quickly moved to upcoming events and Miss Bennet and Mr. Bingley's rapidly approaching wedding. No more was said of the Matlock family.

When the night drew to an end, the ladies agreed to meet for tea in a day or two and exchanged directions so arrangements could be settled later. Mr. Darcy offered to drop the Carringtons at their townhouse so they did not have to walk at night, and Thomas accepted.

As the carriage came to a halt, Miss Bennet gasped. "Oh, I have always been curious about this home. It stood empty for so long. Do you remember, Lizzy?"

"Is this the one? I could not remember which it was."

"That would explain the dust," Adsila told her brother, who simply nodded as he probably hadn't noticed it. "You must join me for tea when your calendars allow. I would be pleased to give you a tour," she told the ladies.

Miss Bennet looked longingly at her sister, who nodded and accepted. "We would be delighted."

The Carringtons said goodnight and entered the house as the carriage began moving once more.

"Did ye have a nice evening?" Mrs. Gallagher asked while accepting their outerwear.

"We did," Thomas replied before turning to his sister. "Though I was worried when we entered the drawing room following dinner because you appeared so pale, Adsi, but you seemed to recover. Was something said which upset you?"

Adsila turned towards the stairs. "No. We were discussing the *ton*, and Lady Matlock was mentioned. It simply surprised me." She took the first step. "If you will excuse me, Thomas, I am tired and will retire. Good night."

Without waiting for his response, she climbed the stairs. Only when she had gained her bedroom and was leaning against the closed door did she allow herself to think about what had been said earlier. Lady Matlock was pressuring her son to marry her niece, but *which* son?

Adsila shook her head and pushed away from the door. What did it matter? She was still the girl from America with Indian blood. A tear rolled down her cheek, but she swatted it away and blinked fiercely to dispel any other that might dare escape.

CHAPTER EIGHT
MAYFAIR
JANUARY

"Good morning, Ashton."

The viscount did not look up from his book. "It is afternoon, Anne."

Hoping she would go away, Ashton turned the page and allowed his gaze to move over the lines, though he did not actually read the passage. In truth, the book had been a prop in the event someone entered the library. Unfortunately, Anne did not show any sign of leaving; instead, she settled on the edge of the settee directly across from him. He could feel her watching him but refused to react. He turned another page.

"You are either reading rather quickly or you are attempting to ignore me."

"How do you know how fast I am able to read?"

"I don't, but I have not been here long enough for you to have finished two pages."

Ashton sighed and set the book aside. "What do you want, Anne?"

"I understand you have no desire to marry me, but that

does not mean we cannot be civil to one another. *I* have not intentionally placed you in this position." She huffed. "No one even asked *me* who I might want to wed."

"Is there someone you hold in affection?" Ashton asked, ashamed it was the first time he had considered the possibility.

"No." Anne slid back in the seat. "Mamma had complete control over my society, and young, eligible gentlemen were rare at Rosings. The only possible opportunity to meet anyone was when I would drive my phaeton, but Mrs. Jenkinson was always with me and reported back to Mamma, so I normally remained within Rosings Park and Hunsford."

"I cannot imagine such a limited life." Ashton ran a hand through his hair. "How can you forgive us for not coming to your rescue sooner?"

His cousin laughed. "You make me sound like a damsel in distress. I am certain I never thought of myself as such. If that were the case, then Mamma would have to be an evil witch or ogre." She met his gaze directly. "You would not want her to believe you thought of her as such."

Ashton swallowed. "Have you been in contact with Lady Catherine?"

"Oh Ashton, do you believe I remain under my mother's influence?" She laughed once more when he did not respond. "You do." Anne shook her head. "Mamma writes to me, but I do not give credit to most of what she says. I have met Mrs. Darcy and found her to be a perfectly lovely lady, and a far better wife to Darcy than I would ever have been. He and I spoke about it years ago. Did you know Uncle Darcy was against the match?"

"Darcy said something of it about the time he befriended Bingley."

"He thought we were too similar in nature," Anne said with a nod.

They fell silent. The ire which had filled him following breakfasting with his father eased. As she had said, Anne was as much a pawn in this cockup as he.

In a calmer and kinder voice, he asked, "Did you have a purpose in seeking me out?"

A hesitant smile lifted the corners of her mouth. "I have heard from my cousins. They are expected to arrive in London in a few weeks, and I want to meet them."

"Anne," Ashton said as he began to shake his head.

"Before you say I should not, you must hear me out. I realize Sam and Tabby are not my cousins, but they are the closest family I have. Papa wanted us to know each other. He hated that Mamma had no other children."

"Can you blame her, Anne?"

A blush covered his cousin's cheeks. "It is not my place to judge either of my parents for their sins. Nor can I blame Sam and Tabby for their parentage." She sat taller, and her pleading eyes met his. "You have Philip and Demi, Ashton. It was always me and Mamma; sometimes Darcy and Philip visited, but that was but once a year."

He closed his eyes and breathed out very slowly. "What do you have in mind?"

"Well," Anne began in a stronger voice, tinged with glee. "Aunt Esther will never allow them to come here, and we cannot meet in public, so I thought Mrs. Darcy could entertain them, and I could arrive unexpectedly."

"And you believe Darcy will allow his wife to invite the Evans sisters to their home?"

She brushed her hand over her skirts. "I doubt he denies her anything. A simple smile from her and he is ready to act the part of footman, maid, or whatever else she desires."

Ashton chuckled despite himself; she was not wrong. "Perhaps," he said as he tamped down his amusement. "But that does not ensure that Darcy would allow two ladies with questionable pedigrees to enter his home."

"Do not speak of them as if they are dogs or horses." Anne sniffed. "Mrs. Darcy is already friends with them. Surely he would not force her to end the relationship."

"Elizabeth is taking her first steps into London society as Mrs. Darcy." He leant forwards in his seat. "She is being scrutinized by everyone who, like your mother, believes she is unworthy of the position. We know she is the best thing to happen to Darcy, but they only see the fact that she is not of the first circles and has taken one of their own from their daughters. Inviting the Evans sisters into her home would be seen as a major misstep, Anne. You cannot ask her to do it."

"But how shall I ever see them otherwise?" Tears glistened in her eyes, and her lip trembled.

With a sigh, Ashton fell back in his seat and considered the situation. "Perhaps," he began, but when he saw his cousin's eager expression, he held up a finger. "I am not saying it will happen, only perhaps."

Anne nodded and appeared to make an effort to conceal her anticipation.

"Elizabeth and her sister frequently visit their aunt in Cheapside. Members of the *ton* would not be witness to any visitors there."

"Ooh." Anne clasped her hands before her. "That would suit perfectly. Do you believe they would agree?"

"We can only ask and see."

Anne leapt from her seat and rushed towards him but stopped short and dipped a curtsey instead of whatever she might have first considered. "Thank you, Ashton." She smiled brightly and rushed from the room.

Poor thing. Anne was not a bad sort; she had simply been sheltered from society. Indeed, though he felt no passion for his cousin, she could be a good match for him if he was not still visited by visions of another.

****

A few days later, Ashton entered his mother's sitting room and bowed to her and his cousin.

"It is a lovely day, do you not think? Quite mild for

winter," he commented as he pointed towards the window. "I believe I should like to take a walk. I wondered if my cousin wished to accompany me."

"What a wonderful idea," his mother replied with narrowed eyes. "I wonder that you did not decide to go out alone."

"A day such as today should be shared. Tomorrow we very well might see freezing rain." He smiled at his mother. "We must take advantage of the chance to breathe fresh air, even if it is London air. It should put a rosy glow in Anne's cheeks. Are you not expecting callers later, Mother?"

"We are indeed." She still watched him suspiciously but finally nodded. "Very well. Anne, you may accompany your cousin, but Ashton—do not overtire her. I will not allow this to be an excuse for her to avoid company."

Ashton bowed and offered his hand to assist Anne to rise from the settee. Once they were in the hall, he asked, "What was that about?"

"Oh, Aunt Esther has invited the Lady Patronesses of Almack's to tea."

A shudder ran through Ashton. "Thank you for the foreknowledge. Once we return from our walk, I shall find business outside the house."

"To where are we walking?" Anne asked as a maid approached with her outerwear.

"Oh, just a short distance. I thought we might visit Darcy and Elizabeth."

Her eyes gleamed, and he quickly shook his head with a glance at the maid. Understanding filled her chocolate eyes and she sniffed. "I suppose that will do."

Ashton offered his arm once she was ready, and they made their way outside. The weather was unseasonably warm, but the wind which sporadically gusted about them held a hint of moisture, making it quite chilly. By the time they had walked the short distance to the Darcy townhouse, they were both anticipating a hot cup of tea.

"Ashton! Anne!" Darcy stared at them from the doorway of his study as they removed their outerwear in his front hall. "Whatever are you doing here?"

"It is good to see you as well, Cousin," Ashton said with a laugh. "We were taking a walk and decided to stop in to see you."

"A walk? Today?" Darcy frowned. "It is January."

The door burst open behind them, and Elizabeth rushed inside with her sister and Mr. Bingley.

"How invigorating!" Elizabeth cried. "Oh, Ashton, Miss de Bourgh, what a surprise. Were you out walking as well? You must come warm yourself with tea and chocolate." She approached her husband and clasped his hand between hers.

"Elizabeth!" He jerked his hand away, then took her hands between his own. "You are like ice. Mrs. Colter!" he called as the housekeeper entered the hall, followed by a maid carrying a tea tray.

"Tea and chocolate, Mrs. Darcy, just as you requested." Mrs. Colter motioned everyone into the nearest drawing room, where a healthy fire burned in the grate.

Ashton, Anne, Miss Bennet, and Bingley took the seats nearest the blaze while Darcy drew Elizabeth onto the settee and continued to rub her hands between his as he blew upon them.

"You should have told me you were going out," he reprimanded his wife.

"You were busy. Besides, you would have only dissuaded us from doing so." Elizabeth laughed as her husband kissed her knuckles.

"You are absolutely correct."

"My husband is becoming a mother hen," she said to the others before meeting his gaze once more. "You must release my hands, sir, or I will be unable to pour our tea." Her brow arched expectantly over her left eye.

With a final kiss to her knuckles, Darcy released her, and Elizabeth began pouring out the steaming brews.

"Miss de Bourgh, why did you allow Ashton to talk you into walking out today?" she asked as she passed the cups around.

"How do you know it was not her idea?" Ashton asked.

No one spoke, but they all looked at him with varying degrees of disbelief on their countenances.

Upon receiving her chocolate, Anne replied, "Ashton and I spoke recently, and I suspected his reason for wanting to walk was to speak to you regarding our plan."

All eyes turned to her, and Ashton groaned.

"Plan?" Darcy asked, his eyes pinning his cousin to his seat. "What plan would that be which involves my wife?"

Elizabeth patted Darcy's knee. "Would anyone like some gingerbread? Cook has outdone herself."

The plate was passed around, and everyone accepted a piece of cake, each exclaiming over it in turn. Darcy's eyes never left Ashton.

"Well?" he asked when everyone was once more enjoying the refreshments.

Ashton had intended on speaking to Elizabeth without Darcy, but his cousin would not allow that to occur now. He resisted the urge to frown at Anne and instead smiled at his hostess.

"Anne has heard from the Evans sisters."

"Oh," Miss Bennet cried. "I am so pleased. What did they have to say?"

"They are coming to town in a few weeks," Anne replied as she looked to Elizabeth.

"No," Darcy said in a low, firm voice.

Elizabeth's hand once more patted his knee. "They have not asked anything, Fitzwilliam."

"Yet."

Ashton cleared his throat. "I have explained to Anne that it would be unthinkable to ask Elizabeth to invite the sisters into your home as she is under such scrutiny from members of the *ton*."

"Good."

"But . . ." Ashton began.

"You were correct in your original thinking, Ashton. My wife is unable to assist Anne in seeing her . . . cousins."

"We are not asking Mrs. Darcy to invite Sam and Tabby here." Anne set her cup aside and folded her hands in her lap. "Ashton suggested Mrs. Darcy's aunt invite them to her home in Cheapside."

Miss Bennet and Elizabeth exchanged a glance.

"I could not invite them, as I do not maintain contact with them. Jane does," Elizabeth replied.

At her words, Darcy visibly relaxed, taking her hand and raising it to his lips as they exchanged a smile.

"I would be pleased to invite them if Aunt Gardiner is in agreement." Jane looked to her sister once more. "We could ask her when we have tea with Miss Carrington."

The smile which had begun to form when Ashton realized the Bennet sisters were willing to assist Anne vanished at the sound of *her* name. But it could not be her; she would be Mrs. Croome now. Even if the bastard had died, she would not revert to her maiden name. It could only be another Carrington, most likely no relation.

"Ashton?"

He looked up to find everyone staring at him. "I beg your pardon, I was woolgathering. What was said?" he asked no one in particular as he was uncertain who had called his name.

All of the ladies had taken on a motherly appearance; their heads were tipped to the side and their brows pinched together. Anne was frowning.

"Aunt Esther will be expecting us," his cousin reminded him.

Taking the opportunity, Ashton leapt to his feet and offered her his arm. "You are correct, dear cousin. Forgive us for bursting in on you, Darcy."

His cousin arose and shrugged. "You need not have dragged poor Anne out in this weather, Ashton. We are to join you for dinner this evening."

"But we could not have spoken then, Darcy," Anne responded. "Aunt Esther and Uncle Henry will be there."

"You are correct, of course," Darcy said with a bow before turning back to Ashton. "I will see you this evening."

Ashton had a sinking feeling Darcy would expect an explanation for his sudden distraction. Upon seeing Anne safely back to Matlock House, he called for a carriage and made his way to White's, hoping for a moment of peace so he could think of an excuse his cousin would not eviscerate.

CHAPTER NINE
MAYFAIR
JANUARY

Ashton felt Darcy's eyes upon him as the ladies slipped from the room and the door closed behind them. In an effort to avoid the coming conversation, he moved to the seat next to his brother.

"I must say, Philip, Miss Bingley is becoming a genuinely amiable young lady. Whatever is your secret, and can you not work your magic on our cousin Anne?"

A smile lit his brother's countenance, surprising Ashton. He truly had not believed Philip's heart to be so engaged.

"It is not me. Miss Bingley has been freed by reconnecting with the Bennet sisters. She frequently bemoans the separation from Miss Bennet as she was the only truly kind young lady at her school. The others were much more ambitious and too impressed by status, particularly their own."

Darcy took the seat across from the brothers, watching Ashton closely. "Elizabeth says little of her time at the abbey, but she always frowns when it is mentioned."

"I disliked the changes which overcame my sister while at school and am pleased to see her becoming the delightful girl I knew beforehand," Bingley said. "I agree that the Bennet sisters began the transition, however, it is the colonel who has made her smile more recently." He raised his glass to the officer.

The conversation was dying off, and Ashton sensed Darcy's intent to change the subject.

"Father," he suddenly cried. "Have the Lords accepted your new measure?"

His cousin frowned but sat back in his seat and silently sipped his port as the earl and Lord Bedlington pontificated on the shortsightedness of their colleagues. By the time the duo had spent their ire, it was time to return to the drawing room. Ashton smirked as he stepped into the hallway.

"Do not think I will forget what I saw," Darcy whispered as he stepped up beside Ashton. "You went positively white this afternoon."

Ashton frowned. Perhaps he had, being faced with a ghost from his past, but he had not realized his reaction had been so visible to his companions. If Elizabeth and Miss Bennet had befriended a Miss Carrington, he would have to become immune to the mention of that name. After all, there was only madness in thinking of *her* when it was an impossibility for anything to become of it.

The door to the drawing room beckoned, and he entered, looking to his mother for another chance to avoid his cousin's inquiries. Unfortunately, she sat silently, an odd expression upon her features.

"Are you well, Mother?" he asked as he bowed over her hand.

Her eyes met his, and he knew the topic of the new Miss Carrington had been covered in his absence. Unable to hold her gaze, he smiled at Anne, who sat beside her. His cousin returned the gesture, and Ashton took the opportunity to claim the seat on her left. It was time he moved beyond this hopeless phantom and bowed to his father's wishes.

"How was your tea this afternoon, Anne?" he asked.

The lady rolled her eyes. "Much like tea with Mamma."

Lady Matlock sniffed. "I daresay some of the ladies would not like that comparison."

"No matter how accurate?" Ashton asked, causing his mother to purse her lips.

"Anne received her voucher," she said in a composed tone. Her arched brow allowed Ashton to anticipate her next comment.

"Then we will be attending this coming Wednesday?" he asked his cousin.

Anne's eyes narrowed. "You will accompany us?"

"Of course. Am I not your escort while you are in town?" he asked with a wink, which appeared to fluster her.

"I did not believe you were pleased with the role." Her eyes darted toward her ladyship and back.

Ashton shrugged. "My knowledge of the character and propensities of many of the gentlemen will ensure you are not pressed to dance with someone unsuitable."

Lady Matlock's surprise at his acquiescence was amusing. Her jaw fell ever so slightly, but she quickly covered it by thanking him for the service. "Though I pride myself on my discernment, your more intimate knowledge of many of the gentlemen of your circles would be greatly appreciated, Ashton. Do you not agree, Anne?"

"My cousin is all politeness."

"Please excuse me; I must speak with Lord Matlock." His mother rose and crossed the room to her husband. The couple proceeded to whisper while casting glances back at Ashton and Anne.

Knowing she had recognized his actions for what they were, a sign of resignation, Ashton turned his attention to his cousin once more. Before he could speak, the lady assaulted him in a harsh whisper.

"Whatever do you think you are doing?"

"I beg your pardon?"

Anne's gaze darted to the married couple watching them closely and back to him. "Your mother and father will believe you intend to court me."

"Yes. Is that not what everyone desires?"

An exasperated sigh escaped her lips. "It most certainly is not—neither by me, nor by you."

"Anne . . ." Ashton turned his back to the rest of the room and reached for her hand, but she snatched it away. "I have come to realize in the past few days that my parents are correct. There is no other lady whom I hold in esteem." *And is available to me.* "We are not too similar, as Uncle Darcy said of you and his son. I believe we could rub along well enough."

Her jaw fell open, and she sat speechless for a moment before finally finding her voice. With a quick glance to the others, she leant forwards, her whisper even harsher than before. "And what if I want more than simply *rubbing along well enough?* I have no desire or ability to be the force Lady Matlock is and must be, therefore, you are the last man in the world whom I could ever be prevailed on to marry."

It was Ashton's turn to gape at her. "I believe that is a bit strongly spoken."

"I do not." She drew a deep breath and ran her hands down her skirt. "Now, I must insist you stop this behaviour and go speak to Darcy. He has been watching you most intently and clearly has something he would like to discuss with you." Without another word, Anne rose from her seat and joined Miss Bennet and Mr. Bingley on the sofa.

As Ashton considered how he had erred with his cousin, he failed to see Darcy's approach until the man settled into the seat vacated by Anne.

"It appears your attempts to stir up distractions have come to an end, so would you prefer to speak here or in the library?"

"I have nothing to say," Ashton replied and turned his attention back to the room. Elizabeth was watching them with intense curiosity while speaking with Demi. Most of the others were absorbed in their own conversations.

"I cannot remember ever seeing you as you were this afternoon. If I am not mistaken, it occurred precisely when Jane mentioned a Miss Carrington."

Ashton held himself in check, determined not to flinch in any manner.

"We met the lady and her brother at dinner at the Gardiners' last week. We intend to introduce him to Mr. Bennet. Nice enough chap, but easily distracted by scholarly pursuits. He is spending a few months in London before returning to America."

Darcy leant closer after Ashton's sudden intake of air.

"His sister has seen to his home while he studied at Oxford."

"Sounds like an interesting fellow," Ashton managed in a dismissive manner before rising. "I believe Mother wishes to speak with me. If you will excuse me." He made his way to his mother's side before Darcy could respond.

"Son," her ladyship said as he approached. "Are you well?"

He smiled. "Of course. Why would you think otherwise?"

"I have never seen Darcy carry a conversation before. It appeared the two of you had switched places." She gave the affected society laugh, proper for every lady. It made his skin crawl.

"He was telling me of encountering a new acquaintance." He frowned. "I believe I should speak with you and Father regarding Anne."

Her eyes brightened. "That is not necessary at the moment, Ashton. We shall simply see how things progress."

"I'm afraid they will not, Mother."

The society mask fell away from her features, and she

frowned at him. "What precisely do you mean?"

With another glance about the room filled with family, Ashton shook his head. "I would prefer not to do it now. Demi and her husband have not been part of previous discussions, and I do not wish to ruin a lovely evening."

Lady Matlock considered his words as she returned her expression to that of the perfect hostess. "I am certain whatever it is can wait until tomorrow when the earl returns from the House of Lords."

With a tip of his head, Ashton agreed. He spent the remainder of the evening avoiding Darcy and his wife and was grateful when he was finally able to find his bed. He hoped the glass of brandy he imbibed would suppress any dreams of stormy grey eyes.

****

"What do you mean she will not marry you?" Lord Matlock demanded.

Ashton took a deep breath and pinched the bridge of his nose. "Anne has no desire to fill Mother's role in society," he explained for the third time.

"But she has not refused *you*, per se." Lady Matlock tapped a finger to her chin as she considered the situation.

"Her exact words were, 'you are the last man in the world whom I could ever be prevailed on to marry.' I will allow you to interpret as you see fit."

His mother turned to her husband. "Demi is fully capable of stepping into my shoes. Ashton's wife would not have to do so."

Lord Matlock turned from his wife back to his son. "The last man in the world? She actually said that?" His surprise seemed to have vanquished his anger.

"Well, she may have taken offense to something else I said." Ashton felt his cheeks warm.

"Which was?"

He looked to the side and murmured, "I thought we

could rub along well enough."

His mother groaned. "Oh, Ashton, tell me you did not . . . No woman wants to feel as though she is better than *nothing.*"

"I no longer wonder why you have not married." His father began to chuckle.

"Henry, this is not a laughing matter," Lady Matlock scolded before turning away, her shoulders shaking suspiciously.

"I do not see the humour in this." Ashton crossed his arms over his chest.

"No," his mother said as she turned about. She appeared about to continue, but she snorted in a most unladylike manner, then clapped a hand over her mouth.

By this time, Lord Matlock was nearly falling out of his chair.

Ashton rose from his seat. "It appears our views of this situation are at odds."

Lady Matlock collapsed into the chair beside her husband, fully engulfed in childlike giggles.

Ashton left the study, passing his brother in the hall. "Do not go in there; it is quite unseemly."

Philip raised his brow, but Ashton continued walking. He was not surprised when the sound of his parents' hysterics grew louder a moment later. Philip's curiosity was bound to get him in trouble one day.

The freezing rain Ashton had predicted had arrived, forcing him to retreat to his room. He sat in a chair by the fireplace and stared at the flames. How had he come to find himself in this position? A laughingstock to his own parents. All because someone mentioned the name Carrington. And, he reminded himself once more, it could not even be *her* as *she* was surely married by now.

There was a quick tap at the door before it opened and his brother entered, biting his lips.

"If you are going to laugh, do it in your own room." Ashton returned to staring into the flames.

Philip took the seat opposite him, and they sat in silence for a few minutes. "You never told me her name," he finally said in a calm, sober voice.

Ashton shook his head. "It is unimportant."

"This new acquaintance of the Gardiners?"

He shrugged. "Perhaps a relative."

"Are you not curious?"

"I am the eldest son of an earl, Philip. My choice must be from the prospects Father sets before me."

"And I never believed he would consider me marrying outside the first circles."

Ashton's head snapped up. "You are truly considering marrying Miss Bingley?"

It was his brother's turn to focus on the mesmerizing flames. "I have reached an age I doubted I would see." His haunted eyes met Ashton's. "I have outlived Uncle Anthony. There are younger men eager for a fight I no longer wish to pursue."

"But if you resign, what would you do?"

Philip leant forwards, resting his elbows on his knees. "Several members of our family have offered me the use of properties. I have contacts with breeders and could make a living in horseflesh."

"Would Miss Bingley be agreed to this?"

"That is the question, is it not?" He sat back in his seat once more. "Father has suggested I make a bid for a seat in the House of Commons."

"Father would." Ashton sighed. "I have put my foot in my mouth several times, so I hope you do not take offense when I say I do not see you being content in politics."

Philip smiled as he shook his head. "I take no offense as you are correct. I do not know how you do it. And Bedlington was clearly born to it." He shook his head again. "I dislike the disguise and the manipulations." He smiled. "A horse will never lie to you."

"If there is ever anything you need . . ." Ashton met and held his brother's gaze.

"I thank you, and I offer the same. I know I have been away more than I have been home, but I am in your corner, no matter the fight."

They continued staring at the flames a few minutes longer before Philip arose with a sigh.

"It is a gloomy day outside. What say I beat you at billiards?"

Ashton grunted. "What say *I* beat *you* at billiards?" he responded as he stood.

Philip shrugged with a mischievous grin. "If you can."

The brothers elbowed each other as they hurried towards the billiard room.

"Where is the good cue?" his brother asked as he looked over the selection. "Have another fit?" He frowned at Ashton.

"Ask Father," Ashton replied as he racked up the balls.

CHAPTER TEN
CHEAPSIDE
3 FEBRUARY

Adsila sat in the dining room window seat, her cup of tea forgotten in her hand as she stared at nothing in particular. Mrs. Darcy, Miss Bennet, and Mrs. Gardiner were expected for tea that very afternoon. Upon waking, she had checked every public room to be certain it was ready to be viewed. They would not enter Tom's study as it remained the disorganized jumble he preferred. A sigh slipped from her lips.

"Adsi?"

She turned to find her brother watching her from the doorway. "Yes, Tom?"

He approached, an unfamiliar frown altering his features. "You have been out of sorts since we dined with the Gardiners. Are you certain you are not ill? Perhaps the ladies should not come today."

"Nonsense!" She forced a smile. "I have been looking forward to seeing them again. Perhaps I am simply in need of fresh country air. London can be so oppressive, particularly in the winter."

"Perhaps." His voice held a hint of doubt.

Thomas took his seat at the table, and Adsila joined him after ringing for their breakfast.

"Have you any plans for today?" she asked as the food was set before them.

"Mr. Bingley and Mr. Darcy have invited me to their club, therefore I shall be out of your way while the ladies are visiting."

She nodded, a slight sense of relief calming her agitated nerves. Perhaps with his absence, she would have the courage to ask after Lord Grayson. Not that it mattered. They were from different worlds, and she would be returning home soon. Just a few more months now. Then she would be back in Virginia with her mother and would be able to cry away her heartbreak. She huffed at her foolishness, drawing her brother's attention once more.

"Adsi?"

"Nothing, Tom, I was simply thinking of something I read last night."

She turned her attention to her meal and ate silently. Her brother finished eating, picked up a muffin and his cup of tea after she refreshed it, and kissed her forehead.

"Should you need me, I will be in my study," he said but he did not leave.

Adsila looked up to find him studying her. "Yes?"

"You are certain you are well?" He appeared discomfited. "I only ask because you appear pale, and your eyes are . . . troubled."

She took a sip of tea and settled her cup in the saucer. "You know I dislike London. I suppose I am simply anxious to be travelling home."

He frowned. "Is that truly what you desire, Adsi?" He set his cup down and regained his seat. "Father expects me home as I am to take my place at his side, but . . ." He shook his head and did not finish.

"What is it?"

"I just never . . . you never seemed to *fit* back home.

You are like a tropical plant growing out of a cold mountain crevice. I marvel that you survived as long as you did."

Her shoulders lifted. "And you thought I would thrive here in England?"

His hand covered hers. "I hoped you would find a gardener who would know what to do to make you happy."

"I believe I hoped for that as well." Her voice was soft and held a hint of sadness.

He smiled and patted her hand. "Well, we have a few months yet. Who's to say you won't?"

Adsila stood and kissed his cheek. "Thank you, Tom, but I am certain I will be accompanying you on that journey home."

She left the room before he could see the tears filling her eyes and climbed the stairs to her room. Once the door was closed, she leant her forehead against the solid oak and allowed one or two tears to escape.

"I did find him, or thought I might have, but he was beyond my reach."

****

By the time the Darcy carriage stopped before their home, Adsila had banished her melancholy and was truly looking forward to having tea with Mrs. Gardiner and her nieces. Tom joined her in the drawing room as the ladies entered, followed by Mr. Darcy and Mr. Bingley.

"Have no fear, Miss Carrington," Mrs. Darcy said as she rose from her curtsey. "The gentlemen are simply here to collect your brother. They will return to claim us after they do whatever it is that gentlemen do when we are not about."

"We count the moments until we can be in your presence once more, my dear." Mr. Darcy kissed his wife's hand, causing a blush to cover her cheeks. "Shall we, gentlemen?"

Once they were gone, Miss Bennet teased her sister. "You have met your match, Lizzy. Darcy is learning how to tease you back."

A brilliant smile covered the lady's face, but she turned to Adsila instead of her sister. "I am so pleased to see you again, Miss Carrington. I have learned that we have friends in common."

"Oh?" Adsila managed as she clasped her hands behind her back so no one saw them shaking.

"Yes. We had a family dinner last week at Matlock House. I understand you have been there."

The ladies settled into their seats, and Adsila acknowledged that she had. "I was there for Lady Demetria's wedding breakfast."

"She said as much. Demi and her mother remembered you fondly."

"They did?" she asked, so startled she was unable to hide her disbelief.

Mrs. Darcy nodded. "Oh yes, they both said you were lovely, and they were sorry they had not gotten to know you better."

"Oh." She smoothed her hands upon her skirt. "I thought much the same of them. I saw Lady Demetria several times as she was close friends with Lady Gertrude, the daughter of my mother's friend." She swallowed and pressed onward though her mind told her it was foolish. "She and her brother, Lord Grayson, would visit for tea."

Her guest's eyes sparkled as though they had located a lost treasure. "I wondered if you might have known Ashton."

"Briefly. Is he . . . well?"

"For the most part. He has appeared somewhat out of sorts lately, but I am certain he will rally."

The party looked to their hostess expectantly, but Adsila's mind kept repeating Mrs. Darcy's last comment. Finally, she was able to push it to the side to consider later and asked, "Would you like the tour first or tea?"

The ladies decided upon the tour, and Adsila showed them about. All the furnishings had come with the house and were a bit outdated. Though the landlord had given them permission to refurbish items as necessary, Adsila had not felt it her place, and Tom barely noticed a chair until he sat upon it. She told her guests as much.

"Well, if you ever change your mind, I am certain Mr. Gardiner would be pleased to welcome you to his warehouses." Mrs. Gardiner settled onto the faded sofa in the drawing room. "He has just received several bolts of material which would look lovely in this room."

"Oh, yes!" cried Mrs. Darcy. "Why, you must join me on Thursday. I have arranged to meet with my uncle and plunder his wares for my bedroom and sitting room."

Adsila laughed as she imagined the spirited Mrs. Darcy ransacking Mr. Gardiner's warehouses. "You paint a picture I must witness."

Miss Bennet nodded. "My sister never liked shopping until she had a bottomless purse."

"That is not true." Mrs. Darcy's eyes sparkled with mischief. "I never liked shopping with Mamma." She dipped her head towards Adsila. "The woman is far too enamoured of lace for my liking."

Looking over the lady's ensemble, Adsila realized it was rather plain considering her standing in society, but the elegance of the materials and their patterns disguised this from the passing eye.

"I have never seen you anything less than beautiful, Mrs. Darcy." She too leant forwards in a conspiratorial manner. "I have never preferred an abundance of lace. My mother's friend pressed it upon me, but once I was away from her home, I removed the majority of it."

Mrs. Darcy laughed as she clasped Adsila's hand. "I have found a kindred spirit. You must call me Elizabeth or Lizzy, as my family does."

A warmth filled Adsila's chest. "I would be pleased to

do so if you will call me Adsila."

"I have longed to do so since I first heard it," Mrs. Darcy—Elizabeth—confided. "Jane, will you join us? You will have to redecorate the mistress's chambers at Bingley's home."

A blush covered Miss Bennet's cheeks. "No, I think not. Charles and I have decided to focus on Netherfield Park for the time being. We will purchase what we require in Meryton."

"Very well," Elizabeth replied in a teasing tone. "Adsila and I will simply have to purchase enough to cover your absence."

"Lizzy," Mrs. Gardiner scolded lovingly. "Do not make Miss Carrington feel as though she must purchase from your uncle's warehouses."

Elizabeth squeezed Adsila's hand. "I am certain she would not allow me to do so." She turned her sparkling eyes upon her new friend. "I give you permission to speak your mind and berate me for becoming anything remotely resembling my mother or your mother's friend."

Laughter bubbled up within her, and Adsila allowed it to flow freely. "How I wish we had met when I was last in London. Perhaps I would not have grown to dislike it so."

"Dislike London? Why, there are so many magical places here. Do you not agree, Jane?"

"There are," Miss Bennet began in a judicial tone. "However, I can understand how Miss Carrington may have felt discomfort when dealing with members of the *ton.*"

"Miss Bennet," Adsila began hesitantly, "will you not also call me Adsila?"

"Yes, you must, Jane. We must consider Adsila as another Bennet sister since her family is so far away."

Miss Bennet smiled warmly. "I would be pleased to do so if you will call me Jane. Lizzy is correct; you require family in England, and the Bennets love to adopt others into our clan. Mamma will be so pleased to meet you. You must come to Hertfordshire with us in a few weeks for my wedding."

"What a wonderful idea." Elizabeth clapped her hands together. "You and your brother can stay at Netherfield Park. Mr. Bingley will be pleased to host you."

"Oh, we could not. Will you not have family there?"

"But I have already stated you *are* family, and this will give you an opportunity to leave London for a few days."

"Please say you will, Adsila," Jane said with an earnest expression.

Reluctantly, Adsila nodded. "I will discuss it with Tom and see what he says."

The ladies finished their tea just as they heard the front door open and the gentlemen return. They stood to greet their menfolk and were pleased to see their smiles.

"Adsi, you will not guess," Tom said as he squeezed his sister's hand. "I was telling Darcy and Bingley how you disliked London in winter and they suggested we accompany them to Hertfordshire for Bingley's wedding."

"Well," Elizabeth said with a laugh. "It is settled then, as Jane suggested the same."

"I suppose it is." Adsila felt her cheeks warm.

The ladies received their outerwear, and Tom and Adsila walked them to the door.

"I will call for you Thursday at noon," Elizabeth said before embracing her hostess. "We shall have such fun."

Mr. Darcy handed his wife and her aunt into the carriage while Mr. Bingley saw to his betrothed. Both waved before they entered the carriage and it rolled away.

Tom closed the door and followed Adsila back to the drawing room.

"If the *ton* is anything like those fine individuals, I am surprised you disliked it."

"If I had met individuals like our new friends, I would not have." Adsila hummed a tune as she fell into her seat. "Did you enjoy your time at the gentlemen's club?"

"I did. I met a Colonel Fitzwilliam, Darcy's cousin,

who is courting Bingley's sister. Nice fellow, much like Bingley. His brother was to join us as well, but he sent a footman with his apologies." He tilted his head as he observed her. "You are in a far better state of mind. I am pleased you have made friends, Adsi."

"Yes, I am as well." As the words left her mouth, she realized how true they were.

CHAPTER ELEVEN
CHEAPSIDE
6 FEBRUARY

Elizabeth and Adsila walked arm in arm down Gracechurch Street. Their excursion to Mr. Gardiner's warehouses had been quite successful. Though she had not planned to do so, Adsila selected a few fabrics to re-cover furniture in the drawing room. Mr. Gardiner suggested a man who could do the work for a reasonable price and return the pieces in a timely manner. What Elizabeth purchased would have been enough to re-cover everything on the first floor of Adsila's townhouse, though it was meant for only a bedroom and sitting room at Darcy House. In addition to the material, she had found wallcoverings which gave the feel of being in a garden.

"Mr. Darcy will be pleased the shopping is finished," Elizabeth said as they made their way towards the Gardiners' home. "Once everything is in the housekeeper's hands, I will stop asking what he prefers." Elizabeth's laugh was light and pleasing.

As they approached, a grand coach pulled away from the curb, and Elizabeth tugged upon Adsila's arm.

"Oh, Miss de Bourgh must have arrived."

Adsila's chest suddenly felt as though it were clenched within a vice. "Miss de Bourgh?" she managed in a soft whisper.

"Yes, did I not tell you?" Elizabeth shook her head. "I was so excited about our plans, I must have forgotten. Jane and I attended school with two members of her family. She has not seen them in some time, and we arranged for them to meet at our aunt's home."

"Why would they not meet at Matlock House?" Adsila asked in a suspicious tone.

Elizabeth's cheeks pinked a bit more than what was caused by the chill February air. "Lady Matlock is not in favour of Miss de Bourgh furthering the acquaintance. Ashton suggested they meet here so none of the *ton* would hear of it."

Adsila stopped walking, her gaze locked on the front door of the Gardiners' home. "Ashton? Lord Grayson?"

"Yes." Elizabeth's countenance was bright and expectant. "I believe he was to escort her here today."

With a supreme effort, Adsila forced herself to relax. "Then it will be a family reunion. I should return home." She slipped her arm from Elizabeth's. "I thank you for thinking of me and extending the invitation to join you. It has been a joy seeing you today. Please do not concern yourself with me. I will walk the rest of the way home; I find I require a bit of exercise."

She was about to turn away when the door of the townhouse opened and Mrs. Gardiner called out to the ladies.

"There you are! We thought you were still shopping." She laughed and waved them forwards. "The ladies are within becoming reacquainted. You are just in time for tea."

Adsila attempted to escape once more, but neither Elizabeth nor her aunt would hear her excuses. Finally, she accepted her fate and entered the house. Her hands shook as she removed her gloves, bonnet, and pelisse. Mrs. Gardiner and her niece led the way to the parlour, where they could hear ladies' voices. She delayed her entry as long as possible, and when she finally entered the room, her gaze searched every corner, but there was no gentleman present. The sinking feeling in her stomach took her by surprise.

She was introduced to the ladies, took a seat, and accepted a cup of tea. There was a certain similarity between Miss de Bourgh and her cousins, though their dresses were of a decidedly inferior material to that of the heiress. It soon became clear that these ladies were not relatives of the Matlocks, but of Miss de Bourgh's father. The sisters blushed frequently and spoke in softer tones but appeared delighted to be in company with Miss de Bourgh again. She, on the other hand, ignored everyone else in the room and made demand upon demand on her relatives to tell her everything they had done since the three had last met some thirteen years prior.

Elizabeth excused herself from the group and took a seat beside Adsila.

"Though I attended school with the Evans sisters, it has been over a decade, and we have not kept in touch. They correspond with Jane once or twice a year, which was how Miss de Bourgh was able to reach out to them once more."

Adsila nodded and continued to sip her tea as she observed the others. Miss de Bourgh was petite, her skin holding that translucence which spoke of years spent inside away from the sun. Her speech, though cultured, was that of a girl half the lady's age: demanding with the ability to turn petulant when told she was incorrect or should not speak so. A child in a woman's body given every advantage but allowed, possibly encouraged, to be proud and conceited.

Unbeknownst to her, a frown had crept over Adsila's countenance as she watched the lady. Before she could consider the propriety of it, she turned to Elizabeth and asked in a low voice, "Who was Lady Matlock pressing to marry Miss de Bourgh?"

"Lord Grayson," Elizabeth replied before turning her gaze back to the others. "Though they are friendly towards one another, I do not believe it would be a wise match."

"Why not? They are both of a noble line. I am certain society would approve." Adsila hoped her friend did not hear the bitterness in her tone.

"Perhaps, but I believe they would be strangers at best." Elizabeth shrugged. "Maybe I am prejudiced by my own happiness, but I have never agreed with marriages of convenience."

"You have been blessed to find a husband who cares little for society's opinion."

Adsila swallowed around the lump which had formed in her throat. Her vision blurred as she suddenly felt overcome by a longing she had suppressed for so many years. Turning away from her friend, she coughed into her handkerchief and dabbed her eyes.

"Forgive me," she said as she turned back. "I fear I am not feeling myself. Pray excuse me. I believe it best if I return home."

The concern overtaking Elizabeth's features nearly undid Adsila again. "If you insist, allow me to call my carriage for you. You should not walk if you are ill."

Adsila shook her head. "The fresh air might bring improvement."

"If we were in Hertfordshire, I might agree with you."

Elizabeth rose and left the room before Adsila could stop her, and Mrs. Gardiner took her niece's seat.

"Would you like to refresh yourself?" her hostess asked.

A glance told her Jane had watched the exchange as concern was also etched upon her features. The Evans sisters looked her way when possible but were still undergoing Miss de Bourgh's interrogation. That lady was oblivious to the scene playing out across the room.

"Yes, please," Adsila agreed and rose to follow Mrs. Gardiner.

Once in the hall, Elizabeth joined them to report the carriage would be ready in a few minutes.

"I was just escorting Miss Carrington to your uncle's study. Please have Mercy bring a cool cloth."

"Pray, forgive me for being such a bother," Adsila whispered to Mrs. Gardiner as they entered the masculine room.

"Nonsense," the matron said, pressing her guest into a wingback chair. She opened a cut-crystal decanter and poured a bit of the crimson liquid into a glass. After adding a touch of water, she offered the wine to Adsila. "Sip this."

The initial burn forced the tears from her eyes, but the warmth which filled her chest had a calming effect. She sat back in the seat and took another sip.

"I do not know what came over me," Adsila whispered into the glass.

Mrs. Gardiner patted her shoulder. "Whatever it was, you will feel better once you are able to lie down. Are you certain you wish to return home? You could rest in our guestroom."

"Thank you, but it is not far to my home, as you know. I am certain nothing dire will befall me before arriving there." She sipped the wine once more and handed the glass to her hostess. "You have provided precisely what was needed. I thank you again."

She slowly rose from the chair, bracing herself with a hand upon the back of it as Elizabeth entered the room. "Please give my apologies to the ladies."

"Of course," Mrs. Gardiner replied with a frown.

"The carriage is ready, if you are certain you should leave," Elizabeth said as she held out the dampened cloth.

Adsila accepted it and pressed it to her heated cheeks and most likely puffy eyes. The coolness finished what the wine had begun, and she once more felt sufficiently herself to give her friends a tentative smile.

"You have been so wonderful to me, but I would simply like to return home. I will rest and am certain I will feel well by this evening."

Taking Adsila's hand, Elizabeth walked with her to the front of the house. Once they were properly attired, she slipped an arm about Adsila's waist and aided her to the waiting carriage.

"I thank you for your attentions, Elizabeth," Adsila said with a small smile, "but you need not leave the others on my account."

"Nonsense," her friend replied. "I cannot help but think this is my doing. Did I say something to discompose you?"

Not trusting her voice, Adsila shook her head and patted her friend's hand.

"Very well," Elizabeth reluctantly said. "I see you are determined."

Adsila hugged Elizabeth, whispering her gratitude before allowing the footman to hand her into the carriage. Her friend remained as the carriage drew away, a troubled expression drawing her brows together.

The journey was blessedly brief, and Adsila, by biting the inside of her lip until it bled, was able to hold her emotions at bay until her bedroom door once more closed behind her. Tearing her gloves from her hands and the bonnet from her head, she raced for her bed, dropping upon it and clutching her pillow to her chest as unrestrained sobs tore at her throat.

****

Sometime later she awoke, noting the fading light outside her window. Rising, Adsila removed her pelisse and day dress before dipping a cloth into the washbasin and cleansing her face, arms, and chest. A glance in the mirror confirmed that her eyes were swollen, so she wet the cloth again and returned to her bed, placing the blessedly cool cloth over her eyes. After a few minutes, a soft knock forced her to sit up as she called for the individual to enter.

"Forgive me, miss," Sinead said as she entered the room. "Maimeo told me ta check on ye as your maid has the day off. She was worried when ye returned earlier than expected." She set a small tray with a cup of steaming tea and a plate of biscuits upon the side table. "This will refresh ye, miss."

A smile tugged at Adsila's lips. "Thank you, Sinead. You and your grandmother are very kind." She sipped the tea but winced when the heat touched her injured lip. Returning the cup to its saucer, she sat a bit straighter. "What time is it?"

"Near dinner, miss. Will ye be joining Mr. Carrington?"

Missing dinner would only upset her brother, so Adsila nodded. The maid gathered her discarded clothing and entered the dressing room, returning with Adsila's favourite evening gown. The material was older, but it was soft and felt like a warm hug when she wore it. She smiled, being cautious of her lip.

Once Adsila was dressed and seated so Sinead could brush and set her hair, the maid dipped the cloth in the cold water and handed it to her mistress. The coolness felt good upon Adsila's eyes, and she set her elbows on the table before settling her chin in the palms of her hands. The maid hummed a soft tune which had a lulling effect upon Adsila.

"There ye are, miss," Sinead said in a soft voice as she laid a hand upon Adsila's shoulder.

Reluctantly, Adsila lifted her head to stare at her reflection in the mirror. Her hair glistened in the candlelight, and the whites of her eyes seemed a bit brighter, her tears having washed away the red from sleepless nights. The skin about them remained a touch puffy, but overall she believed her brother would not be *as* concerned as he might have been seeing her upon her arrival.

"You have worked a miracle, Sinead." Adsila smiled at the young girl who grinned back at her.

"Ye're beautiful, Miss. It makes the work easy." With that, she gathered the tray she had brought earlier and slipped from the room.

Adsila looked into the mirror once more and sighed. If only they could leave for home sooner. She did not regret meeting and befriending Elizabeth, Jane, and Mrs. Gardiner, but hearing the viscount's name and mentions of his activities might destroy her a bit at a time. She shook her head and squared her shoulders. Tom wanted to enjoy the London season before returning home. Perhaps he might meet his future bride.

She rubbed her tongue over her tender lip as she wondered what would happen if he delayed their journey in order to court a young lady. Adsila could not sail alone, but she disliked the idea of lingering in England longer than necessary.

The clock in the downstairs' hall chimed the hour, and she gathered a shawl about her. With one last glance in the looking glass, she made certain a contented smile set upon her lips before she went below. She ignored the storm brewing in her grey eyes.

CHAPTER TWELVE
HERTFORDSHIRE
10 FEBRUARY

"That little rise," Elizabeth said as she pointed out the carriage window, "is Oakham Mount. It is one of my favourite places to walk."

Adsila turned back from the window in time to see Elizabeth wink at her husband, who sat across from her. She suspected the location held special memories for the couple.

"The countryside is lovely, Mrs. Darcy." Tom continued looking out the window. "It reminds me a bit of home. Does it not, Adsi?"

"Virginia is such a vastly varying state, I suppose it is similar to some parts of it."

"Oh, do tell us of it. It borders the ocean, does it not?" Elizabeth asked as she took Adsila's hand and squeezed it.

"It does," Tom responded. "But there are also mountains as well as farmlands. No matter your desire, I am certain you could find it somewhere in Virginia," he said with pride.

"Do you miss it?" she asked, this time looking directly

at her friend.

"Tom does, I am certain." Adsila gazed out the window at the passing scenery. "I suppose I miss the mountains. What I have seen of England in recent years has been a bit too tame for my tastes."

"You would love Derbyshire," Mr. Darcy replied. "If not for family demands, Elizabeth and I would already be there." He glanced at the dormant fields. "Pemberley, our home there, is most likely covered in snow."

"It sounds lovely. Though I dislike that you have not been able to visit your new home," Adsila said as she smiled at Elizabeth, "I am pleased you were in London so we could become friends." She turned towards Mr. Darcy. "I believe I travelled through Derbyshire many years ago on my way to Yorkshire."

"Depending on your route, it is possible."

"Are you certain you wish to return home so soon?" Elizabeth asked. "I would love for you to visit us at Pemberley."

Adsila laughed. "So soon? It is still several months away."

Tom grinned at her. "I am pleased you changed your mind, Adsi. I believe this is the happiest I have seen you since my arrival in England."

"Changed your mind?" Elizabeth asked with wide eyes. "Were you considering not accompanying us?"

A warm blush covered Adsila's cheeks as she frowned at her brother. Before she could respond, Elizabeth asked, "Was it due to your sudden illness at Aunt Gardiner's?"

Her throat constricted a bit, and Adsila simply nodded before clearing it. "I did not wish to cause you further worry should I have a similar episode. It is nothing serious; I was simply struck by a moment of wistfulness, but it passed as I suspected it would." She once more turned to stare out the window.

"I am no stranger to wistfulness, as you call it," Mr. Darcy said to the suddenly silent coach. "I believe it comes from being on one's own for too long."

Adsila turned back to see him looking at his wife with affection. "Yes, you are probably correct. Being separated from loved ones can make you feel alone in a crowded room."

Once more, Elizabeth looked to her with only concern in her features. "I will cease pressing you to stay beyond the time you have set and will not keep you from your family longer than necessary."

"Please, dear friend," Adsila said with a smile. "Do not believe you have caused any of my distress. Quite the opposite, actually; you have brought me joy when I doubted I would find it in London."

The carriage turned into a drive, and Elizabeth's smile grew broader. "I can only hope you feel the same after you meet my family."

Amusement danced in Mr. Darcy's dark eyes as he reached to take his wife's hand. "I shall not ask if you believe they will be here to greet us this time."

The carriage rolled to a stop, and the doors of the manor house opened to allow for a sea of ladies to flow onto the steps. Elizabeth laughed as she squeezed her husband's hand.

"I will never doubt you, my love." The gentleman kissed her fingers and stepped out of the carriage when the footman opened the door. "I thought we were to stop at Netherfield, not Longbourn," he called up to the driver.

"Mr. Darcy, do not be silly." The eldest lady fluttered her lacy handkerchief at him. "Help my Lizzy from that massive carriage of yours."

"At once, Mother Bennet," he replied with a bow before turning back to hand his wife out of the equipage. "Carrington, it is for your own sake I hand my wife out before allowing you to stretch your legs. Mrs. Bennet can smell a bachelor at a hundred paces."

Elizabeth lightly slapped her husband's shoulder. "Fitzwilliam, you will frighten the poor man." She turned to look at her friends, her cheeks becoming rosy though the cold air had not yet nipped them. "I did tell you my family can be a bit excitable," she offered before allowing Mr. Darcy to assist her from the carriage.

A barrage of female voices began, all speaking over one another as the group encircled Elizabeth and led her into the house. Mr. Bingley appeared at Mr. Darcy's side, shaking his hand as he called out to Tom that it was safe to emerge. Tom joined the gentlemen outside the carriage before reaching back for his sister. With a quick intake and release of air, Adsila accepted her brother's hand and joined them outside.

The manor house sat upon a slight rise, and the trees which most likely shaded it in the summer did nothing to block the gusts of cold air in the winter. The foursome hurried to enter the home before they might be blown away.

"Welcome to Netherfield Park," Mr. Bingley said with a bow once the doors closed out the cold. "My sister, the Bennet ladies, and Miss Darcy and her companion have arranged tea for you in the drawing room, but if you would prefer to refresh yourselves, I will have Mrs. Nicholls show you to your rooms."

Adsila was torn between the choices until Mr. Darcy offered a compromise.

"Perhaps it would be best if we joined the ladies long enough for introductions so we can allow Elizabeth the opportunity to refresh herself."

All agreed and followed their host towards the voices, which grew louder upon their approach.

Elizabeth remained in the midst of them, laughing and hugging each in turn. "Oh, you must meet our friends," she cried as she spotted the new arrivals.

Breaking away from her sisters, she took Adsila's hand and drew her forwards. "This is Miss Adsila Carrington from Virginia in America and her brother, Mr. Thomas Carrington. They have been in England several years and will be returning home this summer but have not yet seen our part of the country."

Elizabeth introduced the ladies, and everyone offered the proper obeisance.

"Adsila, what a lovely name," Mrs. Bennet exclaimed as she moved closer. "The two of you have been here for years without your family?"

"Adsi actually came a year before me," Tom offered.

"Why, you must have been ever so young. Did you travel alone?" The matron took her hand and led her to a sofa, drawing Adsila down next to her. "Have you a large family? You must have missed them dearly."

"My father accompanied me when I first arrived in England, but I stayed with my mother's friend until Tom came to attend university."

"Which one?" An older gentleman asked from the doorway.

"Mr. Carrington, Miss Carrington, this is my father, Mr. Thomas Bennet," Elizabeth said before she placed a kiss on his cheek. "He was most likely hiding in the library until the noise died down."

The man smiled fondly at his daughter as he patted her hand upon his arm and then returned his gaze to Tom.

"Oxford, sir."

"Ho, ho," the man cried as he grasped Tom's hand. "Well done, Lizzy, you have brought me another true scholar as opposed to these Cambridge men who have infiltrated my family."

Mr. Darcy and Mr. Bingley did not appear to take offense. The party settled down, and Adsila soon realized Mrs. Bennet was looking at her expectantly. Thinking back, she realized she had not answered all the lady's questions.

"Tom and I have only one more surviving sibling. Arthur is but twelve years old." She looked to her brother, but he appeared distracted and was not attending her conversation. "I am certain our mother will not allow him from her side when it is time for his schooling. He will have to attend the College of William and Mary, for I fear she will not even allow him to leave Virginia. Is that not correct, Tom?"

Her brother startled and turned to meet her gaze. "Of course," he replied, though she was certain he had no idea to what he agreed.

"And you are returning to Virginia?" one of Elizbeth's sisters asked Adsila's brother.

"Yes," he replied. "As the oldest, it is time I returned to assist my father."

"Do you own slaves?" the plainest of the sisters asked.

"No," the siblings replied in unison.

"Our father freed the few we owned when he inherited. We were blessed that most wished to remain with us," Tom explained. "Our land is set up similarly to an English estate, with tenant farms."

"Are their Indians in Virginia?" the first young lady asked.

Glancing at his sister, Tom smiled. "There are, though not as many as there once were. Our great grandmother was Cherokee, as is the name Adsila. It means blossom."

"You're Indian?" the girl's eyes widened, and she stepped closer. "How fascinating! Do you live near them?"

Tom shrugged. "The tribe has moved, so we rarely saw them before coming to England."

"Lydia, leave the man be," Mrs. Bennet said, drawing shocked stares from her eldest daughters. "I am certain he has no interest in being interrogated."

"I do not mind, madam. It has been some time since I have spoken of home." His gaze returned to the young lady before him. "Ask me what you wish, Miss Lydia. I am at your service."

The girl blushed and bit her lower lip.

"Have we time to refresh ourselves before tea?" Elizabeth suddenly asked.

"Oh dear, how silly of us." Mrs. Bennet patted Adsila's

hand. "I am certain you must all wish to wash off the dust, and here we are asking a hundred questions."

Miss Bingley, who Adsila had not had the opportunity to meet while in London, stepped forwards. "If you will follow me, Mr. Carrington, Miss Carrington. Elizabeth, you and Darcy are in the rooms you used before."

They followed the hostess from the room and had begun up the stairs when they heard a feminine voice say, "But he is so handsome, Mamma."

A glance at her brother revealed a blush covering his countenance. He met his sister's gaze for a minute before turning away to hide his smile.

"You have an admirer, Mr. Carrington," Elizabeth said. "I fear it is only the prospect of her daughter travelling so far which keeps my mother from speaking vivaciously on the merits of marriage."

"You are saying that if Pemberley had been in Ireland, perhaps . . ." Mr. Darcy began, leaving the end unsaid.

"Oh no, sir. I am her least favourite daughter, or I *was* until I married a wealthy gentleman." The couple giggled as they turned to the right at the top of the stairs.

Miss Bingley shook her head as she looked after them. "It amazes me when I hear him tease her." She turned back to the siblings. "Mr. Darcy was always such a quiet, proper gentleman before he married Lizzy. No one who sees him now believes he is the same man." She opened a door to the left. "Miss Carrington, you will be in here. Mr. Carrington, you are just across the hall. We have other guests arriving in the coming days, including my sister and her husband." Her cheeks reddened. "I will apologize in advance for anything she might say or do. Lizzy told me your first foray into London society was . . . unfulfilling, Miss Carrington. I fear Louisa's ambition in life is to be a revered member of the first circle."

"I am certain one such person in a sea of companionable individuals will not affect me, Miss Bingley. You have no reason to apologize for her."

Their hostess smiled and dipped a quick curtsey. "If there is anything you require, simply ring and it will be provided. Tea will be served in half an hour." She glanced at the hall clock and laughed. "Forgive me, we spent more time speaking than I thought. The tea will be brought out in one quarter of an hour, but do not rush on our account."

The siblings thanked her and entered their rooms. Adsila found herself humming as she allowed the maid to assist her with changing her clothing. She was suddenly very pleased that she had agreed to come to Hertfordshire.

CHAPTER THIRTEEN
MAYFAIR
10 FEBRUARY

"What do you mean you aren't attending Bingley's wedding?" Philip demanded as he followed Ashton into the library.

"I should remain in London and escort Anne to events." He poured a finger then two of brandy and sat in his favourite chair before the fire. It seemed he could not get warm.

"Bingley is expecting you."

"He will be so busy following his bride about, he will not notice my absence." He drained the glass and debated rising for another, but he could not find the strength.

Philip dropped into the seat across from him. "I do not understand you. First you are to meet us at White's, and instead you send a footman with your excuses; now you are begging off from attending Bingley's wedding. I know you enjoy Hertfordshire more than parading about in town. There is something disturbing you, and I will not leave until I know what it is."

With a heavy sigh, Ashton bowed his head. His brother

had that look of determination—a mixture of Fitzwilliam stubbornness and military bearing—which proved he meant what he said. If Ashton wanted time alone to sulk, it would be at the price of telling Philip the details of his heartbreak.

"I was on my way to meet you when I ran into Croome." The man's name was spoken like a curse.

Philip frowned, obviously not understanding the connection.

Ashton pushed out of his seat and paced the length of the room. "Lord Carlisle had selected Croome to marry *her*," he spat out. "The man is disgusting, leering at ladies as I asked after his wife. So pleased with himself that she had given him a son and another child was on the way. It made me ill."

The look of pity on his brother's face angered Ashton.

"I am not going to Hertfordshire, and that is final. God bless Darcy and Elizabeth, but I cannot bear another moment of their bliss. And Bingley is simply nauseating." He grabbed his glass and returned to the decanter. "Leave me to the society I must court here in London and do not force me to witness what I cannot have," he muttered before draining the glass again.

Philip watched him, his finger rubbing back and forth beneath his lower lip. Finally, he rested his elbows upon his knees and indicated the chair Ashton had abandoned.

"I beg you sit as I have something I must say."

After refilling his glass again, Ashton reluctantly returned to his seat.

This time, Philip stood and began pacing before finally stopping before the hearth and staring into the flames.

"I was told not to tell you, but it is obvious all must be revealed." He turned his back on the fire and met his brother's gaze. "Your lady has been invited to Bingley's wedding."

A surge of joy flooded Ashton's chest only to drain into his gut as a sickening sludge. "How would that even be possible? And, more importantly, what is it to me? She is a married woman beyond my reach."

Philip ran a hand the length of his face and dropped back into his seat. "No, she is not." He leant forwards, one leg bent, his hand leaning upon the knee. "When Elizabeth was here for dinner, she told Demi about her new friend. Demi confirmed it was the lady you had once found so interesting. She is not married. She has been keeping house for her brother while he attended university."

Silence enveloped them as Ashton frowned, trying to comprehend his brother's words.

"I do not understand," he finally said. "Croome spoke of his wife."

"What precisely was said?" Philip asked with an amused smirk.

Ashton thought carefully, the brandy blurring the edges of his memory. He had been on Bond Street, wasting time until he was to meet the other gentlemen, when he had seen Croome approaching.

"Mr. Croome," Ashton said in as civil a tone as he could manage. "May I ask after your wife? Is she enjoying the countryside?"

The man chuckled. "She is, indeed. I am surprised you have not yet married, Grayson. It is an amazingly liberating experience. My wife has supplied me with an heir and is currently with child again. If this one is also a boy, I believe that will do. She is comfortable in the country, and I prefer the city. The rules which apply to the bachelor are useless upon the married man. Yes, yes, liberating is what it is."

He eyed a passing young lady who hurried her step to rejoin her friends.

"Liberating," Croome said in a softer, more sickening manner.

"Your wife has no interest in accompanying you to

London?" Ashton calmly asked, though his stomach felt as though it pirouetted within him.

"No! She is a country girl at heart, as I prefer." He leant towards Ashton, his lips curling in a disturbing grin. "Country girls are hardy breeders. Perhaps we will have another, but it is not necessary once we have two sons." He elbowed Ashton. "An heir and a spare, as they say."

"Yes," Ashton muttered, turning away to hide his disgust. "Give my regards to Mrs. Croome," he said before briefly dipping his head.

Croome had not risen from his bow before Ashton was on his way. A sudden illness had taken him, and he told his footman to make his excuses to Philip, Darcy, and Bingley before he climbed into his carriage and returned home.

"So neither of you mentioned her name."

"I called her Mrs. Croome." Ashton squinted at his brother. Was the man daft? He could not very well call another man's wife by her Christian name, and there would be no reason to call her by her maiden name.

Philip shrugged. "I repeat, it is not her."

"Not who?" Anne asked as she entered the room.

"Elizabeth's new friend," Philip supplied, the damning smirk tugging at his lips once more.

"Oh, I met her. Rude thing. A Miss Carlson, I believe. She entered with Elizabeth, then left with Mrs. Gardiner without excusing herself. She was not with them when they returned." Anne took a seat on the sofa and looked at them expectantly.

With sighs, the gentlemen rose from their seats to join her.

"It is not her," Ashton muttered.

"Anne," Philip said in a patronizing tone. "Do you not mean Miss Carrington?"

Their cousin shrugged. "I need you both to help me persuade Aunt Esther to allow me to return to Kent."

The brothers exchanged a quizzical look before returning their attention to Anne.

"Why?" Ashton asked suspiciously.

"Mamma has done something, and I must question her directly." She folded her arms before her and frowned.

"What has Lady Catherine done?" Philip asked.

With a huff, Anne replied, "Sam, Tabby, and their mother never received their inheritance."

Ashton lowered his head and pinched the bridge of his nose. "How do you know they were to receive an inheritance?"

"After Papa died, I heard Mamma yelling and went to see what was happening. She was in Papa's study with Uncle Henry and she was angry. I heard her say Papa could rot in hell because she would not give any money to his whore and her demon spawn."

Philip was overcome with a coughing spell, and Ashton clasped a hand to his mouth for fear of laughing. Anne eyed them with annoyance until they were both once more composed.

"Uncle said it was out of her hands and he would see that the money was transferred to them."

"As it should be." Ashton leant towards his cousin. "I am certain he did so."

"Then why do Sam and Tabby know nothing of it? They have been forced to move from place to place without the funds they should have received." Her lip trembled and her eyes glistened. She blinked several times before sniffing. "Mamma found a way to keep the money from them, and I want to undo it."

"You should speak to Father." Ashton sat back in his seat. "If he said he would make the arrangements, he did."

Anne pouted and looked to Philip.

"Ashton is correct, Anne. Father would have followed Uncle Lewis's will to the letter. If Aunt Catherine attempted anything to keep the inheritance from the Evanses, he would have been aware of it."

"But she must have! How else do you explain it?"

The brothers exchanged another troubled look before Philip tipped his head towards his older brother. With a sigh, Ashton said, "Perhaps their mother spent the money or lost it in some manner and thought it best not to tell her daughters." When Anne opened her mouth to respond, he continued. "It has been known to happen, Anne. Women like Miss Evans—"

"No! Papa loved her. And she was *Mrs.* Evans. She had been forced to marry a man who beat her and was terrible to her. Papa helped her escape from him." Anne sniffed again.

"Regardless, Anne, it is possible the money repaid debts or was spent on necessities and simply did not last until her daughters were old enough to learn of it."

"Could she really have spent fifty thousand pounds?" Anne asked in a petulant tone.

Ashton's jaw fell open before he stuttered, "Fi-fifty thousand?"

"Yes, the same as my dowry." She leant forwards. "I believe he would have left them more but knew Mamma would try to interfere, just as she did."

"Anne," Ashton said as his hand returned to his nose. "I told you, Father would not have allowed her to interfere."

"Interfere with what?"

They all turned to see Lord and Lady Matlock in the doorway. Ashton moaned as he fell against the back of his seat, knowing Anne would do precisely what she did.

"Mamma found a way to stop the Evanses from getting their inheritance," she declared.

The earl and his wife looked at one another, then back at the others assembled.

"They told you this?" Lord Matlock demanded.

"I asked why they moved so frequently, and they were embarrassed to tell me of their financial situation. If you had truly given them the inheritance as you told Mamma, they would not be struggling."

"How do you know what I told your mother?" Lord Matlock demanded as Lady Matlock asked, "How do you know they were embarrassed? Anne, have you seen those girls?"

"Ashton took me to see them in Cheapside."

A groan escaped him as his parents' attention shifted from Anne to himself. Standing, Ashton held out a hand as he said, "She learnt they were coming to London and was determined to see them. I merely found a way for it to occur away from the *ton*."

"Cheapside?" his mother asked. "Did you enlist Elizabeth to aid you?"

"Miss Bennet was the one who actually arranged it," Anne offered. "Ashton said I could not involve Mrs. Darcy, and Fitzwilliam was adamant that his wife would have nothing to do with it."

"At least *he* had some sense," Lady Matlock muttered.

Lord Matlock sat beside his niece and took her hand. "Anne," he began in a firm voice. "How do you know about the inheritance?"

For the first time, she lowered her head and appeared repentant. "I heard Mamma shouting at you after Papa died."

The earl sighed and patted her hand. "My dear, I assure you, I sent the funds as specified in your father's will. Letters were written and sent to Mrs. Evans instructing her how to access them to receive a quarterly allowance." He took a deep breath as though bracing himself. "Could they have spent the money and are now attempting to receive more by saying they did not receive it?"

Anne snatched her hand from her uncle's and stood. "No! Sam and Tabby would not do that. If you had seen them, you would know they were telling the truth." She pointed a finger in his face. "And do not say Mrs. Evans spent it as Ashton suggested."

Father and son exchanged a harassed look before Lord

Matlock patted the seat beside him. "Anne, I am not saying the money went to something unworthy, but perhaps—"

"No! It was Mamma, I know it. She told you she would see they never received it, and she did."

"Henry," Lady Matlock said and waited for him to look at her. "Did you post the letter to Mrs. Evans from Rosings?"

All eyes grew wide as they realized what had occurred.

"I knew it," Anne declared. "What can we do to right this?"

Lord Matlock considered the matter. "First, I will visit the bank tomorrow to discover if the funds remain in the account I established."

"And if they do, shall we travel to Rosings Park and confront Mamma?" Anne appeared overly anxious to force Lady Catherine to confess.

"If necessary, *I* will speak to my sister. I see no reason for involving you."

Before his father had finished speaking, Ashton could see Anne's countenance turn a disturbing crimson.

"Uncle Henry," she said in the same tone she had used when refusing Ashton. "As we discussed when I first arrived, *I* am the true Mistress of Rosings and all my father's holdings, and I believe it is time to remind Mamma."

The brothers stared at one another as Ashton eased back into his seat. Both shook their heads enough to tell the other they had not been completely aware of this news.

"You *will* be when you turn five and twenty," Lord Matlock corrected.

Anne fluttered her hand as though she had swatted an annoying bug. "A month from now."

"A very important month," Lady Matlock said as she stood by her husband's side. "In the coming month, Lady Catherine is able to make changes which could directly affect you. She could arrange a marriage or empty the coffers. Anne, you must be wise regarding this. You do not want your mother more upset than she already is."

Anne pouted once again. "But you will see if the money is still there?" she asked her uncle as she regained her seat.

"First thing tomorrow, I promise." He patted her hand once more. "Patience, Anne. Your mother will be taken to task if she has done anything to interfere with Sir Lewis's will, but not until *after* you have fulfilled your father's wishes and taken your rightful place."

With an exasperated sigh, Anne agreed.

"Come, Anne," Lady Matlock said as she held out a hand to her niece. "Let us rest a bit before we must prepare for dinner."

As the ladies left the room, Ashton and Philip stared at their father. Before either could speak, Lord Matlock rose and peered down at them as he once did when they were errant boys.

"Forget everything you heard," he instructed before turning on his heel and following the ladies.

Silence reigned for a few minutes until Philip asked, "What were we discussing before Anne arrived?"

"What time do we leave for Hertfordshire?" Ashton replied.

CHAPTER FOURTEEN
NETHERFIELD PARK
11 FEBRUARY

A lone footman stood watch over the repast in the breakfast parlour when Adsila entered. The smells had filled the halls, and her mouth watered as she picked up a plate to begin making her selections.

"I highly recommend the honey butter rolls," Elizabeth said as she entered the room on her husband's arm. "I had to loosen my stays the last time I was here because of them."

Adsila turned to reveal the two rolls already upon her plate. "I see we have similar tastes."

Mr. Darcy seated his wife before joining Adsila at the side table. "Do you like meat, Miss Carrington?"

"Some," she replied as she realized there was very little on her plate.

Mr. Darcy remedied this by adding a slice of ham. "I am determined to learn Bingley's cook's secrets on flavouring. Perhaps it is as simple as Hertfordshire wood versus Derbyshire, but the ham is delicious."

She dipped her head in gratitude before making her

way to the table. Taking the seat across from Elizabeth gave her a view of the open doorway. "Are we the only ones to arise this early?"

"Mr. Bingley and Miss Bingley will be down within the next half hour." Elizabeth accepted the plate from her husband and motioned for the footman to fill their teacups. "Does Mr. Carrington keep town hours?"

"No, but he sometimes becomes interested in something and forgets to eat. If he has not appeared by the time I finish, I will have a plate sent to him." She tucked into the ham and agreed with Mr. Darcy that the taste was sublime, not too salty and with a sweet flavour. "Mmm, you were correct, sir. The ham is delicious, and I suspect the elusive ingredient may be honey. It also appears to be fairly fresh. Ham smoked for a long period tends to be much saltier."

"You are quite the expert, Miss Carrington; I shall take your word on it." Mr. Darcy smiled as he cut a bite for himself.

"Ham is a large business in Virginia. We take it quite seriously." She held a straight face as long as possible before giggling.

"Well, I believe you are correct. Now that you noted it, I do detect a honey flavour."

The gentleman continued to eat while Elizabeth asked Adsila what she might like to do that day.

"I am certain Caroline has arranged several possible activities, but with the weather turning colder, we will be forced to remain inside." She looked longingly out the window. "More of the guests will be arriving today as well, so I suppose it is for the best that we not wander far."

"I am certain you could take the carriage to Meryton for a bit of shopping and to visit your friends," Mr. Darcy offered. "It is not a walk through the fields, but it should meet your needs, my dear." He sipped his tea. "Carrington and I are to visit Longbourn. Mr. Bennet is anxious to continue his debate." He smiled as he cut another bite of ham.

"Your suspicion he would appreciate my brother's company appears to be correct then," Adsila said with a smile.

"It is indeed." He turned to his wife. "It should secure my position as favourite son a bit longer," he said with a wink.

Elizabeth laughed. "I am certain your libraries and your choice of wife took care of that, darling. Though taking her so far from Hertfordshire was a mark against you."

"I have only stolen her away to London to date. Our families have worked against us being able to go farther," he murmured as he returned his attention to his plate.

Elizabeth laughed once more as she patted his arm. "Would you like to explore Meryton, Adsila? It is not Bond Street, but the people are friendly."

"That would be lovely," she agreed. "Is your family expecting to see you today?"

"Oh, we will accompany Fitzwilliam and Mr. Carrington to Longbourn and invite my sisters to join us. Of course, Mamma will give us a last-minute order of some sort for the wedding."

A short time later, Tom and the Bingley siblings entered the parlour as the footman was clearing Adsila's and the Darcys' plates.

"Has there been any sighting of our other guests, John?" Mr. Bingley asked the footman as he fixed his sister's plate.

"No, sir."

"I am surprised. I thought your beau would be dragging us from our beds this morning, Caroline." He frowned, but his eyes twinkled merrily. "Has he lost interest so quickly?"

Miss Bingley sniffed. "Just because the colonel does not behave like a puppy nipping at my heels as you do with Jane does not mean his interest has lagged, Charles." She smiled at her guests. "Have you made plans for today? I wish I could have arranged an outing, but I will be tied to the house until everyone arrives. I am certain Louisa and Hurst will not appear until the sky is darkening as they simply will not rise earlier." She thanked her brother for her plate and salted the eggs.

"We are to visit Mr. Bennet, are we not?" Tom asked Mr. Darcy as he took the seat beside his sister. "The man apparently has a fascinating book collection with several rare selections."

"Then you will be content there while I go to Meryton with the ladies," Adsila replied before stealing a roll from his plate.

"I am ahead of you, Adsi," he replied, picking up the remaining roll and pulling it apart.

Elizabeth sighed. "How I wish I had had a brother. I am so jealous of you and Georgiana."

"You may steal from my plate, my love." Mr. Darcy kissed his wife's hand, causing the familiar blush to cover her cheeks.

The party discussed their plans for the day, Mr. Bingley looking most displeased to be reminded that he must remain at Netherfield while the other gentlemen spent the day at Longbourn.

"Jane will be with us in Meryton, Charles," Elizabeth reassured him.

"And Mr. Bennet will be posing scholarly challenges," Mr. Darcy reminded him, bringing a look of relief to the man's countenance.

"I am certain you and Carrington will be able to entertain him far better than I. I do not believe I have ever met a man who enjoys professing opinions which are not his own merely to see how those about him will respond." Mr. Bingley's gaze returned to his plate, and he missed the humorous expressions of Elizabeth and her husband.

"I believe I might know another of a similar turn," Mr. Darcy said as he kissed his wife's hand yet again. He turned his attention to Tom, who had just risen to refill his plate. "Shall we meet in the front hall in an hour?"

"Adsi, is that acceptable?"

"Certainly," Adsila agreed. "If you will excuse me, I will change into something a bit warmer."

The footman stepped forwards and held her chair as Mr. Darcy rose to do the same service for his wife. The trio left the room together, though the married couple barely acknowledged Adsila's presence until they reached the top of the stairs, where they were to separate. At that time, Elizabeth tore her eyes from her husband and smiled at Adsila before Mr. Darcy's arm slipped about her waist and drew her away.

Having never considered herself a jealous sort of person, Adsila was surprised by the pang which twisted her stomach. She made her way to her room and selected her warmest dress before ringing for the maid to assist her. While waiting, she stared out the window and considered these new emotions churning within her.

The majority of marriages she had witnessed while in England had been what she considered mercenary. Certainly some had grown into more caring relationships between the parties, but until meeting the Darcys, she had not been witness to a true connection between the individuals. Elizabeth and her husband reminded Adsila of the relationship she had witnessed between her mother and father, the relationship she had hoped to find for herself. Her lower lip protruded as she remembered what Lady Carlisle had told her all those years ago when she had arrived in England a naïve, hopeful girl.

Adsila stood before Lady Carlisle, her heart pounding so, she feared the servants would come to determine the source of the commotion. Her mother had frequently spoken of her friend and the season they had shared in London. She had made it sound like a fairyland with beautiful princesses and handsome princes.

Her Ladyship's sighs roused Adsila from her thoughts, and she trembled in anticipation of the lady's evaluation of her. Prior to leaving Virginia, her mother had stressed that she would require a completely new wardrobe in order to be considered fashionable. She assured Adsila that her friend would advise her in how to present herself to find a suitable husband.

"Your complexion is much like your father's, though perhaps a bit paler." Lady Carlisle clucked her tongue repeatedly as she studied Adsila. "Your eyes are so unnaturally light in comparison, and your hair is like ebony. I suppose some might look upon you as having an exotic appearance, but, for the most part, English men prefer the pale, blonde English rose."

"I am certain there are some men who prefer darker hair," Adsila replied, her tongue lashing back in defense of her feelings.

"But the majority do not." Lady Carlisle frowned as her gaze fell to Adsila's skirts. "Are all of your costumes similar to this?"

"Mamma said we would have to purchase a new wardrobe so I could dress in the current London style." Had Her Ladyship not received her mother's letters? "She wrote to you several times over the last year requesting your assistance and specifying what she had dreamt for me." She fought the urge to fold her arms before her but was unable to keep her left brow from arching.

Lady Carlisle frowned. "I see you are much like your mother in personality. She too, challenged everything and everyone until she was fit only for an American." She stood taller, her eyes turning cold as they bore into Adsila. "*If* I am to assist you, you must overcome your conceited independence and obstinance. Ladies of the *ton* speak in a cultured tone on the subjects acceptable for them."

She sat but did not offer Adsila the opportunity to do the same. "Your accent will be noted immediately when you enter a room, so I suggest you speak as little as possible and quietly."

Feeling her anger rising, Adsila inhaled slowly, drawing herself up straight as her grandmother had taught her, with the reminder she was descended from chieftains. "In this manner I will be able to come to know a man to determine if we would suit one another? I cannot see how."

Her Ladyship laughed. "Suit? Marriage is a business arrangement, Miss Carrington, nothing more. My husband and I will see that you are well situated, and that your husband will keep you in a manner to which you are accustomed according to your standing."

"As you have pointed out, as an American, my standing is low indeed."

"But your mother's family was not insignificant. I am certain if your grandparents still lived, they would have arranged a marriage for you as they attempted to do for your mother." She sniffed. "Though I see in your eyes you would most likely react in a similar manner to her."

Adsila had heard the stories of the match her grandparents had wanted for her mother. It was not terrible, but once she met Mr. James Carrington of Virginia, her mother could no longer consider the viscount, no matter the size of his estate or the honour of gaining a title. They had been displeased at first but came to accept the marriage before the newly wedded couple sailed for America.

"My mother followed her heart."

"An organ meant to sustain life, not direct it. Understanding what will bring you the best sort of life is far superior. Had your mother done as her parents expected, she would be a wealthy widow today with much influence, able to live on her own terms."

"Without love. I cannot see that as an improvement. My mother is a joyous woman, and our home is filled with love and laughter. Our needs are met and we are happy."

"Yet you were sent to me to find a husband as your very presence makes life uncomfortable for those you love."

There was no emotion in Lady Carlisle's voice as she cut the girl to the quick, but her eyes held a superior gleam. Adsila suddenly realized the lady was jealous of her mother, who had defied convention and chosen another path. A path that, if Her Ladyship was to be believed, Adsila would not find in England—especially if Lady Carlisle had her say.

The maid entered, drawing Adsila from her remembrances. Within a few minutes, she was ready to join the others, but time remained, so she returned to the window once more. The fields were brown. The only other colour to be seen were the evergreens which stood tall amongst their bare-limbed relatives. Remembering her brother's words, she admitted the landscape did hold some resemblance to parts of Virginia.

Recognizing her thoughts were taking a decidedly maudlin turn, she closed her eyes, took a deep breath, and gave herself a little shake to dispel it. Opening her eyes again, she saw a carriage turn onto Netherfield's drive. A smile crept across her lips.

"It appears Miss Bingley's beau is not remiss after all."

CHAPTER FIFTEEN
HERTFORDSHIRE
11 FEBRUARY

Philip's snores rent the air within the carriage. Normally, Ashton thought nothing of his brother's habit and his ability to sleep wherever he might be. It came from his time in battle, when a soldier stole what moments of repose were afforded him. Today, the sound and the officiousness of his brother leaving him to his destructive thoughts felt like the harshest betrayal.

Staring out the window without seeing the passing farmland, he told himself for the hundredth time that Philip was wrong. Adsila Croome née Carrington could not be in Hertfordshire as her husband had abandoned her in Cornwall with her son and another on the way. He pinched his eyes closed in an attempt to block the vision which arose whenever he thought of her situation: her light, pleasing figure rounded with that rakehell's seed; her stormy eyes dull and red from years of misuse.

"Devil it!" He bit his tongue to keep from spitting.

A low whistle, not sleep related, issued from his brother. "Best get that out of your system before we arrive. I doubt Darcy or Bingley will be pleased to hear such things said around the ladies."

"Slept well?" Ashton's exasperation with himself found a new target in his brother.

"Yes, thank you." Philip grinned as he sat up and straightened his coat. "Father's carriages are immensely more comfortable than supply wagons."

"I cannot believe I allowed you to talk me into this," Ashton muttered as he stared out the window once more.

When he received no response, he turned to find his brother studying him, his features set in a frown, which was exceedingly rare on the amiable man.

"Do you plan to be in a foul mood the entire visit?"

"I believe I asked you to leave me in London."

Philip leant forwards, elbows resting upon his knees. "And I believe I explained that Elizabeth is expecting you."

"Elizabeth and Darcy can bloody well keep their noses out of my life. Not everyone is able to live as happily as they do." Ashton crossed his arms and returned to staring out the window.

The silence filled the cabin as Philip's snores had previously. Ashton's knee began to bounce, but he said nothing more. Finally, his brother sat back in the seat.

"Very well. Should you wish, I will disembark at Netherfield, and you are free to return to London. I will find passage back to town following the wedding."

Though tempted, Ashton felt the fight drain from him. "Do not be ridiculous. I would not put the horses through such useless exercise, let alone the servants." He unfolded his arms and rested his hand upon his knee to still it. "If necessary, I will make my excuses to Bingley in the morning and return tomorrow, sending the carriage back for you the following day."

Philip nodded, a smile tugging at his lips as the carriage slowed to take a turn. "I plan to tease you mercilessly on this by tomorrow evening."

Without responding, Ashton sat up and tugged upon his waistcoat before straightening his coat. The carriage drew to a stop in front of Netherfield, and the footman placed the step and opened the door before the inhabitants had appeared to welcome them. Ashton stepped out, followed by Philip. They were on the bottom step when the door opened, revealing Bingley and his sister.

"Miss Bingley," Philip cried as he rushed up the stairs. "It is far too cold. You must return inside before you become ill."

Ashton and Bingley exchanged an amused glance as the couple disappeared within.

"You heard my brother, Bingley, it is far too cold outside."

"I would not think of stepping inside before you, m'lord."

They laughed as they shook hands and entered the manor house.

"Have you breakfasted?" his host asked.

Ashton waved aside his question. "We ate at an inn on our way here. The *colonel* roused me from my bed at an ungodly hour."

"I will admit to expecting your arrival at least an hour past."

Philip turned his attention to the gentlemen. "And we would have been here had I not been saddled with dragging my brother and his city ways along."

"A task I assured you you need not do," Ashton muttered through clenched teeth.

"What's this?" Bingley asked with a look of concern. "Grayson, you wished to remain behind? You were not going to attend?"

Ashton's cheeks warmed, and he silently cursed his tongue. "There was a bit of a stir at home late yesterday. I thought it best that I remain behind, but Philip insisted all would be well without my interference."

"I hope all *is* well," their hostess offered. "Miss de

Bourgh and your parents are in good health?"

"Yes, yes," Philip replied as he placed her hand upon his arm. "There was some concern that our Aunt Catherine had caused some discomforts, and her daughter wished to correct the situation. Father has everything well in hand."

"I am pleased to hear it." Miss Bingley led the party into the nearest drawing room. "Our other guests are planning a trip to Longbourn and Meryton. Charles and I must remain at Netherfield to greet those who have not yet arrived, but you are welcome to join the excursion."

"We have only just arrived." Ashton forced a laugh. "Are you trying to rid yourself of my brother already?"

A becoming blush covered Miss Bingley's cheeks. "Certainly not, Lord Grayson. I simply wished to alert you both to the party's plans."

"I pray you would ignore my brother. He has been in a foul mood for some time now. I believe a few days in the country will set him to rights." Philip bowed over his lady's hand. "As we have just arrived, I would not wish to leave a layer of dust upon your furnishings. Are Ashton and I in the same rooms as before?"

"No," Bingley replied. "I shall show you to your rooms. Caroline, I see Darcy's carriage being brought to the front." He dipped his head towards the window. "I suspect the others will be down soon."

Miss Bingley nodded, flashing a charming smile at Philip, before her brother led the gentlemen back into the hall.

"You are certain there is nothing I can offer you *now?*" Bingley asked as they approached the stairs.

Placing a hand on the man's shoulder, Philip said in an enigmatic manner, "I believe it best if we see to this quickly."

Bingley gave a nod and led them up the stairs. "One of our guests is in your room, Grayson, and her brother is across the hall. You will be a door down from him.

Colonel, you are in the same room as before."

"You have given away my view of the drive?" Ashton asked. "I shall be unable to surprise all with my foreknowledge of arrivals," he said in a forced jovial tone.

Laughter greeted them as they reached the top step. Darcy and his wife rounded the corner, their eyes going wide as they spied the brothers.

"Philip! Ashton." Darcy stepped forwards and clutched the younger brother's hand. "I had not expected you this early."

"I thought it best we arrive in Hertfordshire before my brother could escape the engagement."

Ashton frowned, his eyes travelling between the party before him. Before he could speak, a door opened, and a young man stepped out.

"Ah, Carrington," Darcy said with a smile. "You remember my cousin, Colonel Fitzwilliam. Ashton, this is our new friend, Mr. Thomas Carrington of Virginia in America. Carrington, my older cousin, Ashton Fitzwilliam, Viscount Grayson."

While Darcy handled the introduction, Ashton studied the man before him. He looked nothing like Adsila. The man's hair was blond, his eyes blue, and his skin fair. Obviously, Philip and Demi were mistaken. The disappointment which settled in the pit of his stomach shocked him. Had he been anticipating meeting Croome's wife?

As the gentlemen rose from their bows, Ashton noted Elizabeth whispering to his brother, who was shaking his head. She worried her lip, looking at Ashton with eyes which moved quickly between him, her husband, and the new gentleman.

"Elizabeth," Ashton said warmly as he bowed over her hand. "It is always good to see you."

A snort from his brother drew everyone's attention. "Forgive me; I was just remembering Ashton's earlier comments regarding you and your loving husband."

The desire to stomp upon his brother's foot or elbow him in the stomach was strong, but Ashton simply squeezed the lady's fingers. "Ignore him. He woke me at a disagreeable hour this morning and appears to be in a most plaguing mood."

The door behind them opened, and a soft gasp was heard. Ashton turned, his heart first ceasing, then racing.

It was *her*.

"Miss . . . Mrs. . . . ." he stuttered.

"Lord Grayson," she whispered as she curtseyed. "I thought . . . that is, I heard voices and . . . You are well?"

"Yes." Ashton stared at her. She was exactly as he remembered her. "And you?" he finally asked. "You are well also?"

Her lips twitched. "As you see, sir."

They stared at one another until her brother came to her side. "Adsi?" he asked in a concerned tone.

"You have met Lord Grayson?" she asked him.

"Only just. You know one another?"

"We met during my season in London. I attended his sister's wedding, and he attended Lady Gertrude's." Her eyes never strayed from his.

"Yes," Ashton said as he tore his gaze from her. "When we parted, we expected never to see each other again as your sister was anticipating her own marriage."

Mr. Carrington frowned. "To a clown unfit for her. She joined me in Oxford instead and kept my house while I attended the university."

Silence reigned for a moment while Ashton considered the man's words. His eyes moved between the siblings as the first spark of hope set his dead heart ablaze. "You did *not* marry Mr. Croome?"

"No, sir." Her lips twitched once more, and he suspected she was about to laugh at him.

Drawing his shoulders back, he frowned. "I was not told."

"Why would you be?" she countered, her amusement

draining away. "As I remember, it was made clear we should not see one another again."

"That does not mean I did not desire it," he spat back.

Her head lifted, giving her a regal bearing. "Yet you made no move to find me."

"You were to be *married.*"

"But I wasn't."

"How was I to know?"

She pursed her lips. "Perhaps you could have read the announcement of Mr. Croome's betrothal to Miss Harris."

"I had no interest in reading of . . . who? Miss Harris? Sir Patrick's daughter?"

The lady shrugged. "I suppose."

Philip's hand landed upon Ashton's shoulder. "I see you are on your way out. As we have just arrived, we should wash away the road dust. Shall we see you when you return?"

"Yes. Carrington and I are spending the day with Mr. Bennet, and the ladies are going into Meryton to explore the shops and visit Elizabeth's friends." Darcy laid his hand upon his wife's back and motioned towards the stairs. "We will return in time for dinner."

Before more could be said, Ashton felt himself propelled down the hall. Bingley opened a door, and Philip ushered him inside. Once the door was closed behind the three of them, his brother withdrew his flask and pressed it into Ashton's hands. Without a word, Ashton upended and emptied it of the burning content before thrusting it back at him.

"I told you it was her," Philip said with a smirk.

Ashton stumbled to the closest chair and fell into it.

"I say, Grayson, you are looking . . . well, a bit grey." Bingley shifted from foot to foot. "Can I get you something? Brandy? Coffee?"

It took a moment, but Ashton slowly realized he was shaking his head. Philip and Bingley exchanged a glance before the host stepped to the door.

"I will see you below," he said in a rush before stepping outside and closing the door behind him.

"I never expected to see her again."

Philip nodded. "I remember. You said as much in your letter."

"You were the only person I confessed—" He drew a finger across his lips. "Our situation has not changed."

"How can you say that?" Philip asked as he dropped into the companion chair. "Neither of you are attached."

"Father will not approve."

"Father be damned."

Ashton shook his head. "Easy for you to say; you are the *younger* son."

"Trust me, Ash."

His brother's voice, low and solemn, caused Ashton to raise his head.

"Mother and Father know."

The air suddenly felt as though it had been sucked from his body as well as the room, and Ashton gaped at his brother much like a gasping fish.

"Elizabeth told Demi and Mother of meeting Miss Carrington."

In an attempt to clear his head, Ashton leant forwards and ran his fingers through his hair. "They know she has returned to society."

When Philip did not respond, Ashton raised his head to find his brother squirming in his seat.

"What are you not saying?"

"The following day, Mother visited Elizabeth."

The silence stretched between them.

"And?" Ashton finally asked.

His brother took a deep breath and looked everywhere but at Ashton. "I was told when we would be travelling here."

Ashton frowned. "I do not understand."

"Initially, we were to travel with Darcy and Elizabeth."

"But after Mother spoke to Elizabeth, you were told we

would arrive the day after them."

Philip nodded. "I know not what was said or how everything was arranged, but during the meeting at White's—that you did not attend—Bingley invited Carrington and his sister to the wedding."

The image of a chessboard flashed through Ashton's mind, and he jumped from his seat, pacing to the window and back twice before he slapped his hand down on the chair's headrest. "Am I to be a pawn, moved about as everyone sees fit? Has my free will been ripped from me yet again?"

His brother's shocked countenance merely angered him more.

"I do not understand," Philip finally said to Ashton's back as he paced away once more. "Do you *not* want to know Miss Carrington better?"

"I *want* to make a decision for myself!" He pinched the bridge of his nose and drew a deep breath before asking in a softer voice, "Were *her* feelings considered?"

"Do you believe Elizabeth would force anyone into a situation they found distasteful?"

Ashton spun about, new fear gripping his chest. "She knew I would be here?"

"No . . . that is, I do not believe so. She appeared as surprised as you when she joined us in the hall."

"Then how were her feelings taken into consideration? Had she spoken of me?"

Philip pursed his lips and hesitated before answering. "Her brother was not aware she knew you, so I would say she had not, at least not in front of him."

A wave of nausea washed over him, and Ashton gripped the bedpost to steady himself.

"Whoa!" Philip cried as he rushed to his brother's side and helped him sit on the edge of the bed. "Perhaps you should lie down for a bit."

Absent-mindedly, Ashton nodded and crawled farther onto the bed. Philip pulled the curtains before slipping from the room, leaving his brother to his thoughts. Thoughts that spun about his head, bouncing off one another until what sense they had initially made was demolished in their robust dance. A door clicked open, and his man sat a glass on the tableside before slipping from the room once more. A short time later, Ashton finally succumbed to a restless sleep.

CHAPTER SIXTEEN
HERTFORDSHIRE
11 FEBRUARY

Nothing was said as they descended the stairs. Well, nothing that Adsila heard until Tom laid a hand upon her arm and looked at her with concern in his eyes.

"Adsi?"

She smiled at him, then turned to look at her friends. "I am well."

"We need not . . ." Elizabeth began, but Adsila stopped her.

"I am looking forward to seeing your family again."

Elizabeth nodded, and the party continued to the front door, then out and into the carriage. As they drew away from Netherfield, Adsila replayed the scene which had occurred in the hall. *Obviously*, Lord Grayson had not known of her presence, but she found she was uncertain if he had been *pleased* by it.

"Odious man," she muttered under her breath.

"I beg your pardon?" Elizabeth asked, her eyes flitting to her husband as she bit her lower lip.

"Forgive me, I was thinking aloud." Adsila reached out

to cover Elizabeth's hand with her own. "Is there a shop Jane prefers over the others? I thought I might purchase a gift for her."

"How sweet," her friend said as she laid her other hand over Adsila's. "Jane loves lace, though not like our mother. Mamma views lace as a way of showing one's station in life. Jane is fascinated by the intricate patterns. We will visit the drapers, and you can see which patterns she lingers over longest."

Adsila nodded before looking to her brother. He sat silently watching her. In order to reassure him, she smiled, but it did not appear to relieve him of his concern. Unable to hold his gaze, she turned to look out the window once more.

As the carriage rolled through Meryton, Elizabeth lamented the lack of a quicker road between the estates.

"Longbourn is to the south of Meryton, while Netherfield is to the north. They share a border and are only three miles apart if walking, but the roads force us to travel the long way around."

"You have walked it?" Adsila asked, expecting a story from the couple due to the way Mr. Darcy looked at his wife.

"Oh, many times when I was younger," Elizabeth replied. "But I already showed you Oakham Mount yesterday. It is the point where three estates come together, Longbourn and Netherfield Park being two of them."

"If the weather permits, perhaps we will ride out one day." Mr. Darcy smiled at his wife. "When I first arrived in Hertfordshire, I climbed the mount to better survey Bingley's land and stumbled upon a dancing lady. I believe I scandalized her when I spoke to her without a proper introduction."

A pleasant blush lit Elizabeth's cheeks. "I was scandalized because I was so eager to respond. After your insult the night before, I should never have spoken to you."

Laying a hand over his heart, the gentleman said, "I am forever grateful you forgave my rude behaviour."

"Only because Sir William had begged assistance on your behalf, saying your head ached."

"For which I am also eternally thankful."

Adsila watched the play between husband and wife with a smile upon her lips. When the couple became lost in each other's eyes once again, she turned her attention back to the window. A moment later, Mr. Darcy laughed as he pointed at the passing woods.

"The cold does not stop your sisters, my dear." He nudged Tom. "The first I saw of my wife, she was walking through these woods with her sisters. I believe we are to find Catherine and Lydia have anticipated your trip, Elizabeth."

His wife followed his hand. "Did they not know you and Mr. Carrington were coming to visit? I had thought they would remain home this morning." She sat back and smiled. "We have been seen. They are turning about."

This time Tom leant forwards, catching Adsila's attention.

"Bennet ladies are descendants of dryads or pixies, I have yet to determine which." Mr. Darcy told Tom in a serious tone. "Perhaps it is a mixture as they show characteristics of both."

"Teasing man!" Elizabeth said with a smile tugging at her lips. "How do you know the connection is not through my mother's family?"

The carriage slowed, finally coming to a stop before an older, charming manor house.

Adsila smiled. "I believe this is everything I ever expected of an English home and had yet to see during my time here."

A warmth entered her friend's eyes. "Longbourn is quite perfect, if I do say so myself, but more importantly, it is filled with love."

"Which is why it is perfect," Adsila replied, drawing a larger smile from Elizabeth.

As they exited the coach, the two youngest Bennet daughters hurried towards them.

"Lord, Lizzy, we didn't know you were coming this morning. We thought the gentlemen were to speak to Papa this afternoon," Miss Catherine cried while Miss Lydia stood beside her, staring at Tom.

"Good morning, Miss Lydia," he said with a bow, adding, "Miss Catherine," after a brief pause.

"Mr. Carrington," Miss Lydia responded in a soft voice.

From the corner of her eye, Adsila saw Elizabeth tilt her head as she observed the girl.

"Are you well, Lydia?" she asked.

"Of course," the girl said, her cheeks flaming.

Elizabeth smiled, cutting her eyes to her husband and back to the girl. "Well, do not keep us outside. Let us go in and retrieve the others before we take the carriage to Meryton."

"Oh!" Miss Catherine exclaimed. "Everyone will be so jealous when they see us."

She led the way into the house with Elizabeth a step behind on her husband's arm. Tom offered an arm to both Adsila and the youngest Bennet sister. She accepted, the blush upon her cheeks deepening. Elizabeth glanced over her shoulder and winked at Adsila, who lifted a hand to cover her smile.

"I am pleased to see you today, Mr. Carrington," Miss Lydia managed as they stepped inside. "I had hoped to learn more about Virginia."

"It would please me to answer any of your questions regarding my home."

They separated as they removed their outerwear, and Adsila made a point of entering the drawing room with Elizabeth in order to give the couple a moment together. They were greeted by Mrs. Bennet, Jane, and Mary.

"Lydia," Mrs. Bennet said in a harsh tone. "Leave Mr.

Carrington be. He has come to speak to your father."

"I do not mind, Mrs. Bennet. Miss Lydia was asking me about my home." Tom did not look to the matron as he responded, so he missed her frown.

Adsila, however, did not. After the encounter with Lord Grayson, memories of the snubs and whispers from her time in London were in the forefront of her mind. Believing Mrs. Bennet to be looking down upon her brother brought pain to her heart. Tom was the kindest man she knew and if this woman could not see it, it was her loss. Adsila would not allow him to be hurt by small-minded prejudices.

"Tom is very proud of our home, as he should be. It is the size of Netherfield and at least as prosperous." She straightened while meeting the matron's gaze directly.

Mrs. Bennet appeared flustered, looking to Elizabeth and back to her youngest. "I am certain you are correct."

"Ah, here you are." Mr. Bennet entered the room. "I had not realized you were bringing the ladies with you." He approached Elizabeth and kissed her cheek. "My dear Lizzy," he said before turning to greet Adsila. "Miss Carrington, it is delightful to see you again. Will the two of you be joining our discussion?"

Elizabeth laughed. "Not today, Papa. I have promised Adsila we will visit the shops in Meryton, and I hope to see Charlotte and Aunt Philips."

"Very well," he said with a shrug. "Shall I call for tea?" he asked the gentlemen as he led them from the room.

Tom bowed to Miss Lydia before following the others, causing Adsila to smile lovingly after him. The sweet man had been oblivious to Mrs. Bennet's cutting behaviour.

"Are you going immediately?" that lady asked her daughter.

"We may sit for a few minutes until my sisters have made themselves ready. I know Kitty and Lydia were prepared to walk to town. Jane, Mary, and Georgiana may join us if they wish, and you, Mamma. We have the carriage, so there is room for all." She took a seat beside her eldest sister and clasped her hand. "Would you like to visit Aunt Philips?"

"Oh!" Mrs. Bennet's hand flew to her chest. "In Mr. Darcy's carriage, you say? Yes, that would be lovely. I shall just go and change. Mary, Jane. Come along."

She chased her daughters out of the room, bringing a light laugh from Elizabeth.

"Come and tell me what you have been up to," she said to the sisters who remained.

Miss Catherine ran to the table in the corner and returned with a sketchpad. "Mrs. Annesley has helped me improve my sketches."

"These are lovely, Kitty." Elizabeth tilted the book so Adsila could see. "Would you like to join us in London at some point so you can work with a master? I am uncertain when we will be in town for a lengthy period, but you could also stay with Aunt and Uncle Gardiner."

"Could I?" the girl asked as she clung to Elizabeth's arm. "Oh yes, please!"

Elizabeth nodded. "And what have you been studying, Lydia?"

"She and Mrs. Annesley only speak in French," Kitty said.

"Is that true?" Elizabeth asked her youngest sister.

"*Oui*," the girl replied with a quick smile. "She has promised to send me books on Italian and Spanish as they are quite similar. She says I am a polyglot."

"A what?" Elizabeth asked with a laugh.

"I learn languages easily, like Kitty can draw without much instruction."

The door opened and another young lady entered with an older woman following her.

"Elizabeth," she cried as she hugged Adsila's friend. "Mary said you were here, and Mrs. Annesley allowed me to stop lessons long enough to greet you."

After returning the girl's hug, Elizabeth made

introductions before addressing the companion. "Mrs. Annesley, I must compliment you on your accomplishments with my sisters. They both seem pleased with your lessons."

"They have all worked hard and excel based upon their natural talents. It has been a pleasure teaching them." Her eyes began to water. "It reminds me of when my husband and I had the school for boys. How I wish we could have taught young ladies as well, but our home was inadequate for the demand."

"If there is anything you require, please send your request to Darcy House, and we will see you receive it."

The lady nodded her thanks. "Miss Darcy, you have neglected your stitching, and the rector is expecting the donations for the poor tomorrow."

The girl nodded before turning back to Elizabeth. "Mary and I have been practising a duet to play after dinner tomorrow evening."

"I am certain it will be lovely." Elizabeth looked to the companion again. "Have all my sisters contributed to the donation?"

"Oh yes," Miss Darcy answered. "Kitty and Lydia remade several bonnets, and Mary made baby blankets. Jane and I have been working on infant clothing."

"Jane has the most even stitches of us all," Elizabeth said with a nod.

"That is because you dislike sitting still," her eldest sister said as she reentered the room.

"You are correct, of course."

Before more could be said, Mrs. Bennet was heard giving orders as she approached the drawing room. Once inside, she announced they could depart.

"Georgiana are you not joining us?" she asked Miss Darcy.

"Thank you, Mother Bennet, but I have not completed my lessons."

"Oh, Mrs. Annesley, can she not miss it this once?"

Mrs. Bennet cajoled like a young girl.

"Now, Mrs. Bennet, she has missed entirely too often during her visit. I do not wish to displease Mr. Darcy by telling him his sister has fallen behind."

"Oh no, you are correct. We must not displease Mr. Darcy." Mrs. Bennet kissed Miss Darcy's cheek. "Return to your studies, my dear. We shall bring you a selection of those candies you like so well."

Elizabeth smiled as she watched Miss Darcy hug Mrs. Bennet before leaving the room. "As I told you in London, Adsila, we Bennets are quite apt to adopt lost souls into our fold. My husband's mother passed when Georgiana was born, and their father left them just a few years ago. Mamma has claimed her as another one of her kittens."

"Mamma," Miss Lydia said, stepping forwards. "May I stay home? I have work I should do as well."

Mrs. Bennet frowned. "What work? You and Kitty have finished the bonnets for Mr. Irving."

"Yes," the young girl replied slowly. "But I have not finished my translation yet."

"Mrs. Annesley gave you extra time due to the wedding preparations," Miss Catherine said, earning a glare from her sister.

"You wish to remain behind to speak to Mr. Carrington, and I will not have it." Mrs. Bennet huffed. "You will come shopping with us and leave that man alone."

All the warmth Adsila had begun to feel for the Mistress of Longbourn washed away. "My brother is a respectable man, Mrs. Bennet."

"Of course, he is," the lady replied. "My husband and Mr. Darcy would not befriend him otherwise."

"Then why do you not want your daughter to speak to him?"

"Yes, Mamma," Miss Lydia asked, mimicking Adsila's stiff stance. "Were it any other man, you would be pleased beyond measure."

Mrs. Bennet became flustered, her handkerchief fluttering between her chest and her mouth. "He is from America, Lydia." She looked to Adsila. "Not that this is bad, it is just so far. If he were remaining in England, I would be pleased for one of my girls to catch his eye, but . . ."

Suddenly understanding, Adsila felt ashamed of her suspicions. "Please forgive me," she said as she relaxed and lowered her head. "When I first arrived in England, I was told I would not be accepted because I am from America. The *ton* was just shy of being unkind to me, which has made me overly protective of my brother."

"Oh, you poor dear." Mrs. Bennet placed a finger under Adsila's chin and lifted it. "You need not apologize. I have seen the looks my daughters have given me. They could not understand why I was discouraging Lydia either. Lizzy will be far enough from home, and I could not bear to lose my Lydia as well. At least Jane will be nearby." She smiled at her eldest, who reluctantly returned it.

"But I do not *want* to stay here," Miss Lydia whined. "I want to travel and see new places."

"And you will," Mrs. Bennet assured her. "Lizzy and Jane will take you to Derbyshire and London, and with them married, my brother and his wife may take you with them when they travel."

Miss Lydia continued to pout until Elizabeth slipped an arm about her shoulders and whispered in her ear.

"Truly?" the girl asked in a soft voice.

"We shall see," her sister replied. "Now smile and come with us to Meryton."

She did as she was told, and the party filed out to the carriage.

CHAPTER SEVENTEEN
NETHERFIELD PARK
11 FEBRUARY

"Did you enjoy Meryton?" Ashton asked Miss Carrington.

"Yes."

He felt as though he had been transported back in time. Though the lady's voice was no longer so quiet he had to strain to hear it, it was the fourth one-worded answer she had given him since they sat down to dinner.

When Ashton awoke that afternoon, feeling more refreshed than he had in months, he decided he was being a fool by questioning the motives of his family members. Instead, he should seize the opportunity before him and come to know Miss Carrington better before they were separated once again. Unfortunately, the lady appeared determined to vex him. The Bingleys had aided Ashton by sitting him beside Miss Carrington at dinner, but he had yet to have gained anything from it.

"What think you of the Bennets?" he asked, hoping she would be forced to respond in more than a few syllables.

There was a pause long enough to make him think he

should repeat the question when she drew a deep breath and answered.

"They are a loving family who look beyond an individual's origins to their heart. They are not false or pretentious. I believe that one could trust them to be exactly what they portray."

Her eyes never lifted from her plate, and her words held a stinging reprimand.

"Which could not be said of the *ton?*" Ashton asked, knowing the answer.

This time, Miss Carrington did raise her gaze, spearing Ashton with the lightning dancing in her stormy depths. "I have yet to meet a true member of the *ton* who did not say one thing while doing the opposite."

"And this is your opinion of me?" Ashton asked, heat rising in his chest. "You would include me with rattlepates who say one thing today and the opposite tomorrow based upon what those about them spew?"

A sharp pain in his shin caused him to jolt, and he turned to find his brother glaring at him from the other side of the table.

"I would not know, sir," Miss Carrington hissed at him. "The few conversations we have held revealed little regarding your character. I am certain we know so little about one another that we are near strangers."

Drawing upon the years of experience at his father's side, Ashton took a deep breath and allowed the hum of his dinner companions' conversations to settle his ire. "You are correct, of course," he finally replied in a low but calm voice. "However, it does not mean we must remain as such."

Her head whipped in his direction, and Ashton met her gaze with what he had always considered his most handsome smile. Her eyes narrowed as a line formed between her brows. Before either could say more, their hostess rose, and the ladies followed her from the room.

As the doors closed behind them, Philip took hold of

Ashton's arm and dragged him to the side of the room.

"What was that?" his brother demanded in a harsh whisper as his eyes flew to Mr. Carrington.

"As I told you all those years ago, the lady rarely speaks. It is akin to drawing water from a rock."

"So you attack her and then flirt?" Philip shook his head. "Father had the right of it."

"What do you mean?" Ashton asked as he shook off the hand which still held him.

"It is no wonder you have never married. Darcy would have done better."

"I beg your pardon?" their cousin asked as he approached with the young newcomer at his side. "I might have insulted my wife before we were introduced, but I never did so afterwards."

"Lord Grayson." Mr. Carrington's voice seemed to have lowered, and his countenance had lost all signs of amiability. "From what I have seen since your arrival, and small things my sister has said over the years, I am beginning to believe *you* are the reason Adsila dislikes London."

"Dislikes?" Ashton frowned. "Your sister *despises* the façade presented by members of the *haut ton,* as do I."

"Do you?" Philip asked, a look of surprise affixing his features.

"Yes."

"But you imitate them so well."

Ashton felt his jaw moving up and down, but no words were heard. Finally, he closed his mouth to consider his response.

"You play a role, Ashton, just like everyone else in the *ton.*" Philip laid his hand upon his brother's shoulder. "Father trained you to do so, but who, besides perhaps me and Darcy, knows the real you?"

Before he could respond, Miss Carrington's brother spoke up once more.

"She wants nothing to do with your world. I beg you to

leave her be."

The thought of losing her now that he had finally found her tore at his soul. "I wish I could," Ashton whispered as he slowly shook his head.

"My sister is a treasure, sir. She is not a commonplace lady who will be content in a role assigned by a man who cares only for his own desires. Such a relationship would kill her."

"All I have ever wished was to know Miss Carrington. Not the whispering creature who stares at the floor, but the bewitching woman who walked with me in the gardens on my sister's wedding day. The one who told me we would never see each other again and then took up residence in my dreams." He ran a hand through his hair. "I do not want to harm your sister, Mr. Carrington. I simply want to learn if she is everything I have built her up to be. If she is the one that could restore my faith that Darcy and Elizabeth are not just the lucky ones. That I would not have to live my father's life if she were at my side."

Philip's frown deepened. "Mother and Father love one another."

Ashton's cheeks warmed, and he could not meet his brother's gaze. "They do now, but there was a time when Mother cried herself to sleep."

"You are only a year older than me; how do you know this?"

Taking a deep breath, Ashton raised his head and looked at Philip. "Do you remember the winter I had the croup?" At his brother's nod, he continued. "Mother had a bed placed in her sitting room so she would be near if I needed her. They thought me sleeping. Father was to travel to London without us, and Mother told him she knew of his mistress. She said he should be glad he had his heir and a spare because he would find her door locked when he returned."

"But that was before Demi was born."

Ashton nodded. "It is my understanding he ended it and pleaded with Mother to forgive him." He huffed. "When I confronted him about it years later, he told me he had only behaved as Grandfather instructed."

Philip dropped into the nearest chair. "I always believed . . ."

"I believe Mother always loved Father and he held her in high esteem, but he allowed the *ton* to influence him."

"And you are his son," Mr. Carrington muttered.

"I would *never* take a mistress. I *have* never taken a mistress."

The two gentlemen stared at one another for a time, as though taking the other's measure, before Mr. Carrington took a step backwards and bowed his head.

"Adsila is insistent that she will return to Virginia with me, but I do not believe it is where she belongs. *If* you truly wish to know my sister and have only *her* best interests in mind, I will assist you." He held up a hand. "I do this for her alone. She has not been herself since she arrived in London, alternating between nervous excitement and melancholy, eager yet fearful. I have been beside myself, not understanding what was causing her distress until today."

He stepped forwards once more, meeting Ashton's gaze with determination.

"If you hurt her, Lord Grayson, you will answer to me."

At that moment, Ashton noted how young the man was and realized he had only just reached his majority, just graduated from university. Yet, even though he was barely a man, he meant what he said and would act on his words.

Holding out his hand, Ashton said, "You have my word; if it is clear we are not good for one another, I will step away and leave your sister be."

Reluctantly, Mr. Carrington shook his hand, giving a single nod.

****

The footman opened the drawing room door as the gentlemen approached, allowing the ladies' voices to spill into the hall.

"I warned you, Louisa. If you are unable to be cordial to our guests, you should retire."

Bingley moaned, and Hurst laid a hand upon his brother's arm to slow his pace.

"I do not know what you mean, Caroline. We were having a perfectly pleasant conversation. I do not know what caused her to behave as she did." Her voice changed to one of derision. "Perhaps she simply misses the colonies."

Mr. Carrington leant forwards, but Ashton held out his hand to stop him and whispered, "Wait."

Hurst and Bingley preceded the others into the room.

"What has my wife done now, Caroline?"

Ashton glanced about from his position in the doorway but did not see Miss Carrington. He looked to her brother, but the man was already moving towards the stairs.

"Come, Mrs. Hurst," her husband commanded. "Bingley, you will forgive us, but we shall be leaving in the morning."

"But the wedding!" Mrs. Hurst cried. "My brother is to be married. We are expected to attend."

"If you cannot be civil to my houseguests whom you have only met today, I shudder to think how you will behave towards my betrothed and her family, whom you have repeatedly derided." Bingley shook his head. "Forgive me, Hurst, but your wife is not welcome in my homes until she is able to treat people respectfully."

Hurst nodded. "Understood. I shall see you at the club?"

"Most definitely."

The gentlemen shook hands, then Hurst led his protesting wife from the room. The doors had not yet closed when they heard the normally quiet man bellow, "Woman, desist!"

"I tried to stop her, Charles," Miss Bingley said quietly.

"I am certain you did, Caroline." He looked about. "Where is Carrington?"

"He is seeing to his sister," Ashton replied as he moved into the room. "May we know what was said?"

Miss Bingley and Elizabeth exchanged a look, but neither would meet his eye.

"Elizabeth?" Darcy took the seat beside her.

When she raised her head to look at her husband, Ashton could see the anger in her eyes. "She alternately accused Adsila of throwing herself at Ashton and being rude to him. It was as though she could not make up her mind which would hurt more, but Adsila merely laughed at her and told her to decide which it was."

"It was then Louisa told her a viscount would never marry an American, but he might set her up nicely."

Philip had taken the seat beside Miss Bingley and placed his hand over hers where it lay upon the cushion. She raised her eyes to his.

"I was too shocked to respond. Miss Carrington excused herself and retired for the night."

"She carried herself like royalty," Elizabeth said as she looked to Ashton. "Her regal bearing when she left was much like a slap in the face to Mrs. Hurst. I will go see if there is anything she requires and assure her the Hursts will be gone in the morning."

The gentlemen all nodded. Darcy rose and helped her to her feet. Once Elizabeth had gone, Miss Bingley rang for tea and coffee, and they waited for at least one of their party to return to the drawing room.

CHAPTER EIGHTEEN
NETHERFIELD PARK
FEBRUARY

"I am well," Adsila said for the fourth time. "Please, Tom, return below and assure everyone I am simply fatigued, nothing a good night's rest won't cure."

"That *woman*—"

"Is not worth the breath to curse her."

Her brother stepped closer, placing his hands upon her arms. "Say the word and we will return to London at once. You need never see Mrs. Hurst or Lord Grayson again."

Adsila's head jerked upward. "What has Lord Grayson to do with this?"

Tom sighed. "I saw the two of you at dinner. He says he wishes to know you better, but I cannot help but think it would lead to disaster. I see now that he was the reason you were reluctant to go to London."

Her cheeks warmed. "No. The *ton* caused my hesitation. The thought of seeing Lord Grayson overcame my reluctance."

"Truly?" Her brother's expression was incredulous. "But you barely spoke to him, and when you did, it was in rebuke."

"You were listening to our conversation?" She stepped backwards, drawing away from his touch.

Tom let his hands fall to his side and slouched. "I was worried."

A laugh caught in her throat, and she stepped closer, laying a hand upon his cheek. "Oh, dearest. It is odd, but it is the way we speak. It always seems we are either scolding or avoiding one another. Only once did we speak openly, and then it was because we believed we would never meet again."

"At his sister's wedding?"

"Yes." She narrowed her eyes. "How did you know that?"

"Lord Grayson mentioned it when I confronted him." His gaze fell to the floor.

"You didn't!" she cried, grasping his chin and lifting it so he was forced to look at her. "What have you done, Tom?"

"I told him to leave you be."

Her heartbeat pounded in her ears. "And he said?"

"No."

A smile tugged at her lips, and she spun away before he might see it.

"Adsi?"

"I am well," she said again. "Please, return below and assure everyone that Mrs. Hurst's words have not caused me to be overwrought; I simply thought it best that I remove myself before I said something I ought not."

"You will not return with me?"

"No." After schooling her features, she turned and held out a hand to him. "Everything will be better tomorrow, I am certain."

A soft knock interrupted them, and Adsila motioned for Tom to answer it. She dared not believe Lord Grayson would come to her bedroom, but she would not be surprised if he did in these circumstances.

Elizabeth entered and rushed to take Adsila's hand. "The Hursts have retired and are leaving in the morning."

"What?" Adsila looked to her brother and back to Elizabeth. "But the wedding."

"Charles does not want her there. In truth, he had considered not inviting her, but Jane insisted."

"I do not want to be the cause—"

"You are not." Elizabeth patted her hand. "Louisa Hurst has been this way from the first day I met her when I was seven and we attended the same school. She is a grasping, bitter woman. She tried to push Caroline on *my* Fitzwilliam and wanted Charles to leave Hertfordshire before he could come to an understanding with Jane. Her brother has simply had enough, and I, for one, am pleased it occurred before the wedding rather than after. It will make Jane's life ever so much easier."

Adsila smiled at her friend's determined expression.

"Shall we return to the drawing room?" Elizabeth asked.

"You and Tom should go, but I believe I will retire." She held up a hand when her friend opened her mouth to argue. "There has been enough excitement for this evening, and I would prefer some time to myself. I will see you in the morning."

"Very well," Elizabeth replied with a huff. "Come along, Mr. Carrington. We shall allow your sister to rest."

Tom looked to her expectantly, and Adsila nodded. Reluctantly, he escorted Elizabeth back to the drawing room.

Adsila closed the door and locked it behind them, placing a hand upon the cool, firm surface. "He would not honour my brother's request to leave me," she whispered. A smile spread across her lips until she felt like laughing. She pressed her hands to her cheeks and spun away from the door, finally dropping onto the bed. It was best she remain in her room this evening. If anyone saw her beaming like a mad woman, they would be concerned.

****

Servants hustled up and down the stairs as Adsila emerged from her chambers the next morning. After timing her descent to remain out of their way, she reached the hall below and turned towards the breakfast room just as the Hursts appeared at the top of the stairs.

"I am certain it was unnecessary to arise this early, Mr. Hurst." Mrs. Hurst's whining carried to any awake to hear her.

"As I told you last night, Mrs. Hurst, I am not above gagging you if you continue your complaints. You have brought this disgrace upon yourself, and I would prefer to leave without encountering the others."

Adsila quickened her pace to slip inside the breakfast room before they might see her.

"Ah, Hurst," Mr. Bingley's voice called from above. "I am pleased we are not too late to see you off."

"I had not anticipated you or Caroline rising so early, Charles." Mr. Hurst's embarrassment resonated in his tone.

Feeling guilty for overhearing their conversation, Adsila moved farther into the room and poured a cup of tea before taking up position by the window. The trees bent in the wind, and it appeared to be the start of a blustering day; not the sort on which one would wish to travel. She shook her head before sipping her tea, refusing to feel sorry for the woman who had secured her family's contempt without aid from any other.

A short time later, the door opened and the Bingley siblings entered.

"Miss Carrington." Miss Bingley's hesitant tone accompanied an embarrassed curtsey. "I am pleased you are joining us this morning."

Adsila smiled warmly. "Miss Bingley, Mr. Bingley. I would like to apologize for my abrupt departure last evening. I feared I would say something untoward had I remained and thought it best that I remove from the gathering instead."

"No." Mr. Bingley stepped forwards. "It was our sister who should have and did retire. Nothing you might have said or done would have diminished you in our eyes."

With a single raised brow, Adsila tipped her head to the side. "You have not heard me at my worst, sir. I would withhold judgement until that day."

The man chuckled and motioned towards the table. "Will you join us or have you already broken your fast?"

"I have only enjoyed a cup of your delicious tea."

The trio filled their plates and gathered around the table, eating in a comfortable silence until the door opened once more, revealing the Darcys.

"Oh dear, Fitzwilliam, have we overslept?" Elizabeth asked her husband as she winked at the ladies.

Mr. Bingley rose and bowed to her. "Caroline and I awoke early to see the Hursts off." He took a deep breath before holding out a chair for her. "But we will not be discussing *them* any further."

Elizabeth patted his hand before taking her seat, and her husband went to the sideboard to fix her plate. "Well, tomorrow we will officially be family," she said with a brilliant smile. "Whatever will you gentlemen do this evening while we ladies are at Longbourn?"

Her husband snorted as he set her plate before her. "Hopefully Charles will not do what he did the night before *our* wedding, my dear, or we might have to prop him up at the altar."

The ladies' eyes widened as a blush covered Bingley's cheeks. "That was in celebration of you and Elizabeth, Darcy. Philip was standing up with you, not me."

"And Philip and I had to carry you, Ashton, and my uncle to bed afterwards."

"And what a racket!" Miss Bingley said as she raised her eyes to the ceiling. "Lady Matlock and I laughed over it the following morning before they arose."

"You should have stayed with us at Longbourn that evening." Elizabeth's cheeks pinked as she spoke. "I should have thought of it as Jane has."

Miss Bingley waved her worries away. "It was amusing to see how grown men can behave like children."

"It was embarrassing," Mr. Darcy mumbled as he took his seat, causing his wife to giggle.

"Lady Matlock and I spent the evening in the music room," Miss Bingley assured Elizabeth. "We were only plagued by raucous laughter and minimal cursing before we decided to retire."

Mr. Darcy and Mr. Bingley both blushed.

"Then it is all for the better that we ladies will spend the night at Longbourn." Elizabeth cut her eye at her husband, who nodded.

Though Adsila was amused by the conversation, she found her gaze repeatedly drifting to the doorway, but no more of their party appeared. When she could no longer find a reason to push the crumbs about her plate and she was nearly full to bursting with tea, she pushed the plate away and looked to her hostess.

"What plans have we for the day?"

Miss Bingley had also pushed her plate to the side and was beginning to rise. "I must speak with Mrs. Nicholls regarding the arrangements for tomorrow and see to last-minute things. We are all expected at Longbourn for an early dinner."

"Do not be surprised if Mother drags Jane here this afternoon to make some last-minute changes, Caroline." Elizabeth pursed her lips as her eyes glimmered. "She was exceedingly pleased to have the wedding breakfast at Netherfield but is now regretting not having complete control over it."

"Mrs. Hill and Mrs. Nicholls have been in constant contact for that very reason." Miss Bingley smiled conspiratorially as she leant towards Elizabeth. "I understand Mrs. Hill has explained which directions to follow immediately and which can wait as they will most likely change again before tomorrow."

Elizabeth laughed. "Hill is a good soul. She knows Mother's whims well."

"Well," Adsila said as she rose from her seat, "if there is nothing required of me until later, I believe I will seek out the library and read for a bit."

"Bingley," Mr. Darcy called to draw their host from his woolgathering. "Have you added to your collection? Or at least replaced the stepstool in the library?"

"You will be pleased to hear I have done both in your absence. Nicholls attended to the stool, and Jane helped me select several titles while we were in London." Their host appeared exceedingly proud of himself.

"There is no longer a reason for any lady to climb upon the furniture to secure a book or a husband," Miss Bingley said as she slipped from the room, leaving the others laughing.

"Climbing—"

"It is a long story," Elizabeth interrupted Adsila's question.

"Which ended happily," Mr. Darcy said as he kissed his wife's hand once again.

Mr. Bingley rose and offered to escort Adsila to the library as he was heading to his study to address what business was necessary before he and his wife left on their abbreviated wedding trip. They had no sooner left the breakfast room than Lord Grayson approached from the back of the house.

"Good morning, Bingley. Miss Carrington." He bowed to her, rising with a smile lifting the left side of his mouth.

"Good morning, sir," she replied as she rose from her curtsey. "We have just finished breaking our fast and were off to begin our day."

"Splendid! And have you considered a walk in the garden this morning?" he asked, ignoring their host.

"Have you been outside, sir?" Adsila asked. "It is not a pleasant day in May." Her brow arched in challenge.

"No, you are correct, but our host has secured nearly a garden's worth of flowers for his lovely bride which have just been delivered and placed in the ballroom."

"They have arrived? Splendid!" Mr. Bingley clapped his hands together. "I must inform Caroline. If you will excuse me, Miss Carrington. I trust Lord Grayson is capable of showing you to the library."

Both Adsila and Lord Grayson nodded as Mr. Bingley hurried down the hall.

"Do you prefer the library, or may I tempt you with a walk through Bingley's indoor gardens?"

Laying her finger to her chin, Adsila tipped her head to the side. "I do not remember ever seeing an indoor garden."

"It is delightful, I promise." He held out his arm, and Adsila wrapped her hand about it.

In silence, they made their way through Netherfield's halls until they reached the double doors leading to the ballroom. Lord Grayson stopped and lifted her hand from his arm.

"Close your eyes."

Her eyes narrowed in suspicion, but she did as he asked. His footsteps carried him away from her, and then there was a sweet floral scent. Though tempted, she kept her eyes closed and waited until he returned to her side. He lifted her hand, placing it back on his arm, his hand lingering to hold hers in place, then he stepped forwards, tugging her along. The aroma increased, coming from every side as he led her farther into the room before he stopped.

"Now open them," he whispered.

The area where they stood was indeed filled with flowers. Roses, lilies, sweet pea, and pansies were surrounded by ivy and several herbs, all waiting to be arranged in vases or bound in bouquets.

"It is breathtaking."

"They have no azaleas," Lord Grayson said with a sigh as he stepped to the nearest collection of roses and withdrew an orange bud just beginning to open, the only one of that color in sight. "But, if I remember correctly, you may like this."

Adsila accepted it, lifting it to her nose and inhaling its perfume. "My mother has a rose garden. The orange rose bush stands at the centre and, when I was young, I believed it stood tall above all the others, much like the sun amongst the planets, forcing them to bow to her magnificence."

"As they should," Ashton agreed, holding out his arm for her once more.

They wandered about the room, admiring the colours and aroma until the doors opened and Miss Bingley entered, followed closely by Elizabeth and Mrs. Nicholls.

"Oh!" she cried upon seeing them. "Miss Carrington, I thought you were reading in the library. Would you like to join us? We will be arranging the ridiculous number of flowers my brother purchased."

Adsila laid the rose upon the nearest group and nodded. "I would love to be of assistance."

Lord Grayson stepped around behind her before moving towards the door. "I will hasten out of your way, so you are able to finish without my interference." He stopped before exiting and bowed to them. "Thank you, Miss Carrington, for walking with me in Bingley's gardens."

As he turned to leave the room, she noted the bloom in his hand and suspected she would see it again. Her cheeks warmed, and she was unable to suppress her smile.

CHAPTER NINETEEN
LONGBOURN
12 FEBRUARY

"Two daughters married!" Mrs. Bennet crowed from her seat beside Lady Lucas, causing said daughters' complexions to redden.

"Not quite, Mamma. You would not wish to tempt fate," Lydia said with a wink at said sisters.

The matron gasped. "Bite your tongue, Lydia."

Lady Lucas appeared to be biting her lips to suppress her displeasure. Adsila suspected the lady might be relieved the wedding was the following morning but doubted it would stop their hostess from exalting over her family's good fortune. Though Mrs. Bennet's bragging was in poor taste, Adsila had kept herself from judging the lady for it. After her previous experience at Longbourn, she did not want to lump Mrs. Bennet in with the backbiting ladies of the *ton*.

"My sister and her friends have been in competition for years over which of their offspring might marry first." Mrs. Gardiner said in a tone low enough for only Adsila to hear. "Lady Lucas thought her Charlotte was going to reach the altar first, but the man was not worth sacrificing her daughter's happiness. I begin to suspect there is a wager of some sort involved."

Adsila's eyes widened. "A wager? As I have heard the gentlemen do in their clubs?"

"Oh yes." Mrs. Gardiner nodded. "No money will change hands, but I suspect Lady Lucas already surrendered a much-desired receipt for fricassee of turnips following Lizzy's wedding."

"The turnips we had at dinner?"

The lady nodded knowingly. "Lady Lucas frowned upon seeing them, and I have frequently heard my sister lament that Longbourn's turnips were never so tasty as those found at Lucas Lodge. That and the fact that Mrs. Bennet offered them to her friend at least twice—and Lady Lucas begrudgingly complimented them once she had a taste—fairly confirms the exchange. I cannot wait for our next visit to see what Mrs. Bennet claims on behalf of Jane."

Adsila laughed as Mrs. Gardiner nodded once more before turning to speak to Miss Bingley. Even in Oxford, Adsila had not found such pleasant companions. There it was mostly professors' wives and daughters who were more interested in securing husbands for the latter. A few of Tom's friends would discuss their studies with her, but for the most part they patronized her responses. Since meeting the Gardiners, she had discovered there were those in society who thought similarly to herself and were not fixated on social advancement.

The drawing room door opened, and the gentlemen joined the ladies—well most of them. Mr. Bennet, Tom, and Mr. Darcy were missing from the group. Mr. Bingley nearly sprinted to his bride's side, bowing over her hand and causing Elizabeth to cough into her handkerchief. Adsila was so focused on her friend's amusement, she only noticed the viscount when he took the seat beside her.

"Utterly ridiculous, is he not? Tomorrow she will be his

wife, yet he kept reminding us of the time in his desire to return to her side."

"Does this mean the bloom has gone from the Darcys' marriage?" she asked.

"On the contrary." Ashton nodded towards the door, and Adsila turned in time to see Elizabeth disappearing through it. "His wife knows he dislikes mindless chatter, and she is intrigued to see what discussion has kept her father and your brother."

Adsila looked about. "And your brother? Was he overly eager to leave his masculine company for that of another?"

Lord Grayson leant forwards and glanced at the colonel, a small frown tugging at his lips for but a moment. "I am uncertain. Philip keeps his hand too well concealed."

"You do not approve?"

He sat back into the seat, pursing his lips as he considered his response. "I would rather say I do not understand." He smiled as he met her gaze. "You see, Miss Bingley's sister pushed her towards Darcy as soon as she was out. Until they arrived in Hertfordshire, we all believed her greatest desire was to become the next Mistress of Pemberley. Yet once Darcy began showing his preference for Elizabeth, Miss Bingley gladly yielded the field."

"You thought her grasping? And now? When she encourages the attention of the son of an earl?" Adsila attempted to school her features but could not keep the coldness from her tone.

Lord Grayson tipped his head to the side as his eyes wandered over her countenance. "Yes, I did think her grasping with Darcy. They had little in common, so her only motive for the match would have to be wealth and position."

"And now?" she repeated.

"I cannot say." He shrugged. "It appears she and my brother are on more even ground. Their personalities are neither too similar nor too different. I suppose we must simply wait and see what will become of it."

"Your family approves?"

He chuckled. "You sound doubtful."

"I would be surprised based on what I have seen."

Lord Grayson nodded. "I understand your apprehension and even share it. However, if it brings my brother home, my parents will treat her like the daughter of a peer."

"You are relieved he is in England." It was a statement, not a question.

He nodded again. "And I want him to remain. He mentioned something the other day I had not considered." He took a moment, swallowing as he tugged at his cuffs. "My brother chose the cavalry as our uncle served there. Philip has now lived longer than Uncle Anthony. I believe he tempts fate each time he steps foot on a battlefield. It must be a disconcerting thought; it is for me."

Adsila laid her hand upon his, squeezing his fingers once before returning it to her lap. "I am grateful that Tom never joined the army. He has not the heart for it."

"Have you other siblings?" he asked.

"Just one other brother still living, but Arthur is only thirteen."

"And what do you think he will become when he grows older?" He smiled, clearly ready to leave thoughts of the colonel and war behind.

"I suspect he will assist Tom. Perhaps if they are able to purchase adjoining land, there will come a time when they divide it between them."

"And where will you be? What will you be doing?" His eyes searched hers before she lowered her gaze.

"I have planned to return and assist as I am able." Her lips twitched as she glanced at him from the corner of her eye. "Perhaps we will divide the land into thirds."

"Or . . ." Lord Grayson nearly whispered but did not continue.

"Or?"

"It was my understanding you came to England to find

your home."

Adsila took a deep breath and released it slowly. "A young girl came to England in search of the fairy tale her mother told her, but she learned that was all it was."

"You no longer believe in such things? What of Elizabeth and Darcy?"

"They do make you want to believe again, do they not?"

"I never dared until I saw my parents welcome her."

"As their niece." Adsila looked about the room. "Where is Miss Lydia?"

"She slipped out after Elizabeth. I must tell you—"

"Oh, she insists on following him." Adsila rose from her seat, Lord Grayson at her side.

"It is sweet," he said for her ears only as he escorted her from the room.

"Her mother does not like it."

The viscount chuckled. "Mrs. Bennet would be pleased to see her daughter settled so well."

Adsila stopped in the hall and shook her head. "No, she wouldn't. Her youngest settled across the ocean in a different country? Mrs. Bennet would be distraught. She has said as much."

He held up a hand before her and she stopped. "If they truly care for one another, Mrs. Bennet would not deny her daughter's happiness."

"Perhaps, but they are both far too young to make such a decision on a few days' acquaintance."

"Are you against it?" he asked, leaning away from her.

"Yes. No. If they truly feel something for one another, then I would want them to learn about each other and determine if it could be more, but Tom is returning home in a few months and Miss Lydia has not had a season in town."

"Would that change her mind, do you think?"

She looked at him, wondering if he spoke of more than her brother and Elizabeth's sister. "Who is to know now?

Perhaps in a few years, it might."

"Could they not enjoy this time they have together before he leaves? Use it to learn more of one another and possibly come to a conditional agreement?"

Her heart became heavy and her breath laboured. "Is that what we are doing? Coming to know one another and hoping others will accept if it grows into more?" Her hand flew to her mouth, but she forced it back to her side. "And what if they do not?"

Lord Grayson stepped closer to her once more. "I was trying to tell you—"

The library door opened, and the missing members of the party exited, laughing and smiling.

"I am surprised Mamma has not shooed you men from the house," Elizabeth said as she wrapped her hand about her husband's arm.

"I believe she might," Mr. Darcy replied as he tipped his head towards Adsila and the viscount.

"We were simply coming to learn what was so fascinating," she said as she stepped away from Lord Grayson and over to her brother.

"We were continuing a conversation from yesterday, and Mrs. Darcy and Miss Lydia were pleasant enough to present their theories as well." He smiled at the girl holding onto his arm.

"But it is time for us to return to Netherfield, I am certain," Lord Grayson said. "Shall we have a go at separating Bingley from Miss Bennet?" he asked Darcy.

"You call yourselves gentlemen," Mr. Bennet huffed. "Leaving your comrade in a house filled with the enemy."

"Enemy?" Elizabeth laughed. "You have Uncle Gardiner, Papa, and I believe he brought a new bottle of your favourite brandy."

"Well, then," Mr. Bennet said with a smile. "I believe it is time for the young men to be on their way." He led them to the drawing room and announced it was time for the ladies to retire. "After all, there is much to be done tomorrow. I promised Mr. Carrington we would ride over the property if the weather holds."

"Mr. Bennet! Tomorrow is your daughter's wedding. You will not be riding about." Mrs. Bennet fanned herself. "You take delight in vexing me."

"Oh yes, that too." He turned to Adsila's brother. "We will ride out after the wedding breakfast."

"Papa," Elizabeth scolded in a soft voice, but her father's smile simply grew.

"I believe it is time we were off," Mr. Darcy said. "Bingley?"

Reluctantly, Mr. Bingley and his betrothed rose from the settee and began saying their goodnights. Though it seemed to take forever, the party finally broke up. The eldest Bennet daughters walked with their gentlemen and the Lucases to the front door and returned shortly after the rest of the party heard the carriages depart. Mr. Bennet and Mr. Gardiner were safely ensconced in the library by the time the ladies reentered the drawing room. Adsila sat quietly, her thoughts drawn inwards.

CHAPTER TWENTY
HERTFORDSHIRE
12 FEBRUARY

The gentlemen entered Netherfield's drawing room in high spirits, except one.

"I feel as though we have done this before," Philip quipped.

"Aye," Darcy cried. "We have only swapped out one, and I daresay Carrington might hold his liquor better than the earl."

"I would not wager on that," the young man responded, causing a cacophony of laughter.

Darcy took up the bottle of spirits and began pouring while Philip approached his brother.

"What has you down in the mouth?" His voice was low enough to not be heard by the others, who had already begun congratulating the groom.

Ashton shook his head.

"Your mood will be noted soon; if you are unwilling to speak of it, I suggest you don your society mask."

"Come, Philip, Ashton," Darcy called. "No serious discussions this evening. Is that not what was said the night before my wedding?" He held out two glasses, his brow rising to let them know he was not unaware of the situation but thought it best not to speak of it at this time.

After several rounds of toasts, Carrington leant forwards, frowning. "Is this what is done then when a bloke gets married? Just sitting about drinking to him and his bride's wellbeing?"

The others looked around, feeling the levity strangely missing from the celebration.

"Billiards, anyone?" Bingley asked as he stood and motioned towards the door.

"Splendid idea, Bingley." Darcy rose and waited for the others to follow.

"We'll be there in a moment," Philip called, a hand to his brother's chest holding Ashton in place. Once the gentlemen's voices became distant, he turned a determined gaze upon his captive. "Now, why are you such a dull fellow this evening? You are normally the one who sets the tone for such events."

Ashton shook his head once again, something akin to fear keeping him from speaking the thoughts running about his mind.

"Your conversation with Miss Carrington appeared . . . off."

"I had thought you absorbed in your conversation with Miss Bingley."

"I am capable of doing two things at once." Philip refilled Ashton's glass. "Was she unwelcoming?"

Ashton swallowed a hearty gulp of the spirits and savoured the burn as it travelled through his chest. Finding a touch of courage in the feeling, he asked, "Have I created a paragon which cannot be realized?"

"Explain."

With a great sigh, Ashton turned and studied the room without seeing it. "I have imagined this woman for years, always knowing she was out of my reach. Did I build her up to be the woman of my dreams without truly knowing anything about her?"

"Oh, most definitely."

Ashton turned and gawked at his brother.

"Well, let us examine the situation. You met this woman—who you yourself admitted rarely spoke—a handful of times while in society. Then you had *one* conversation with her where you caught a glimpse of her true self before being separated for years. The woman fascinated you from the moment you first saw her, so your mind pieced together what you knew of her, and your imagination filled in the gaps. Yes, I would say the woman you believe her to be is far more fiction than reality."

"And you believe I should give up this charade and seek someone Father would find more acceptable." He ran a finger around the rim of his glass.

"I did not say that." Philip placed a hand upon his brother's shoulder and met his gaze squarely. "It is undeniable that the two of you have some stunted interest in one another which was not given an outlet to mature or die off. What I would do in your situation is explore it." He emptied his glass and refilled it.

"Explore it?" Ashton asked in some confusion.

"Court her, you jolterhead. Shall I assist you?"

Ashton frowned. "I am uncertain that would be wise. Will it not take time from your own courtship?"

Philip waved away his hesitance. "I know just what to do." He grinned and clapped an arm about his brother's shoulders. "Come! Let us join the others and play a few games while we muck out the details."

****

"Oh, Adsila," Jane said as she embraced her friend. "Thank you." She held the length of lace up for her sisters to see. "This is precisely what was needed to finish my yellow dress."

"May I have the leftovers?" Kitty asked as she fingered

the delicate material.

"Kitty!" Mrs. Bennet cried. "It is a gift for your sister."

"But the pattern is exquisite. I want to sketch it," the girl said in a near whisper, her lips pouted and her shoulders slumped.

"Well, why did you not say as much?" the woman scolded. "I am certain Jane will save a scrap for you."

"Of course, I will." Jane smiled at her sister. "In fact, I would love it if you did a special drawing for me. Perhaps my wedding bouquet with the lace beneath it?"

Without a word, the young girl scrambled to her feet and ran from the room, returning moments later with her pad and pencils in hand. After shooing Miss Lydia from the window seat, the items were arranged there in a pleasing manner. With Miss Kitty sitting with her legs folded beneath her on the floor, the others filled the few empty places about the room and helped Jane finish her packing while asking about her wedding trip.

"Oh, Darcy and Elizabeth have offered us the use of their townhouse for a few days, but we will wait until the weather warms to travel more extensively."

Elizabeth held up a shawl, and the sisters exchanged a warm glance before Jane took it from her and laid it over Mary's shoulders. The young girl gasped as she ran her fingers over the beautiful old garment.

"Grandma Bennet's shawl?" she whispered reverently.

"You will now be the eldest Miss Bennet," Elizabeth said. "It is only fitting it be yours."

Mary pulled the shawl about her like a hug, then embraced both her elder sisters. "Thank you," she said before moving to the side and dabbing her tears with a corner of the wrap.

Miss Darcy joined her, and the two whispered as they examined the worn stitches.

"Our grandmother wrapped each of us in her shawl at one time or another," Elizabeth told Adsila. "Normally if we were feeling ill or sad, she would settle into her favourite chair with us upon her lap and tell us a story while we played with the tassels. She always made us feel better, and now her shawl brings back the memories."

"That is beautiful," Adsila replied. "My grandmother gave me this brooch before she passed." She laid a hand upon her most prized piece of jewellery. "She always reminded me that her grandfather was a white chief—as good as any king—so I should hold my head high as I am a princess."

"A white chief?" Lydia asked.

"Yes, in each Cherokee village there is a white chief and a red chief. The white chief leads in times of peace, and the red leads in times of war. Her comparison is not exactly accurate, but my great-great-grandfather *was* an influential man."

"Do the Cherokee have any special courting traditions?" Lydia asked.

Adsila glanced over the girl's head to find Mrs. Bennet frowning. "Courting rituals are, in many ways, similar between different people. The Cherokee begin with a dance—not a ball, but the single ladies perform a dance before the single men. Instead of speaking to the father, though, the man sends his mother or aunt to talk to the girl's mother."

"The women arrange things?" Mrs. Bennet was suddenly quite interested in Adsila's tale.

Adsila nodded. "Then the man must track and kill a dear. He prepares the meat and leaves it at her door. If she cooks the meat and offers it to him as a meal, she has accepted his courtship. If not, she is not interested."

Kitty scrunched up her nose. "Imagine having dead deer piled up on your doorstep."

The others laughed, but Lydia asked, "Then what?"

"They meet in the evenings, overseen by adults, and come to know each other better as is done here in England. However, once the man is ready to ask her to marry him, he must kill another deer to give to her parents.

If he is invited to join them for the meal, they are engaged."

"How perceptive they are to understand the mothers' intuition regarding their children." Mrs. Bennet smiled at her eldest daughter. "I knew at once how it would be with Mr. Bingley. My Jane could not be so beautiful for nothing! I remember, as soon as ever I saw him, when he came into Hertfordshire last year, I thought how likely it was that they should come together."

"Yes, Mamma," Jane said when her mother drew breath to continue. "You were quite correct regarding Mr. Bingley and me, but what of Mr. Darcy and Elizabeth?"

Elizabeth's eyes widened as she shot a bewildered glance at her eldest sister, who was turning away, her hand rising to her lips. Adsila thought the lady's shoulders shook and had her suspicions confirmed when Miss Bingley also covered her mouth and coughed.

"Oh, well, I dared not hope Mr. Darcy would consider Lizzy! Who would have thought it? But he is such a charming man. So handsome! So tall!"

Elizabeth blushed. "Yes, Mamma." Her eyes narrowed as she looked at Jane, who also blushed but did not appear repentant.

"But what of the viscount, Mamma?" Miss Lydia asked. "Is he not also handsome and tall?"

"Lord Grayson? Why, of course, and he is a *very* important man. I had thought he might be right for you, Lydia, but he is so much older."

"*I* believe he is interested in Miss Carrington," the youngest Bennet replied with an impish gleam in her eye.

All eyes turned towards her, and Adsila found herself gaping like a landed fish.

"Ashton would be ever so lucky to win Adsila's affections," Elizabeth declared with a smile. "I cannot think of another lady who would be so perfect for him."

"I am certain there are many his parents would select," Adsila demurred.

"None that he has not already rejected." Elizabeth slipped onto the bed beside her friend and squeezed her hand. "Lady Matlock herself encouraged me to introduce him to my friends in the hope he might show some interest."

As the lady finished, her brow lifted in a manner which spoke more than her words, causing Adsila's eyes to widen.

"Truly?" Adsila whispered, to which her friend nodded.

"Mamma, will Jane not be wearing your pearls tomorrow?" Elizabeth asked.

"Oh, oh dear," Mrs. Bennet leapt from her place in the only chair. "I had quite forgotten."

She rushed from the room, causing the others to laugh, but Adsila was still in awe of what had been revealed.

"We are to spend a few weeks at Netherfield, but Lady Matlock requested I host a tea when we return. It is my turn, after all, since you hosted us first, and she asked to be included. Lady Demetria voiced her eagerness to attend as well." Elizabeth rose to help her sister fold a lap rug.

"Will there be anyone else there?" Adsila asked, forcing her voice not to quiver.

"Jane, if she remains in town, and Caroline." Elizabeth smiled. "Just family."

"Are Lady Matlock and Lady Carlisle still friends?" Adsila picked at a loose thread on her sleeve.

Elizabeth frowned. "Forgive me, but there are so many ladyships, I could not say for certain. Lady Matlock is cordial to all, but I do not know which she might consider friends."

Taking a deep breath, Adsila lifted her head and nodded. "I would enjoy seeing Lady Matlock and Lady Demetria again."

The smile which spread across her friend's countenance would make one believe she had just been given her heart's desire. "Then it is settled. We will decide upon a day once we return to Netherfield Park tomorrow.

After the wedding breakfast, of course."

CHAPTER TWENTY-ONE
NETHERFIELD PARK
13 FEBRUARY

Ashton stood in the doorway of the drawing room, watching his brother, Miss Bingley, and Miss Carrington, who were seated on the far sofa. He wanted to cross the room and join their conversation, but he was under strict instructions to wait for the sign.

"I must say, you look remarkably better than you did on *my* wedding day," Darcy said as he joined his cousin.

"Yet I cannot admit to feeling any better." Ashton tugged at his waistcoat then his coat.

Darcy laid a hand upon the viscount's shoulder and looked him in the eye. "It is a good plan, Ashton. Forget what you thought you knew and begin again." His gaze darted to the side, and a smile spread across his features. "Ah, here is my lovely wife."

The gentlemen bowed as Elizabeth approached. "What are the two of you up to, lurking in doorways? Why are you not mingling?" She slipped her hand about Ashton's arm. "My husband has informed me you require an introduction to my particular friend from America."

Before Ashton could respond, he found himself approaching his brother and the ladies. Philip's smile and nod had a surprisingly calming effect upon him, and the tension left his shoulders.

"Ah, Ashton," his brother cried as he rose. "I am pleased you have joined us. Mrs. Darcy, will you do the honours of introducing your friend to my brother?"

Miss Carrington's brow cocked at this, but she said nothing.

"I would be delighted," Elizabeth replied.

Ashton thought he had seen her wink at her friend, and it appeared the lady relaxed a bit as she stood. He took a breath and hoped this would work.

"Ashton, I am pleased to introduce for you notice Miss Adsila Carrington of Virginia in America. I believe you are acquainted with her brother, Mr. Thomas Carrington. Adsila, this is my husband's cousin and Colonel Fitzwilliam's brother, Ashton Fitzwilliam, Viscount Grayson of Matlock in Derbyshire."

"I am pleased to make your acquaintance, Miss Carrington." Ashton performed a perfect bow and was thankful his voice had not shaken.

The lady rose from her curtsey, her eloquent eyes clear and searching his. "The feeling is mutual, Lord Grayson." Her gaze shifted to the orange rosebud in his lapel.

"Are you enjoying your visit to England?" he asked as the party took their seats and he patted the flower.

"I have found the last month to be the highlight of my time in this country."

"That must certainly be due to the presence of my new cousin. Mrs. Darcy has a way of putting everyone at ease and making them feel welcomed."

"She does, indeed," Miss Carrington replied as she smiled at her blushing friend. "I will be forever grateful for making her acquaintance during my last months in England."

Ashton nodded. "You are to return soon?"

"In a few months. It is time for my brother to take his place at my father's side."

"I am certain you will enjoy seeing your family again. Has it been long since you last saw them?"

"Over five years have passed since I last saw my father and six since I left my mother and youngest brother."

Her head lowered for a moment, and Ashton feared he had caused her to become melancholy, but then she met his gaze once more.

"I attended your sister's wedding several years ago. How is Lady Demetria?"

"Demi is well. Her son will soon be a year old." Ashton's patience was slipping. His brother's plan for them to meet as strangers frustrated him as strangers were limited to the blandest topics.

"I must remember to congratulate her when I see her. Elizabeth mentioned she and your mother will be joining us for tea when we return to London."

Her lips curved in the softest smile, and Ashton wondered if she had learnt that Lady Matlock would not object to her. He was so lost in thought, he nearly forgot to respond.

"I am pleased to hear you will meet them again."

The lady took a deep breath, releasing it slowly as her eyes rested upon each of their companions before returning to him.

"I fear I have been sitting for some time; I would like to take a turn about the room." She looked to the others again, but they did not immediately respond.

"May I escort you?" Ashton asked as he rose.

She smiled, her eyes softening as she accepted his hand. "That would be lovely, Lord Grayson."

They had walked a short distance when Miss Carrington sighed.

"Are you unwell?" Ashton asked as he looked about for a footman to retrieve whatever she might desire.

"No. I noticed the flower in your lapel. I was given a

similar bloom yesterday and foolishly laid it down."

"Perhaps a lucky gentleman took it up to treasure, as it had been caressed by your hand."

A becoming blush covered her cheeks. "I had seen a gentleman take it up and thought he meant to return it to me."

"I suspect he had considered it but, having made a fool of himself repeatedly, feared you might not accept it."

The lady tsked with a shake of her head. "I had thought him far more courageous."

"If he were not fully vested in the outcome, he might be."

Ashton stopped near the corner where few guests were lingering and turned to face her directly. "Have you thought of me over the years as I did you?"

Though she tore her gaze from his, she nodded. "I have."

"Then I hope you will understand what I must share." He swallowed and waited until their eyes met again. "Our encounters before were . . . odd. If I am correct, you hid your true self except for that day at Demi's wedding. I realize now that I did something similar as the possibility of a connection between us was discouraged. We have never truly met each other."

"Until today."

He smiled. "Until today." His countenance fell as he considered the other thoughts that had tortured him since the previous evening. "I hope your expectations of me are not beyond my abilities."

Her laugh took him by surprise but was as musical as he remembered.

"Oh dear." She tucked her hand back into his elbow and bumped her shoulder against his arm. "Are there expectations I shall be unable to meet?"

They began walking once more as Ashton discretely examined her features. Though she was smiling, her hand trembled upon his arm. He suddenly realized she was just as nervous. "I am certain any imperfections will only make you more endearing."

They were now approaching the newly married couple, and his companion's smile broadened. Ashton slowed their pace so the Bingleys could finish their current conversation before he and Miss Carrington arrived at their side. As Bingley turned his bride towards them, Ashton held out his hand.

"Congratulations, Bingley," he said as they shook hands. "Mrs. Bingley, may I say you are a vision of happiness and loveliness." He bowed over her hand.

"Lord Grayson, you are too kind." Mrs. Bingley smiled at Miss Carrington.

"Oh, Jane, Lord Grayson said precisely what I was thinking. Your happiness radiates from you."

"I am truly a blessed man," Bingley said as he lifted his wife's hand and kissed her fingers.

Ashton found it difficult not to roll his eyes. It seemed that the groom was determined to take up Darcy's habit; the man was forever touching or kissing his wife's hand. He chose to ignore his own desire to cover Miss Carrington's hand with his own.

"I am pleased the two of you have met," Mrs. Bingley said with a sweet smile. "Though I had looked forward to performing the duty myself."

"Elizabeth took it upon herself," Ashton said in a teasing manner.

The bride huffed in faux displeasure. "First she marries before me and now she takes away my joy in introducing the two of you. She is fortunate I love her."

They all laughed, but others were waiting to bestow their well wishes, so Ashton bowed and led Miss Carrington away.

"They remind me of my parents." His companion's voice held a hint of wistfulness.

"Are they as affable as the Bingleys? I imagine your mother is a beauty."

Her smile was soft, and her eyes took on a faraway look. "My father has a certain dark ruggedness about him, but he is as amiable as Mr. Bingley. Mother is quite similar to Jane; she only sees the good in everyone." Her smile slipped away, and she lowered her gaze. "I wish I had taken that into consideration when I first arrived in England. Perhaps I would not have been surprised by those I was led to believe I could trust."

Ashton nodded and, succumbing to the temptation, placed his hand over hers where it rested upon his arm. "I have noted a certain distancing between Mother and Lady Carlisle over the years. Demi and Lady Gertrude have also become more acquaintances than friends. Of course, Father and Lord Carlisle still hold their alliances, so all are in company from time to time, but the ladies are not as open or warm as they were when we were younger."

She lifted her head in a regal manner. "I asked Elizabeth about that, but she appears to be a bit overwhelmed by the number of ladies she has met. She could not say for certain if Lady Matlock retained a close relationship with Lady Carlisle."

"Though Elizabeth is a social creature, I doubt she enjoys the machinations of the *ton*," Ashton said with a chuckle. "I am certain she would appreciate having a friend at her side as she navigates the first waters."

"I would have," Miss Carrington replied as she nodded. "She will have her sister."

"But Bingley is from trade and will not receive the same invitations as Darcy."

They were nearing the subject of their discussion, and Elizabeth was looking at them expectantly. Ashton had no desire to separate from Miss Carrington but knew it was inevitable. Reluctantly, he lifted his hand from hers and removed the rose from his lapel. He inhaled the sweet fragrance as he slowed their pace until they were stopped a short distance from the others.

"I believe this is actually yours." He held the rose out

to her.

She accepted it, lifting it to her nose before lowering it to reveal a warm smile. "Thank you, Lord Grayson."

"I was pleased to hold it for you." His eyes roamed over her countenance taking in her clear grey eyes, the upturned nose, the glowing complexion, and the petal-like lips. "May I call upon you when we return to London?"

A blush covered her cheeks as she nodded. "I would like that." She bit her lip. "Are you aware my brother and I are staying on Gracechurch Street in Cheapside?"

"Near the Gardiners?"

Miss Carrington nodded. "I believe you had just left your cousin there prior to my arrival with Elizabeth last week."

He knew his jaw hung slack, but he was unable to close it. Had he truly come so close to seeing her earlier? What would have been his reaction? Of course, he would have believed her married.

"My lord, are you well?"

Her hand reached out to him, and he clutched it. "Forgive me, I was wondering if I would have made as big a fool of myself there as I did here."

The smile which lit her face flooded him with hope. "You could have done no worse. Indeed, I am certain Miss de Bourgh most likely holds an unfavourable impression of me as I left rather suddenly and rudely."

"You? I do not believe it."

She nodded, manoeuvering her hand back to his arm and moving them forwards once more. "I feared seeing you again and became discomposed."

"But now?"

"Now I am quite looking forward to returning to town."

The smile she bestowed upon him drew a similar response. By the time they reached the others, he was surely beaming like a fool. His brother's expression told him he would be teased mercilessly once they were alone, but he cared not. Miss Carrington had accepted his request to court her and was even anticipating it. Suddenly, his future no longer held the bleak loneliness he had dreaded.

CHAPTER TWENTY-TWO
LONDON
9 MARCH

The Gardiner carriage drew to a stop before an impressive townhouse. Adsila glanced across the square to the Matlocks' home opposite as her stomach did a small flip, causing her to press her hand against it. Luckily, it had not voiced its concerns for all to hear.

Mrs. Gardiner gave her an encouraging smile just before the door opened and a footman handed her out. Adsila followed and the pair hurried up the front steps, clutching their bonnets to keep the wind from stealing them away. Instead, a gust pushed them through the door when it opened. They were laughing while they handed their outerwear to the waiting servants and followed the butler to the drawing room.

Elizabeth rose as they entered, her smile welcoming. "I am so pleased you were not blown away," she said as she took her aunt's hands and kissed her cheek. "Spending most of my time in the country, I thought the buildings blocked the wind in the city." She took Adsila's hand and pulled her towards the settee she had just vacated.

"It channels it instead," Mrs. Gardiner replied after greeting Lady Matlock.

"Adsila, you remember Lady Matlock and her daughter, Lady Bedlington?"

Her voice deserted her, so Adsila nodded as she curtseyed to the ladies.

"Miss Carrington." Lady Matlock's voice was warm and friendly. "You are as lovely as I remember."

"Thank you, your ladyship," Adsila replied as a blush warmed her cheeks.

"I was pleased to hear you had returned to London," Lady Bedlington said as they took their seats. "When we first met, I was so distracted by planning my wedding that we did not spend much time together. I hope you will remain for some time, and we can know each other better."

"My brother and I are planning on returning home next month, but I would like to know you better as well." Adsila hesitated, then decided to continue. "When we last met, I thought it possible that we might become friends in time."

"Do you miss your home and family?" Lady Matlock asked.

It was a question frequently asked of her, but the lady's warm tones took Adsila by surprise. They reminded her of her own mother when she knew the subject could be emotional. It brought tears to her eyes as she nodded.

"I do. My little brother might be a grown man by the time I see him again."

"We did not speak of it when we met before, but I knew your mother and father."

Adsila's eyes widened. "I did not know, though it should not be surprising."

"Your father was the talk of the *ton* that season. Every young lady wanted to catch his eye, though most had no desire to leave England; but once he saw your mother, they primped and preened in vain." She pressed her hand to her chest. "How he looked at her."

"He still does," Adsila said. "Theirs is an uncommon love." She smiled and looked to her hostess. "Though I believe Mr. and Mrs. Darcy have something similar."

"I would have to agree with you." Lady Matlock smiled at her new niece. "And, like your parents, the Darcys are envied by many of the *ton*."

The tea arrived, and Elizabeth served her guests. Once the servants had left, Adsila chose to further the conversation.

"My mother never told me about the *ton*, not in any real detail. I only knew that her parents did not want her to leave England, but eventually they recognized the love Mother and Father had for each other and gave their blessing."

Lady Matlock sipped her tea before studying Adsila. After a moment, she set her cup and saucer aside and folded her hands in her lap. "Your mother was a rare young lady. I doubt she saw the *ton* as they truly were, or perhaps she chose to see them as she wanted them to be. Even those she called her friends." The lady's brow rose upon this last bit, and she held Adsila's gaze.

Slowly, Adsila nodded. "I came to realize that to be the case once I was here."

"It is a shame your grandparents passed before you came to England. They would have given you a coming out that would have rivalled a princess's."

"Mother has only heard from her extended family twice since her marriage, and that was to notify her when her father and then her mother passed. Unfortunately, she was with child when my grandfather died, or she would have returned to England. I believe she wanted Grandmother to come live with us." Her shoulders were back and her head held high. "She never considered asking her cousins to sponsor me, and I have not been introduced to them since I have been here."

"No, I dare say that is for the best." Lady Matlock

shook her head as she took up her tea once more. "The Codringtons are quite firmly set in their ways."

"Codringtons?" Elizabeth asked. "Are they not the ones who gave me the cut at the theatre?"

"They did what?" Lady Bedlington demanded. "As if they are so very high and mighty. Why I have half a mind––"

Lady Matlock laid a hand upon her daughter's arm. "They are not worth the effort, Demi. We are above that."

"Did you not give them a bit of a cut yourself, Aunt?" There was a mischievous twinkle in Elizabeth's eye as she hid her smirk behind her teacup.

"Did I? It is quite noisy following a performance, as you are aware, and I doubt I would have heard if anyone called my name as I passed them."

"I am certain you are correct, Mamma." Lady Bedlington exchanged a wicked smile with their hostess. "I doubt I shall be able to hear her if Lady Codrington should address me in such a setting as well."

"Has my son called upon you?" Lady Matlock asked, causing Adsila to nearly choke upon her biscuit.

"He has," she replied when she had regained her composure.

"The viscount has also attended dinner at our home along with the Carringtons," Mrs. Gardiner offered.

Lady Matlock nodded. "Demi, are you not holding a musicale next week?"

"On Tuesday," Lady Bedlington said as she too nodded. "I gave Ashton an invitation to deliver to the Carringtons as I did not have their directions. Do you play, Miss Carrington?"

"Oh, I am certain she must," Lady Matlock said with a smile. "Her mother was quite a proficient."

"To my mother's vexation, I do not." Adsila felt her cheeks warm. "I have always blamed my inability on small hands," she said as she wiggled her fingers. "Instead, I would sing while she accompanied me."

"Oh, we must practice something together," Elizabeth cried. "I am not a proficient, but your voice would surely cover any of my slurs."

"You must take advantage of Georgiana's music instructor now that she has returned to town, Elizabeth" Lady Matlock advised. "I will not have the *ton* speaking ill of your abilities."

"They dare not," came a male voice from the doorway.

The ladies turned to find Mr. Darcy and Lord Grayson had entered the room. The viscount kissed his mother's cheek and nodded to his sister before bowing to rest of the ladies. As he rose, he smiled at Adsila.

"When Darcy told me you were having tea with Elizabeth, I forced him to invite me."

"Ashton, did you not give Miss Carrington the invitation to my musicale?" Lady Bedlington asked in a petulant tone.

"I have not had the opportunity. You only gave it to me yesterday, Demi, and this was the first I have seen the lady since then. I had planned to deliver it tomorrow when we are engaged to visit Montagu House."

"You are interested in the museum?" Lady Bedlington asked Adsila.

"Oh yes," she replied. "I did not have the opportunity when I was last in London. My brother and the Darcys are to join us."

"I have been looking forward to it," Elizabeth said. "I have not been since the year before my coming out."

"Georgiana is to accompany us as well," Mr. Darcy added.

Elizabeth nodded. "She has agreed to sketch anything she thinks my cousin would like to see as he is too young to attend."

"Has your eldest begun his schooling?" Lady Matlock asked Mrs. Gardiner.

As the matrons discussed the advantages and disadvantages of educating boys at home as compared to a school, Lord Grayson selected the seat nearest Adsila and drew it even closer.

"I am pleased to see you here today," he said with a soft smile she knew was for her alone.

"We have been having a lovely tea," she replied, causing his brow to arch.

"Until Darcy's and my arrival?" he asked with a devilish grin.

Adsila cocked her head to the side. "I did not say nor infer such a thing."

"Though it is true," Lady Bedlington said. "I hope you are not apt to follow Darcy's example and demand every moment of every day from Miss Carrington as he does from Elizabeth. I dare not think what I would do if Lord Bedlington was as attentive to me. It would drive me to Bedlam."

"Does Bedlington abandon you, Demi?" Lord Grayson asked with a frown.

"Heavens no," the lady replied with a laugh. "He simply allows me to spend my day as I choose. We are together in the evenings for dinner and any events. It is perfectly companionable without being suffocating."

Adsila noticed Elizabeth's brow crease before she forced a smile and said, "And young Herbert must take up much of your time." She turned to Adsila. "The Bedlingtons' son will be a year old next month."

A soft smile lifted Lady Bedlington's lips. "Herbert is a dear. I visit the nursery several times during the day when I am not making social visits."

"I do not know how you are able to be separated from him," Elizabeth said. "I just want to squeeze his chubby little cheeks every time I see him."

Her Ladyship laughed. "From the portraits I have seen, he is the very image of my husband's father, who, though he was a fit man in his youth, is once again a bit portly."

A distant look entered Elizabeth's eyes as she glanced at her husband. "I am impatient to see the gallery at

Pemberley to learn who our children may one day resemble."

Mr. Darcy's gaze softened as he regarded his wife. "I hope they inherit your features, my dear, though it would be best if our sons have my height."

Elizabeth laughed. "You would not be as proud if they were my height?"

"They may not be given the same esteem," Lord Grayson said before his cousin could respond. "I am certain if Darcy were not such a great tall fellow, he should not be paid half so much deference."

Mr. Darcy's eyes narrowed as he frowned at the viscount, but he was unable to respond as Lady Matlock had risen from her seat.

"I fear Demi and I must be going. We have a dinner this evening we are forced to attend."

Lady Bedlington scrunched her nose but rose to stand beside her mother. "Whether we wish to avoid it or not."

Their carriage was called, as was the Gardiners', and the party moved to the hall for the visitors to don their outerwear. Lord Grayson bowed over Adsila's hand before helping her into the carriage, then joined his mother and sister in theirs.

As she sat back against the squabs, Adsila decided it had been a pleasant afternoon, and she looked forward to being in company with the ladies again.

CHAPTER TWENTY-THREE
LONDON
MARCH

"My mother asked if you and your brother are available for a family dinner this Thursday," Ashton said as they paused before another landscape painting.

He had lost interest in the museum shortly after arriving, having been there with his cousin Anne a little over a month prior. Watching Adsila's reactions to some of the odder collections had been amusing, but he preferred sculptures to paintings and portraits to landscapes.

His companion turned from the artwork and studied his expression. "We are, but we shall only attend if you tell me your honest opinion of that piece." She pointed at the artwork behind him.

Without glancing at the work, Ashton replied, "It is much like every other landscape in this collection. I find nothing exciting nor inspiring about it."

"I am pleased to see our thoughts are comparable." A smile tugged at her lips as she began walking towards the exit. "What time are we to arrive?"

"I shall send a carriage to collect you at a quarter past four."

She nodded. "Who will be included in the party?"

Ashton slowed their pace. "Unfortunately, my Aunt Catherine will be in attendance as the party is in honour of her daughter's birthday. I was quite surprised Mother invited you at first, but I have been considering her possible reasons." He saw a look of concern cross Adsila's features and discreetly patted her hand which rested upon his arm. "My aunt will *not* be on her best behaviour as I suspect my father will make an announcement that evening which will displease her. Mother is either exposing you to the worst of our family to see if you are strong enough to withstand the harpy or—and I believe this to be more likely—so Elizabeth has additional support."

"Does the announcement have something to do with Elizabeth?" Adsila asked, her concern replaced by curiosity.

"No, but Aunt Catherine will blame her for it. You see, Darcy was supposed to marry Anne, according to her mother."

"Ah," she said with a nod. "If Elizabeth had not usurped the title of Mrs. Darcy, whatever is being announced would not have the same effect." She lifted a finger to her lips before leaning closer to him. "Is Miss de Bourgh coming into her inheritance? That would unseat her mother, which, had she married Mr. Darcy, would have been immaterial."

Ashton laughed. "You are too quick, my dear."

"Lord Grayson," a feminine voice called, and they stopped to look about.

Ashton frowned as he saw Lady Carlisle and her daughter approaching. "Your Ladyships," he said with a bow. "I believe you know Miss Carrington."

The look of surprise upon the ladies' countenances was fleeting but still amused him.

"Miss Carrington, it is a pleasure to see you in town,"

Lady Gertrude said with a modicum of sincerity as she curtseyed.

"I had not realized you still lived in England," her mother added with a nod of her head and the look of having eaten a lemon.

Adsila curtseyed. "My brother finished his schooling last term and we decided to spend the remaining time in London before returning home."

"You are not remaining in England?" Lady Carlisle's eyes darted to Ashton before returning to Adsila.

"It has fallen to me to change Miss Carrington's mind and convince her to stay with us longer." He purposefully held Adsila's gaze, not sparing the others a glance for a moment before reluctantly returning his attention to them.

"Will you be attending Lady Bedlington's musicale?" Adsila asked.

Mother and daughter exchanged another glance before the elder said, "I do not recall seeing the invitation."

"It must have slipped her mind last evening at dinner," Lady Gertrude replied.

Ashton's companion cocked her head to the side and caught his eye, her brow arched as she pursed her lips. Before more could be said regarding the event, Lady Carlisle held out her hand to Adsila.

"It was pleasant seeing you, Adsila. Please give your mother my best when you see her."

"Thank you, Lady Carlisle. I will."

After the ladies had left them, Ashton rested his hand upon Adsila's once more. "Shall we find the Darcys?"

She nodded, saying nothing.

They entered another gallery where they had arranged to meet with the others, but he guided her to an area mostly devoid of visitors, drawing her to a stop by a window.

"Are you well? Did meeting them upset you?"

Adsila raised her head to look directly into his eyes. "I was merely lost in thought. Were you aware your mother and sister were not looking forward to their dinner last evening?"

"They did say as much, did they not?" Ashton asked with widened eyes. "You believe it was due to the Carlisle ladies?"

She shrugged. "They were not invited to the musicale."

A strand of her hair had slipped from its pin and framed the side of her face. Ashton's fingers itched to tuck it behind her ear, but they were in too public an area. "I suspect Demi did not want you to feel uncomfortable."

"Lord Grayson, please tell your sister that Lady Carlisle and Lady Gertrude's presence will not unsettle me, but if *they* felt slighted due to my unintentional comment, it might make things more difficult for us all."

Her sudden silence was now explained; she had been attempting to find a way to undo the tension between the ladies. Ashton smiled and, surrendering to the temptation, tucked the silky lock of hair behind her ear.

"Miss Carrington, dare I ask that you call me Ashton when we are alone?"

Her cheeks reddened as she glanced about. "I had not realized we were alone, sir." Her brow arched and her lips twitched.

Having not heard his approach, Ashton jumped when Darcy's hand fell upon his shoulder, effectively stopping him from kissing Adsila in public and removing the lady's choice in the matter of a betrothal.

"Georgiana is finishing her last sketch. Have you seen enough art for today, Miss Carrington?" Darcy asked.

"Yes, Lord Grayson and I decided we had given the display of landscapes our share of attention."

"Splendid. Elizabeth had asked to visit Gunter's. Her sweet tooth is being very demanding of late."

"You truly cannot refuse her, can you?" Ashton asked with a shake of his head.

"Could you?" Darcy replied with a fleeting glance towards Adsila, causing Ashton to laugh.

"I suppose not," he conceded.

Darcy nodded. "I will find Carrington and see the carriage is readied," he said before leaving them.

"It appeared you were about to say something before Mr. Darcy approached us," Adsila said as they began walking towards the Darcy ladies at the far end of the gallery.

"Did it?" Ashton replied, searching for a diplomatic answer.

She nodded but said nothing more, forcing him to respond.

Ashton diverted her to a painting of children at play with no observers standing nearby. "Do you truly want to know where my thoughts had gone in that moment?" he whispered.

"I would," she responded, raising her stormy grey eyes to his.

"I considered how you would respond if I kissed you here, forcing you to accept my hand. I wondered if you would be terribly angry with me."

The blush returned to her cheeks, and lightning flashed in her eyes. "I am to leave London soon, sir, so I could not be forced to accept what I might not want."

"Might?" he asked, his heart in his throat.

"You asked if I would be angry with you."

Ashton nodded.

"For a time, I would have demanded a penance, I am certain. No lady wishes to have her choice taken from her; it is the only thing we have."

"And then?"

"I would not have allowed you to forget your *faux pas*."

"For how long?" he pressed, his hopes rising with every statement.

"Until we were separated." Her lips twitched.

"Tease," he whispered as he saw the ladies approaching them.

Adsila's musical laugh brought a lightness in his chest,

and he wondered how long she expected him to wait before asking for her hand.

****

The library door opened and closed just before Ashton heard his cousin's soft footsteps approaching him. She was once again attempting to sneak up on him, so he waited until she had nearly reached her goal before asking, "May I be of service, Anne?"

She dropped onto the sofa across from him with a soft huff. "Yes."

When she said no more, Ashton closed the book and met her gaze with expectancy.

"Have you proposed to Miss Carlton yet?"

With a small sigh, Ashton said, "Miss Carrington. No, I want to be certain she will not refuse me."

"What lady would refuse a future earl?" Anne asked before realizing what she had done. Giggling, she covered her mouth with her fingers.

"Yes, what lady, indeed?"

"Are you now not pleased that I did? You are free to court the lady of your choice." She folded her arms across her chest and smiled at him in a superior, Lady Catherine manner.

"Why do you want to know if I have proposed?"

Anne's posture relaxed a bit, and she brushed some lint from the cushion beside her. "I was thinking you could announce your betrothal before Mamma can begin her tirade tomorrow evening."

He frowned. "Her tirade will begin the moment Father gives your birthday toast. You want me to upstage you and steal your moment?"

"Oh." Anne giggled again. "Not then. I mean later, when I tell her of my plans for Rosings Park."

Ashton felt a sinking in his stomach. "What plans?"

"Once Mamma is removed to the widow's cottage, I

will invite Sam and Tabby to come live with me, along with their mother."

"What of your coming out and finding a husband from the *ton?*"

The corners of her lips turned upwards in a disturbing smile. "I never truly had any interest in marrying. You are not the only man I would have refused, Ashton. The doctor told me years ago that it was unlikely I would survive childbirth, so why would I chance it?"

"Does Lady Catherine know that?"

Anne shrugged. "I suppose, though she rarely believes anyone that disagrees with her. Shortly after that, a new physician began handling my care."

Pinching the bridge of his nose, Ashton asked, "Are Mother and Father aware of your plans?"

She tsked. "Of course not! You are the first I am telling as I require your assistance." Her eyes widened. "And I forbid you to tell anyone!"

Reluctantly, he nodded. "Anne, if you do not marry, who will inherit Rosings after you pass?"

"Well, at this time it is Philip, but that might change in the future. After all, it will be mine to do with as I see fit."

Suddenly remembering the last scene which had played out in the library, Ashton leant forwards and asked, "What did Father learn regarding the Evans sisters' inheritance?"

His cousin appeared a bit ill at ease for a moment. She glanced at the door, but then turned towards him. "It has not been touched."

"Then Lady Catherine merely destroyed the letter?"

"We can only suppose that is all. Perhaps she made an attempt to do more but was thwarted in some manner."

Ashton settled back in his seat and crossed his legs. "Do you truly think so little of your mother, Anne?"

"Does not everyone?" Her eyes glistened, tugging at Ashton's heart.

Standing, he joined her on the sofa and took her hand in his. "I am sorry it seems that way. Lady Catherine can be overbearing and demanding, but I daresay everything she has done has been for your benefit." The words surprised them both, but Ashton believed them to be true. "Had she not been so autocratic in her delivery, perhaps others would have been more receptive to her requests. Not that they would have given into them, but there would have been conversations instead of arguments."

"But Mamma *is* demanding and overbearing. I am not saying she is a terrible mother, only that I have earned my position as Mistress of Rosings. I will decide from here on how I shall live and who will be in my life."

Ashton bowed his head. "You are correct, of course."

"Then you will propose before tomorrow evening?" she asked, her eyes wide and hoping.

Ashton dropped her hand and stood. Gathering his book, he bowed to her. "I will decide when I propose based upon Miss Carrington's reception."

"But you will see her before the dinner?" Anne pressed.

Ashton turned and left the room. He heard his cousin call his name as the door clicked shut, and a moment later something hit the door with a solid thud. He shook his head, hoping the book had not been badly damaged and was not one of his father's favourites.

CHAPTER TWENTY-FOUR
LONDON
12 MARCH

It was early, but Ashton had to speak to Darcy and Elizabeth before arriving at the Carringtons' door. Anne's encouragement to propose, albeit for her own purposes, had unsettled him the entire night.

Since their time in Hertfordshire, he had come to realize that Adsila was more than what he had once believed her to be. Like their moment in the museum, she was quick to see his disinterest and force him to admit it. During an evening at the opera, she noted his discomfort with the attention they were receiving from patrons and redirected him to the performance. For the remainder of the act, it was the two of them holding hands while fully enraptured by the music. Even after the lights came up, they spoke quietly to one another while the others in their party dealt with visitors to the box. She made the *ton* disappear.

Then there was her concern regarding the Carlisles. Ashton knew they had not treated her as her mother had wanted, but Adsila would not revel in their being excluded from Demi's musicale. As she requested, he asked his sister, who confirmed she had omitted the Carlisle's to avoid Miss Carrington's discomfort. Though Demi no longer considered Lady Gertrude her particular friend, she did send around invitations to the family. He was certain Adsila would be pleased when he told her.

How could he explain to her that he wanted to marry her *because* she was not part of the *ton?* Because she disliked their intrigues as much as he did, but remained compassionate to their feelings? She had been hurt by them, but she would not hurt them in return. For this reason, he wondered if asking her to be his wife, subjecting her to *their* criticism, was not selfish. Would she have any desire to accept such a role? He was the eldest son of an earl; he could not turn his back on his position and responsibilities.

The sitting room door opened, and Elizabeth entered with her husband just behind her, interrupting Ashton's pacing.

"Good morning, Ashton." Her words were friendly, but her expression was concerned.

Darcy was more to the point. "You look to be in a pelt. What has you in such a state?"

"Good morning, Elizabeth," Ashton said as he bowed over her hand. "I apologize for interrupting your breakfast, but I must speak with you before I depart for Gracechurch Street."

Her brows rose. "Be at ease, we had finished eating. How can we be of assistance?" She motioned to the settee, but Ashton was too agitated to sit.

"Have you spoken to your friend? Regarding me?"

Elizabeth and Darcy exchanged a glance as they took their seats. Her husband took her hand in his before addressing his cousin.

"Has something occurred? Have you changed your mind regarding courting Miss Carrington?"

A harsh laugh burst from Ashton's lips. "No!" He fell

onto the settee. "I am fearful it is too soon to ask for her hand. Will she refuse me if I ask now? Anne suggested—"

"Anne?" Darcy interrupted him. "What has Anne to do with your proposing to Miss Carrington?"

He leant forwards, placed his elbows upon his legs, and plunged his fingers into his hair. "She will be making an announcement tomorrow evening and hoped I could distract her mother by announcing my engagement to Adsila." He sat back, waving away his cousin's questions and exclamations. "I know it is not a reason to propose, but the thought of having her as my wife has been with me ever since Anne mentioned it; before, if I am truly honest with myself." He looked to Elizabeth. "Do you think she would consider accepting me, or should I wait a bit longer?"

"I have not discussed it with her," Elizabeth replied with a slight shrug. "From what I have seen, the two of you are quite compatible."

Darcy snorted. "They abandoned us at the theatre, forcing us to speak to all who came specifically to see his lady."

Elizabeth nodded. "They were quite inattentive to other people and wholly engrossed by one another. Is not general incivility the very essence of love? I am certain you and I have been accused of it on occasion."

"Occasion?" Ashton asked with a shake of his head. "Had I not been announced, the two of you would not have seen me upon entering the room, I am certain." He had been about to continue berating his cousin when Elizabeth's words struck him. "You believe Adsila and I are on par with you and Darcy?"

The couple exchanged a loving look as their lips curled upward. Ashton began to wonder if they remembered his presence when Darcy turned to him.

"It is not for us to say, Ashton. *Ask her!*"

****

Ashton stood upon the Carringtons' stoop in a light drizzle, still debating the motives of his presence. The door opened, though he had not knocked, and the lady of the house smiled up at him, effectively removing whatever conflicting thoughts bounced about his head.

"I found Mrs. Gallagher tapping her foot in the hall as she had work to do, but she was waiting to admit you." Her lips pursed and her eyes danced in amusement.

Ashton stepped inside, closing the door behind him. He just stood, staring at her for a moment. His eyes caressed her features, drinking her in as though it was the first time he had seen her since they had separated years prior.

"Ashton," she scolded in a soft voice, "you are wet."

The thrill of hearing his name on her lips warmed him, and he barely noticed she had removed his hat and was tugging at his coat.

"March is still too cold to be walking in the rain," she tsked.

He surrendered to her ministrations but remained where he was when she tugged on his arm to lead him to the parlour.

"Where is your brother?" Ashton asked.

"Waiting for us."

"May we have a moment?" He laid his hand upon her upper arm, turning her to face him fully.

Adsila's brow arched. "In the hall?"

"No." He looked about, seeing their surroundings for the first time.

With an easy laugh, she slipped her hand about his arm and led him to the parlour.

"I have rescued Lord Grayson from the misty London rain, Tom. Will you ask Mrs. Gallagher to bring the tea tray?"

Her brother's brows knit together. His gaze drifted to the bell pull, but he rose when Adsila placed her hand upon her hip.

"I shall return quickly," he said to Ashton before leaving the door open as he exited the room.

Once again, Ashton found himself staring at the lady beside him. Her eyes, which could appear so stormy, now looked like the sky on a foggy morning, hiding everything——a dangerous situation if one were unfamiliar with the terrain. He wondered if he was familiar enough to avoid any misstep.

"My brother will return soon, sir." She lowered her eyes. "Did you have something to ask me?"

"Yes," he breathed. Suddenly feeling afloat, he reached out and grasped her hand. "I realize you have no love for the society to which I belong, but—"

"Ashton." She lifted her free hand and cupped his cheek. "Do you truly wish to speak of *them* now?" Her lips lifted on one side.

"Minx," he whispered as he drew her into his arms.

Her brows lifted as she placed her hands against his chest. "Are you attempting to remove my choice again, sir?"

"Forgive me." He released her and dropped to his knees before her. "I would never dream of forcing you into anything you do not desire. However, if you are of a similar heart, would you consider becoming my wife? I find I cannot think of my life without you at my side."

Her smile spread as she squeezed his hand. "Yes," she whispered. "Yes," she said again as she leant towards him.

Ashton was on his feet in an instant, wrapping his arms about her and pulling her close. "I promise to protect you from the fools who are unable to see your worth."

Her fingers covered his lips. "Again, you mention them. Ashton, I am marrying you, not them."

"But in becoming my wife—"

"I am ensuring my happiness."

"Adsila," he said reverently, "how am I so fortunate?"

Her teasing smile returned. "I took pity on you."

Ashton pulled her flush against him, kissing her soundly until he heard a woman's gasp and felt a hand upon his shoulder.

"I will assume I am to wish you joy, as I have no interest in challenging you," Carrington said as they separated.

"You may," Adsila replied, causing the housekeeper to squeal and rush from the room.

"Shall we speak?" her brother asked Ashton.

Adsila huffed. "I am of age and older than you."

"But I am your only male relative in England," Tom said with a smug smile.

Lifting her hand to bestow a kiss, Ashton smiled. "Forgive me, Adsi, but he is correct."

Her eyes narrowed. "Very well, *Ash.*"

With a chuckle, he kissed her hand once more, realizing why Darcy did so frequently. He bowed formally before following her brother from the room.

Upon entering the study, he felt as though he had been transported to Longbourn; clutter covered every surface steady enough to support it. The main difference was that every seat other than the master's held something preventing it from being used for what it was intended. He thought in Bennet's case it was his daughters who maintained a semblance of order and could not suppress the frown which followed when he feared Adsila had no interest in entering the room.

"Forgive me." Carrington moved a stack of books from the chair positioned in front of the desk. "I fear Adsila has completely given up on this room. When she first arrived in London, she forced me to keep at least one chair open, but she has decided the study has insufficient windows and forces me to join her in the drawing room for any discussions." He settled the stack on top of another, which teetered but did not topple, then motioned for Ashton to sit in the cleared seat. "Have you—?"

Ashton drew the settlement papers from his breast

pocket and placed them before the young man. "You will see the areas where you need enter your sister's dowry, which will be hers always."

"You were certain you would be accepted?" Carrington asked as he sat back in his seat without examining the document.

"No. When we returned to town, I had my solicitor draw up the papers based upon my father's and my cousin's. Being pleased with what he had provided, I found no reason to make any changes. I brought them with me today hoping Adsila would accept me despite my own feelings of unworthiness."

A smile pulled at Carrington's lips on one side. "Good. Even with a title, you understand she is far superior."

"I do."

"Then I will have my man determine the current value of Adsi's dowry and return these to you as soon as may be." The slight smile turned into a full grin. "It has been amusing to watch you bungle your way through. I have learnt much, and I thank you. Though there is one thing you should know." He leant forwards in his seat. "Do not think that my being on the other side of an ocean will save you should you hurt my sister, Grayson."

Ashton sat taller in his seat. "I am certain you will have allies in my brother and cousin, so I do not doubt you. Indeed, I might never forgive myself if I were to injure her in any way."

The younger man nodded. "We are agreed. Shall we return to Adsi before she storms in here to find us?"

They could hear feminine voices as they approached the drawing room, entering to find the housekeeper and her mistress.

"'Tis 'bout time!" Mrs. Gallagher cried when she spied them. "I opened a bottle o' wine to celebrate."

"I was telling her it was too early, but she insisted," Adsila said with a laugh.

"Pish," the woman responded. "'Tis never too early to

celebrate a joyous moment. Lord knows there is enough sadness in this world, so we must rejoice when we are able." She poured out four glasses and handed them about.

Ashton exchanged an amused look with his betrothed as he moved to her side.

"Well, Master Carrington, have ye nothin' to say to your sister and her beau?" Mrs. Gallagher prodded.

"I have said what was needed to Lord Grayson." He dipped his head towards Ashton before facing his sister. "Adsi, I wish you joy; there is no one, in my estimation, who deserves it more, and I am pleased to know that Grayson agrees with me."

They drank, then the housekeeper raised her glass before looking sideways at Carrington. "Well done, sir, but in this the Irish will always excel." Clearing her throat, she looked to the couple. "May ye always have walls for the winds, a roof for the rain, tea beside the fire, laughter to cheer ye, those ye love near ye, and all your heart might desire. *Sláinte!*"

They drank once more, then the lady gathered the bottle and tray. "I'll be givin' the others a sip in your honour if ye approve, miss."

Adsila laughed. "Of course, Mrs. Gallagher. We are to dine with Lord Grayson's family this evening, so you may celebrate my happiness then as you see fit."

The woman dipped a curtsey to all and left the room as Adsila turned to Ashton.

"Please tell me we have a property where Mrs. Gallagher and her granddaughter may work. I shall miss them dearly when Tom returns home and we leave this house."

"Whatever you desire, my love." He lifted her hand and kissed it. "If need be, I will purchase one."

She laughed once more, and Ashton was certain he had never heard a more beautiful sound.

CHAPTER TWENTY-FIVE
LONDON
12 MARCH

The Matlock carriage made its way from Cheapside to Mayfair with relatively little impeding its progress. Inside, Adsila hummed to herself as she watched the buildings pass without noting a single detail. Her brother watched her with a smirk lingering upon his lips, much as it had been all day.

Ashton had only departed when it was absolutely necessary in order to prepare for dinner and took a hackney, leaving his carriage so the driver was not forced to traverse the distance numerous times. With only one forward facing seat, it was the smallest of the Matlock carriages, for which Ashton apologized profusely, as though such a thing would upset her.

With a shake of her head, she thought of all the times she would have to remind her betrothed that she was not a demanding member of the *ton,* just before a disturbing idea replaced it. *Would* she become like them? Having whatever one required when one required it—or worse, having whatever one *desired* whether it was a necessity or not—

could change a person.

"I believe that is the first time I have seen you without a silly smile upon your lips. What has caused you such distress, Adsi?" Tom nudged her arm with his. "You are not regretting your decision, are you? Though I was reluctant at first, I do believe Grayson is a good match for you."

With a shudder, Adsila pushed the disturbing thoughts aside. "I was being silly for a moment. No, I am not reconsidering. It looks as though you were correct; you will be returning home alone."

Her brother's expression transformed from teasing to horror stricken as his jaw fell open and his eyes widened. "Oh, I forgot. Oh, Adsi, forgive me; it completely slipped my mind. While you were preparing for this evening, I received a letter from Father."

"Father?" Her heart began to race. "Has something occurred? Are Mother and Arthur well?"

He patted her hand before reaching into his pocket. "They are. They have decided to join us. We are to expect them on the ship we were to board the end of April."

Tom handed her the missive, and she opened it quickly, greedy to read it for herself. It began with praises for Tom's completing his studies ahead of schedule, but the next section caused her frown to return.

"Why is Father concerned for my wellbeing?" she asked her brother.

Tom's countenance reddened, and he rubbed the back of his neck. "Adsi, I know you were pleased to see me when I arrived in England, but you were not happy. In the years that followed, you tried to appear content, but I knew something was wrong. I wrote of my suspicions to Father, and he discussed them with Mother. Apparently, your letters to her were equally lacking in your normal spirited ways."

"They are coming to England because they do not wish me to return but want me to be happy here?" Her eyes fell back to the page which now shook slightly as she continued reading.

"No! You know we all want what is best for you, and you have found it. Grayson loves you, as you do him. You will be an important lady of the *ton*, perhaps even changing some of its members for the better." He said the last with a huff. "They are already at sea. Can you not see how happy they will be when they arrive to learn that you are engaged?" He smiled. "Perhaps we should not announce the engagement until they arrive and Grayson has asked Father for your hand."

The smile returned to Adsila's lips. "I am certain the only reason he will not announce it this evening is because we are gathering to celebrate his cousin's birthday. You may try to forestall him further, but I doubt it will work."

The carriage slowed, and she tucked the letter into her reticule to read again later. Tom exited when the door was opened, but the hand which reached back for her was not his. Her smile spread as she took Ashton's hand and stepped out of the equipage.

"I missed you," he whispered as he lifted her hand to his lips, causing warmth to flood her cheeks.

"It has only been a few hours."

"An eternity." He slipped her hand about his arm and escorted her into the townhouse, where Tom was already greeting the Darcys, who had arrived a few minutes prior.

Elizabeth's grin was enough to tell Adsila her friend was aware of the change in her circumstances. Mr. Darcy shook his cousin's hand a bit harder than normal.

"Have you been inside?" Ashton asked, to which the couple replied in the negative. "Lady Catherine has not yet descended. One might think it was *her* birth we celebrated."

With a soft jab of her elbow, Adsila noted, "I believe she had an active part in the day."

Her betrothed's cheeks pinked. "You are correct, of course. Forgive me."

"Oh, he does that well." Elizabeth slipped her arm about Adsila's free arm. "Come, let us join the others before we can be accused of lingering too long in the hall."

The ladies preceded the gentlemen into Lady Matlock's drawing room, though not her favourite, Elizabeth noted. "When all the family is here, it is the most comfortable. However, for smaller gatherings, she prefers the green room which overlooks the gardens. It is a lovely view, and I am always pleased when led in that direction." She nodded further down the hall towards the back of the house.

Adsila could not help but think her friend provided this information knowing one day she might be living in this very house. She pursed her lips, wondering if she and Ashton would be sharing the townhouse with his parents. It was nothing against Lady Matlock; Adsila had simply become accustomed to being the lady of the house.

A pat on her arm recalled her to the present, and she smiled at Elizabeth just before they entered the drawing room.

Lady Matlock rose and approached them with what appeared to be a genuine smile. "Welcome," she said before placing a kiss upon Elizabeth's cheek and then Adsila's.

Lady Bedlington also approached and took a hand of each of the ladies, pulling them to a sofa large enough for the three to share. "Aunt Catherine arrived this morning, but she has not come below. I suspect she is anticipating making a grand entrance. Miss Carrington, I apologize for anything you see or hear from my aunt this evening."

"Your brother has already warned me," Adsila said with a reassuring smile. "Do not forget, I am accustomed to the ways of . . . certain types of people."

"What a polite way to say it." Her Ladyship shook her head. "Unfortunately, one cannot choose family."

Elizabeth laughed. "Oh, Demi, do not be so dramatic. I can attest, everyone has a member or two of their family who can be somewhat embarrassing."

"But my brothers have told me how delightful your family is, even if they are not fashionable. At least they do not reprimand and lecture complete strangers." She shuddered.

"And where is Miss de Bourgh?" Adsila asked.

"Papa asked to speak with her. They should return shortly." She giggled as she clasped Adsila's hand. "My brother is quite displeased with me for stealing you away, but he must become accustomed to it. Ladies and gentlemen rarely speak in the drawing room unless they are single."

Lady Bedlington's eyes sparkled, making Adsila blush. Glancing across the room at her betrothed, she wondered if he had told his family or if they were simply able to tell. At least they appeared pleased.

The doors opened, admitting the exasperated-looking earl and Miss de Bourgh, who wore a decided frown. After greeting the company, the pair claimed seats by Lady Matlock and began a hushed conversation.

"Oh dear," Lady Bedlington said under her breath. "I had hoped we would have a few moments of pleasantness this evening, but it appears doubtful. I suppose we will have to make the most of this time." She turned to Elizabeth. "When is Miss Bingley to arrive in town? I believe the four of us should have an outing. Perhaps a visit to the modiste and a few other stores before taking tea."

"I believe her arrival is dependent on your brother's presence."

"I do wish Philip would resign from the army," she said with a sigh. "He would be so much happier if he were settled."

"Is the colonel not a man of action?" Adsila asked. "Will he be able to settle into domestic life? I have heard of men who are unable to leave soldiering behind them."

"Oh, not Philip." Her Ladyship shook her head, her

eyes wide. "He loves society and is quite at ease in any setting. He will have no trouble transitioning; he is only an officer as he is a second son and it is expected."

Elizabeth frowned as she looked at her cousin but said nothing, so Adsila followed her example. Instead, she glanced about the room. Ashton, Tom, Mr. Darcy, and Lord Bedlington were gathered nearby and seemed to be having a debate, though the others frequently had to recall her betrothed to the conversation. She smiled at him, and he appeared about to rise and come to her side when the doors opened once more.

The woman who entered was tall and rather large, with strongly-marked features which might once have been handsome. Her air was not conciliating, and she seemed to view them all, the earl included, as of an inferior rank. She ignored Elizabeth completely and merely looked Adsila and Tom over from head to toe following the introduction before turning to her brother and demanding he resign his seat to her as it was her preference.

"Dinner is ready, Catherine," Lady Matlock said. "We have merely been waiting for you to join us."

Without acknowledging her hostess, Lady Catherine reached for her brother's arm, but he stepped away.

"Anne is our guest of honour this evening, so I will be escorting her." Lord Matlock offered his arm to his niece, who accepted it without meeting her mother's eye.

Lady Matlock followed the earl on the arm of her son-in-law, followed by Ashton, who quickly bowed to his sister, sending a longing look at Adsila while his aunt huffed.

"Aunt Catherine," Mr. Darcy said as he held out his arm.

Though she frowned, she accepted, but she said nothing to him as they traversed the hallway.

"I believe I am the luckiest gentleman present this evening," Tom said as he bowed to Elizabeth and Adsila.

They each accepted an arm and followed the others

into the dining room.

"Fitzwilliam and I have a wager on how long it takes his aunt to complain about the odd number of guests," Elizabeth whispered loud enough for both her companions to hear. "If he carries the conversation at dinner, you will know I have won."

They entered the room in time to hear her ladyship proclaim in a disparaging tone, "Esther, you were unable to find another gentleman to fill the table?"

"Philip was to join us, but I received word in the last hour that his general required his presence."

Mr. Darcy sighed as he took his seat. "We shall simply have to muddle through without my cousin's wit this evening." He turned to his hostess. "Your table is elegant as always, Aunt."

Lady Matlock looked at him suspiciously. "Thank you, Darcy." Her eyes flashed towards his wife and narrowed.

Adsila looked across the table to find her friend trying unsuccessfully to suppress a grin. Tom, to her left, cleared his throat, and she realized he too appeared highly amused.

"Bedlington," Darcy said, taking the man by surprise. "Have you had the duck at Matlock House? If not, you are in for a treat."

"Why, yes, I believe I have." The man turned to his right but quickly looked to his hostess instead of addressing Lady Catherine. "I cannot think of a meal at Matlock House that has not been delicious."

"I shall pass your compliments on to Cook." Lady Matlock nodded once. "Though I believe I should wait until you actually taste this evening's fare."

As the first course was served, Adsila looked across the table at Ashton and smiled. She was pleased to have amiable companions in Tom to her left and Lady Bedlington to her right, but having her love before her stole most of her attention.

Conversation flowed as it normally did, however everyone at the table slowly began casting odd looks at Mr.

Darcy. Adsila noted Elizabeth employing her glass and her serviette frequently to hide her amusement. With a look to her brother, she gave a knowing tip of her head, and they too were forced to utilize the same techniques.

"What did I miss?" Lady Bedlington whispered to Adsila.

Lifting her serviette to her lips, Adsila replied, "Mr. Darcy has lost a wager to his wife."

Her companion tittered. "And his punishment is speaking?"

Adsila nodded. As she lifted her head, she found Ashton watching her with a soft look in his eyes. Warmth rushed up from her chest, and she knew her countenance must appear quite red, but she could not look away.

The dinner began to come to an end, and Lord Matlock rose from his seat. Everyone quieted as he cleared his throat.

"We are gathered together this evening to celebrate our Anne's birthday, a very special birthday indeed. Everyone, raise your glass. I hope that we are able to celebrate many more such days with her, either here or in her home, as I am pleased to announce that Anne is now the Mistress of Rosings Park and the remainder of her father's estate."

The group wished her a happy birthday and drank to her health. Adsila felt as though everyone, not just herself, was fighting the urge to look at Lady Catherine.

Shortly after, Lady Matlock rose and led the ladies back to the drawing room, but not before reminding her husband she expected the gentlemen in less than half an hour. Laughter was heard after the dining room door was closed. Elizabeth, who had slipped her arm about Adsila's, giggled.

"My poor husband," she whispered. "If you had not guessed, I said his aunt would complain before we had even been seated. He thought she would have been complaining regarding something else—most likely having to do with either him or myself—at that time and would only have the opportunity to mention the seating after the first course was served."

Adsila shook her head. "Must he continue speaking for the entire evening?"

"Oh heavens, no." Elizabeth's smile grew. "Mr. Darcy has always been reticent. His cousins found ways to encourage him to speak when he was younger, and my family and I have continued their practices, but he would become quite cross if he were forced to speak all night. In truth, I allowed him to stop after the fish course, but by then Lord Bedlington and Aunt Esther were expecting him to continue, so he was forced to do so."

"Perhaps if you had alerted them to the circumstances, they would have allowed him to fall silent," Adsila suggested.

"If I were not afraid Aunt Esther would frown upon the wager, I might have," she said with a laugh as they entered the drawing room and drew to a stop at the scene before them.

"Anne, this is ridiculous. You are far too weak to be Mistress of Rosings. I insist you return home with me tomorrow. You look pale," Lady Catherine decreed from a chair turned to encompass the entire room.

"I will be returning to Rosings tomorrow, Mamma, but I am not weak. Papa wanted me to be the Mistress of Rosings, and so shall I be." Miss de Bourgh's posture was rigid as she confronted her mother. "A letter has already been sent to the housekeeper to have your things removed to the dower cottage. Those servants who prefer to remain with you will do so."

"You what?" Her Ladyship demanded. "How dare you make such arrangements behind my back?"

"There has been nothing secretly done. Uncle Henry told you months ago that I would inherit Rosings today and you would remove to the dower cottage. Repairs and modernizations have been made over the time I have been in London. Everything was done directly beneath your nose to make ready for this day, so I cannot fathom you being unaware of it."

"And this is how you would treat me? This is your final resolve! I am your mother, and I have a say—"

"*Had* a say, until today." Miss de Bourgh took a deep breath as she smoothed her hands over her skirt. "I had thought we could be rational regarding the changes, but you have proven me wrong."

Lady Matlock laid a hand upon her niece's. "This need not be discussed now."

"Oh, shut it, Esther," Lady Catherine shot at her brother's wife. "We are not your society friends, eager to bow to your demands in order to gain a seat at your table."

"No, you are not." Their hostess stood. "Were you such, I would have you removed from my home due to your boorish behaviour. Unfortunately, you are family, which you have always believed gave you the right to behave as you like. In this instance, I am pleased to disappoint you. If you are dissatisfied with the way the evening is progressing, I ask that you remove to your rooms until the morning, when you may return to Kent."

Lady Catherine also rose, standing toe-to-toe with the countess. "How *dare* you speak to me in this manner? I shall speak to my brother—"

"And say what, Catherine?" Lord Matlock asked from the doorway.

"Uncle Henry," Anne said as she rose from her seat to join the other ladies. "I believe it best that all is brought forth at this time."

"What are you speaking of?" Lady Catherine eyed her daughter suspiciously, a fierce frown upon her features.

"You must be removed from Rosings, Mother, as I have asked my sisters to come live with me there."

Lady Catherine sputtered, her colour rising until Adsila feared for her wellbeing. Ashton, Darcy, and Lord Bedlington moved closer to the woman, possibly to catch her should she collapse. Lord Matlock closed his eyes, a pained look crossing his countenance.

"You managed to keep them from their inheritance since Papa passed, but now they will have the life they should have had. We will be happy as a proper family." There was nothing cruel about Miss de Bourgh's expression. Her eyes might have held a hint of victory, but she also appeared on the verge of tears.

"You would bring those demon spawn into *my* house?"

"*My* house."

Her Ladyship turned on her brother. "You knew this?"

"Anne made me aware of her plans just before dinner." The earl appeared a bit defeated.

"And you allowed it?" his sister demanded.

"It is her home, Cathy, as Lewis desired."

Lady Catherine snorted. *"Lewis desired."*

"I warn you, Mother." Miss de Bourgh took a step closer. "Say *nothing* against my father."

"Your father was not a saint, Anne!"

All in the room remained pinned to their places. No one sat, moved, or even breathed, except Lord Matlock.

"Catherine, this subject is closed for this evening."

"Indeed," Anne said as she looked over her mother's shoulder. "We have had enough of my birthday. Let us truly celebrate something joyous. Ashton, is there not something you have to tell us?"

All in the room inhaled as one, and Adsila turned wide eyes towards her betrothed, praying he would not join their happiness with this degradation.

"Now is not the time, Anne," he replied without looking away from Adsila, allowing her to breathe once more.

Lady Catherine spun about to face her nephew. "Of what does she speak?" She turned back and looked at Adsila, her eyes narrowing. "What have you done?" She spun back once more to face Ashton. "You are a viscount and will be earl. You cannot marry *her*. She is a half-breed Colonist."

Elizabeth, Tom, and Lady Bedlington surrounded Adsila, but it was the look in Ashton's eyes which supported her the most. The fire which burned there was by far the warmest, safest place she had ever beheld. Without a thought, she crossed the room and took her place beside him, lacing her fingers with his.

"Miss Adsila Carrington has more character, class, and good breeding in her smallest finger than you have in your entire body, and I am blessed to have won her regard. She will be Lady Grayson and, when the time comes, Lady Matlock, and there is nothing a bitter old woman such as yourself may do about it."

He turned to Adsila. "Forgive me for having to announce our happiness in this manner, my love." He lifted her hand to his lips and pressed a lingering kiss to her fingers before turning to his mother. "Forgive me, Mother, for being disrespectful, however, I can see no reason why we may not have *this woman* removed from *our* house."

Lady Catherine turned upon her sister by law. "You would not dare remove me from my family's home."

"It appears you have estranged yourself from your family, Catherine." Lady Matlock nodded once towards the door, and two footmen stepped forwards. "Please escort Lady Catherine to her rooms and alert her maid they will be leaving at first light for the dower cottage at Rosings Park."

The woman's shouting could be heard through the solid oak doors until only distance quieted them. Once everyone was convinced she would not return, the shock of the situation began to wear away. The first to recover was Tom.

"I say, Grayson, I thought you understood the change in circumstances I conveyed to you following dinner."

Many of those gathered paled as their eyes darted between Adsila, Ashton, and Tom.

"I had no intention of making an announcement this

evening, Carrington. I was forced to it to defend Adsila." Ashton lowered his gaze to her. "I had no desire to connect our engagement to *this.*"

"I know you did not," she told him.

"But what has changed?" Lady Matlock asked.

Adsila smiled at her hostess. "My parents are to arrive in England in a fortnight. Ashton must ask my father for his blessing."

CHAPTER TWENTY-SIX
LONDON
15 APRIL

Mr. Henson entered the breakfast room carrying a letter lying on a silver salver. He paused by Ashton's chair with an almost imperceptible gleam in his eye.

"Lord Grayson," the butler said in his usual formal manner.

Ashton noted the decidedly feminine handwriting and snatched the missive from the tray. Though he attempted to present some semblance of calm, he nearly tore it open in his desire to learn its contents. *"They have arrived,"* the sender confirmed the reason for the early morning arrival. Ashton leapt from his seat, nearly knocking Henson down, and rushed for the door.

"Ashton!" his father called, pulling his son to a stop. "Whatever is it?"

"Adsila's parents have arrived."

Without another word or a backwards glance, he took the stairs two at a time and ran down the hallway leading to his mother's suite. Not leaving sufficient time for his first knock to be answered, he rapped again upon her door. He was about to knock a third time when someone cleared their throat behind him.

"Forgive me, sir," Henson said in a staid voice. "You left before I could inform you a letter was also delivered to Lady Matlock."

"Thank you, Henson," Ashton called over his shoulder as he headed back the way he had come, pausing only a few feet away. "Have a—"

"The carriage will be out front in a matter of moments, and Mr. Carter is gathering your outerwear."

A slow smile spread across his features as Ashton shook a finger at the man. "If you are angling for a raise, it is not yet my decision." As he turned, heading back down the stairs, he thought he heard the servant laugh.

As promised, in a matter of moments, he was in his father's finest carriage, moving ever closer to Gracechurch Street. The moment the regret of not riding while the carriage followed began to creep into his mind, he withdrew Adsila's letter and read it again.

"My dearest,

They have arrived! A storm as they entered the Channel caused the delay, but Mother, Father, and dear Arthur arrived this morning as Tom and I were sitting down to break our fast. We explained that they will not be staying with us as the house is too small, but we will attempt to wait until you arrive to tell them more.

Hurry, my love,
Adsila"

The wait for the Carringtons' arrival had lasted longer than the expected fortnight. It had now been nearly five weeks since the disastrous birthday dinner. The first three weeks were filled with peace as Lady Catherine had left at first light the following morning and Anne a bit later in the day. Demi's musicale had been a success, and the Carlisle ladies had been polite if not overly familiar when speaking to Adsila.

The looks of the *ton* as they slowly came to understand Ashton and Adsila were forming an attachment were humourous. Having Darcy and Elizabeth to draw some of the attention was a godsend. Adsila and Elizabeth had grown closer, if that was possible, while facing society's scrutiny. Miss Bingley arrived in town and joined the others, particularly when Philip was granted leave to attend events.

Ashton frowned. His brother had appeared distracted the last few times they were together. He wondered if something was afoot. Before the thought could fully germinate, the carriage slowed, and Ashton realized they were entering Cheapside. In a few more minutes, he would be meeting his future family.

Taking a deep breath, he looked himself over and determined that, minus a piece or two of lint which was easily plucked away, his appearance was immaculate. If he could keep his hands from shaking or his foot from tapping, he might appear to his best.

The carriage made a final turn and slowed to a halt. Ashton forced himself to wait for the door to be opened and not leap from the equipage like a boy of ten. Eventually, the step was placed, the door opened, and he found himself climbing the steps to Adsila's front door. It did not open at his arrival, so he rang the bell.

Mrs. Gallagher answered, smiling when she saw him. "Lord Grayson," she said with a curtsey. "You are expected, sir."

As he entered the drawing room, he forced himself to tear his eyes from Adsila and greet her parents and younger brother following the introductions. Her father was a rather large man, tall with broad shoulders and striking features. His complexion was several shades darker than his daughter's and spoke of years spent in the sun. In comparison, her mother was small and delicate, one might say fragile in appearance, but her eyes shone with something he had only ever seen in Mrs. Jane Bingley née

Bennet. He could not name it, but it was welcoming. The youngest Carrington appeared to be a mixture of his two elder siblings, taking his height from his father as he looked his sister in the eye at his young age.

"Lord Grayson?" Mr. Carrington asked, his eyes moving to his daughter and back. "Henry Fitzwilliam's son?"

"Yes, sir. My father is now the Earl of Matlock. My grandfather passed in 1790. You were familiar with my father?" His stomach began to churn.

"Yes."

The single-word answer and the cold stare which accompanied it did nothing to eliminate Ashton's ill ease.

"Father." Adsila stepped to Ashton's side. "Ash—Lord Grayson's parents have invited you to stay with them in Mayfair."

If possible, the man's frown deepened.

"Oh, how kind." Mrs. Carrington's voice had a musical quality which might soothe the most ferocious beast. She laid her hand upon her husband's arm. "Do you remember Lady Grayson? Oh, but she would be Lady Matlock now." She smiled at Ashton. "I always admired your mother. She had such a way about her, smoothing over slights and easing tempers."

"Well, Eleanor, she did marry a Fitzwilliam," her husband replied with disdain.

"She remains as you remember her." Ashton met Mr. Carrington's eye. "My mother is one of the leading ladies of society and will not allow disrespect of any sort in her home. She has even gone so far as to have my father's sister removed from the house quite recently."

"Anne?" Mrs. Carrington asked with a gasp.

Ashton dipped his head. "No, Aunt Anne passed many years ago."

"My condolences, she was a lovely lady," she replied, "but I was unaware of another Fitzwilliam sibling."

"Truly? You did not know Lady Catherine de Bourgh

of Rosings Park in Kent?" Ashton asked in astonishment.

The lady's laugh reminded him of her daughter's. *"She* is a Fitzwilliam? I was aware of her reputation, but she was rarely in London during my season, and my family was rarely in town prior to then."

"She is the eldest sibling," Ashton allowed. "I had not considered that she might have already removed from town before you entered society."

"Your parents surely do not remember us," Mr. Carrington said, "and Mayfair is a distance from Cheapside. Perhaps it would be best for us to find lodgings closer."

"My mother remembers you both and would be disappointed if you declined her hospitality. She has also extended an invitation to A—Miss Carrington and her brother."

Ashton felt his cheeks warm as the man's eyes bored into him. A glance to the right encountered the younger Mr. Carrington's amused smirk. Screwing up his courage, Ashton turned to Adsila's father and met his gaze directly.

"I understand you have arrived a short time ago, sir, but I would appreciate a moment of your time."

Mrs. Carrington smiled beatifically at her daughter and stepped to her side while her husband's eyes widened.

"Tom, may we have the use of your study?" Mr. Carrington asked.

"Of course, Father."

The three men left the room with the youngest leading the way, his father directly behind him. Ashton wondered if there were seats available for the meeting as he remembered his last visit to Carrington's study.

"In four years, your habits have not improved?" he heard Mr. Carrington ask as he entered the room after his son. The question was sharp but held a hint a humour.

"They have," Carrington replied. "The stacks are organized by subject."

Ashton entered as the younger man removed books

from two chairs, placing them in a corner before turning to face his father, whose brow had risen.

"I would like to be present as I had spoken to Grayson before learning of your impending arrival."

"Grayson?" his father asked as he looked at Ashton again. All humour had disappeared from his features.

"Yes, Father."

The man nodded once, then stepped behind the desk and sat. Carrington smiled at Ashton as they too were seated.

"You wish to marry my daughter?" the man asked before Ashton could say a word. "Why?"

The question took him by surprise, but he collected the strands of his composure and straightened. "I met Miss Carrington during her first season in London, and I will admit to being fascinated by her, but we did not come to know one another before the season ended."

"And in the following five years?"

Ashton swallowed. "I assumed she had wed."

Mr. Carrington's brow furrowed. "The basis for your assumption being?"

With a glance at the younger man, Ashton took a deep breath. "I was under the impression that Lord Carlisle had brokered a match with a . . . gentleman . . . whose home is in a distant part of England. Mr. Croome, the man in question, had told me he intended to install his wife in his home but spend most of his time in London."

"Croome?" Mr. Carrington asked as he rose and leant menacingly over the desk.

"You know him?"

"Most likely I knew his father, a cur who attempted to court her mother but was discouraged by my late father-in-law." He regained his seat and waved his hand. "Continue."

Ashton nodded. "My father and Lord Carlisle have been friends as long as I can remember. They both discouraged me from coming to know Miss Carrington better. Being a young man of five and twenty, I did as I was told." He lowered his head. "But she returned to my thoughts frequently and I bemoaned the opportunity I had let slip away. Recently, my family began pressing me to marry as I have reached the age of thirty."

"And your cousin was in need of a husband," Carrington reminded him in a quiet voice.

The senior Carrington's brow arched. "Cousin?"

"Miss Anne de Bourgh," Ashton supplied.

"Lady Catherine's daughter," Carrington added as Ashton shot a glare in his direction.

"Shortly after my cousin's wife made Miss Carrington's acquaintance. She suspected, based on things that were said, that your daughter was familiar with my family and confirmed her suspicions by speaking to my sister, who had assisted me in meeting Miss Carrington years prior."

Mr. Carrington placed an arm on the desk and stroked his chin. "They matched you?"

"Mrs. Darcy arranged a moment when they might meet away from London," Carrington offered.

"We were both invited to a friend's wedding in Hertfordshire. Our initial meeting was . . . not what I would have wanted it to be, but I remained under certain misunderstandings." He was not certain, but he thought he saw a bit of amusement in the man's dark eyes. "We were able to move beyond it, and I began courting her—with your son's permission. Five weeks ago, I proposed to her and was accepted."

"I gave my blessing, Father, as I witnessed the change which overcame Adsi. Their affection is genuine and they, well, they strengthen each other." He looked to his friend. "Grayson is not a bad man, and he dislikes the *ton's* intrigues. Adsila helps him to see what is important. She makes him a better man."

Mr. Carrington stared at Ashton. "And what, beyond a title and unwelcome attention from society, do you offer her?"

"My heart. She stole a piece of it five years ago, but I did not realize it until recently. I offer her the protection of my name and my position. No one would dare speak against Lady Grayson as she will one day be Lady Matlock." He drew a deep breath. "Miss Carrington and I have spoken of what is expected of us. We are in agreement to fulfil our obligations, but in our own way. We will accept advice from my mother and father but make any decisions together and base them upon our own beliefs and principles."

"Principles?" Mr. Carrington huffed. "I have seen Fitzwilliam principles."

Ashton suddenly understood the man's aversion to his suit. "My father is not a saint, sir. From a young age, I was aware of his dalliances, but that changed when I was still a small child. My mother and father have a genuinely loving relationship. I beg you would not base your opinion of me on what you knew of him decades ago."

"Father," Carrington chimed in, "I assure you, I would not have given my approval if I did not believe it was in Adsila's best interest."

The man looked from one to the other. Releasing a sigh, he wiped a hand over his face. "I have only just arrived, expecting my daughter to be in some state of despondency." He eyed his son before returning his gaze to Ashton. "Instead, she was glowing with happiness. Now I learn it is due to you, and she is to be wed."

"Once we learned of your imminent arrival, we made no announcement nor any plans." For the first time, a sense of hope filled Ashton's chest. "I am not pressing for your blessing at this time, but I wanted to make you aware of our circumstances. Once you have come to know me, I hope you will accept me as a suitable husband for your daughter."

Mr. Carrington studied him but said nothing for some time. Both Tom and Ashton began to fidget in their seats like schoolboys.

"Are we to remove immediately to Mayfair?" he finally asked.

"My mother is prepared for your arrival, sir, but we will leave when you are ready to do so."

The man rose, causing the others to do the same.

"Then let us go."

CHAPTER TWENTY-SEVEN
LONDON
15 APRIL

"Eleanor Carrington," Lady Matlock exclaimed. "You do not look a day older than the last time we met. Have you found the fountain of youth in America? If so, I hope you brought a vial to share."

Adsila's mother laughed as she curtseyed. "As if you require it, Lady Matlock. You remain one of the loveliest ladies of all my acquaintance."

The ladies were seated in the green drawing room towards the back of the town home. Adsila and her mother sat on a settee to their hostess's right. The gentlemen had disappeared shortly after arriving at Matlock House.

"I apologize for arriving at such an unfashionable time, but we were so anxious to be on land again. When we arrived at Tom and Adsila's home, they told us of your offer." She looked to her daughter and smiled. "We were surprised until your son arrived."

Lady Matlock laughed. "Yes, when the two of them are together, it is obvious, is it not?"

"I fear my husband is determined to make it difficult on Lord Grayson. Adsila is our only daughter, so he will only have one opportunity to intimidate a young man."

Adsila was about to voice her concerns regarding her father's intentions, but servants arrived to deliver trays of tea, toast, rolls, and preserves. She waited until they were gone and Lady Matlock had prepared the tea.

"Mother," she said in a soft voice. "Father will give his blessing, will he not? I am of age, but Ashton and I do wish to have his approval."

"Oh, Adsi." Her mother laid a hand upon her cheek. "Do not fret. Once your father understands that you have feelings for Lord Grayson and he has determined the young man's sincerity, he will give his blessing."

"And your mother and I will help him along," their hostess chimed in with a wink at Adsila's mother.

"It truly is good to see you." Adsila's mother looked about the room. "I can hardly believe I am back in England. It is all so strange yet familiar."

"I am certain there are many who will be anxious to see you again." Lady Matlock's brow rose. "Some will even be pleased to see you looking so well."

"Oh, the *ton* and their ways." She shook her head. "I suppose I do not miss everything about England, but people are people no matter where you are in the world." She sipped her tea. "Are you friends with Lady Carlisle?"

For a brief moment, Lady Matlock's eyes locked with Adsila's before she replied. "Our husbands are allies, bringing us together frequently, and our daughters attended seminary together." She looked out the window. "I understand I have you to thank for my lovely flame azaleas. Adsila made me aware of it when she attended my daughter's wedding some years ago."

Adsila's mother looked between the ladies. "Yes, I sent a plant to Margaret. Did she share a cutting?"

"It appears, Mother," Adsila said in an even tone, "Lady Carlisle found it too exotic for her tastes and gave it to Lady Matlock."

Her mother's lips turned downward, but rebounded to their normal smile so rapidly Adsila nearly missed it. "She always was very particular regarding her tastes. I should have known it would not be to her liking. Though I am pleased it found a home with you."

"And several ladies who have seen it have requested cuttings to add to their own gardens. It truly is lovely." Lady Matlock set her cup on the table. "Mrs. Carrington, I realize it has been a long time and we were not particular friends all those years ago, but would you consider calling me by my Christian name, Esther?" She smiled at Adsila. "After all, if our children have their way, we will be family."

"I will do so only if you do the same."

From that moment, the slight feeling of unease lifted, and the older ladies began sharing memories of their time in London over twenty years prior. As they spoke, Adsila began to realize her mother was aware of the shortcomings of the *ton* but would not lower herself to their level. When a subject became distasteful to her, she simply asked of another individual she had once known. Only when they began speaking of Lady Carlisle, however, did she ask more questions, even of her daughter. Once Adsila had reluctantly admitted the lady had not been particularly kind towards her, her mother looked to her with an air of sadness.

"I always suspected Margaret was jealous of me, though I could not understand why. It did not occur to me that she would treat my daughter poorly because of it. Will you forgive me, Adsi?"

"Of course, Mother." Adsila kissed her mother's cheek. "Though I wish I had been better prepared for the Ladies Carlisle, they were unable to disturb me. I found humour in them and their pretenses."

Her mother patted Adsila's hands. "Your grandmother instilled that in you." She turned to their hostess. "My husband's mother told our children they were descended from royalty and no one was above them. James said it was not true but could not hurt."

Lady Matlock's eyes brightened. "Your daughter is a diamond, Eleanor. We are pleased she and Ashton have found one another."

****

Ashton prowled about the edges of the room. The ladies had removed following dinner, leaving him, his father and brother, Bedlington, Darcy, and Carrington and his father. Bedlington and the earl had begun speaking of politics, as always, and Mr. Carrington had joined the conversation. Surprising to all, the three men were in agreement on most things. As promising as it was to see the elder men getting along, Ashton remained anxious to rejoin the ladies.

"Is your son always so distracted?" he heard Mr. Carrington ask.

"Only since your daughter entered his life," Lord Matlock replied with a laugh. "When they first met, I am embarrassed to say I attempted to direct him away from her." He sighed. "I was a different man then. These young men have opened my eyes. Darcy there"—he motioned with his cigar—"has married a delightful girl who will revive society with the joy which emanates from her. Had I only considered ancestry, I might have frowned upon the match, but she was able to do something no other lady could." He leant forwards in his seat. "She made him smile."

"Then they are happy and will continue to be so, though life brings storms." Mr. Carrington smiled at Darcy, raising his glass in toast.

Darcy nodded, raising his glass in like manner. "And your daughter has given my cousin a new outlook. For years, he has played a role because it was expected of him, but I realize now there was little happiness in his life. Since being reunited with Miss Carrington, he has been a grinagog, amusing us all with his grins in unguarded moments." He turned to Philip. "Did I tell you how he ignored us at the opera and we were forced to speak to the visitors to *his* box?"

"More than once," Philip replied. "And I believe it was Father's box."

"Forgive my nephew, he dislikes speaking to individuals with whom he is not particularly acquainted. His wife is trying to assist him, but it appears that is one new trick the old dog will not learn."

"Mr. Darcy and I held a fascinating conversation earlier, after only just meeting. She has done him some good, I am certain." Mr. Carrington glanced at the clock. "Forgive me, gentlemen, but it has been a long day for me and my wife. Will we be joining the ladies soon?"

Ashton had reached the door by the time his father announced the time had come. The others followed him, laughing, but he ignored them. He had nearly reached the drawing room door when Mr. Carrington stopped him.

"Lord Grayson, may I have a moment?"

Eying the portal, he reluctantly agreed and hung back while the others entered.

"My wife and I spoke earlier this afternoon. She pointed out to me that, had we not travelled to England, you and my daughter would already be engaged and planning for your wedding day." He clasped his hands before him. "I trust my son's judgement, but as Adsila's father, I must decide for myself."

Ashton glanced at the door. "Forgive me, Mr. Carrington, but I am uncertain of what you are saying."

A smile spread across the man's lips. "As am I." He paused. "Adsila is my only daughter. It was hard leaving her here in England with strangers, and not my original plan. I do not want to make that mistake again."

A sudden understanding came over him. "It might have

only occurred recently, sir, but I assure you, Adsila is no longer without friends. My family and I have fallen in love with her. Mrs. Darcy introduced her to her family, the Bennets. They adopted her, as such. She is an honorary sister, and there are five originally."

"Five?"

"And no sons. Which is most likely the reason Mr. Bennet spent most of the visit with Tom."

Mr. Carrington's smile grew, and he placed a hand upon Ashton's shoulder. "I am pleased to hear it and look forward to possibly meeting Adsila's friends while I am here. For now, she is probably wondering where we are."

Relieved, Ashton nodded and led the way into the room. Adsila's eyes met his the moment he entered, and her smile lit her countenance. Ignoring the others, he crossed to her side.

"I was speaking with your father."

"I thought as much. Has he made a decision?"

Before Ashton could respond, Mr. Carrington cleared his throat, drawing the room's attention.

"Forgive me, Lord Matlock, but I hope you will not begrudge my making an announcement."

The earl nodded his approval, then winked at Ashton.

"Though I have not learnt everything which has occurred while my daughter resided amongst you, I have been able to discern one important detail: she is happy. More importantly, she appears happiest when she is with Lord Grayson. As my sudden and unexpected appearance delayed the announcement of their engagement, I have decided to not force them to wait longer. Lord Grayson, you have my blessings in marrying my daughter."

Ashton smiled at Adsila as the family began wishing them joy. Mr. Carrington approached and shook Ashton's hand before hugging his daughter.

"We will remain in England until July. I leave it to you to decide how soon you wish to marry."

The couple exchanged a look before Adsila answered.

"We would like to marry once the banns have been read, but we will delay a wedding trip so we can spend time with you, Mother, and Arthur."

"That seems to be the fashion this year," Philip quipped. "Darcy and Elizabeth have yet to leave for their wedding trip, and the Bingleys married in the winter, so they decided to wait for warmer weather before travelling."

"Or perhaps they were anticipating being needed to chaperone or discuss another wedding," Elizabeth said with a smirk.

Both Philip and Miss Bingley blushed, but neither responded, avoiding meeting the eye of any in the group. Ashton's suspicions from earlier in the day returned, and he decided to speak to his brother at his earliest convenience.

Everyone began speaking at once, some giving advice while others declared that as family, they should drop honorariums. Ashton drew Adsila to the side and took her hand in his.

"Are you happy, my love?"

"Happier than I believed I could be. Is three weeks too soon?"

"Not soon enough." He lifted her hand to his lips. "We have lost five years, and I have no desire to lose a minute longer than necessary."

"I agree." She leant closer. "Who would have thought all those years ago that we would be here now?"

"A dream I dared not acknowledge became reality, but only because we followed Darcy and Elizabeth's example and defied propriety."

The End
Watch for the third book in the Defying Propriety Series, A Soldier's Life

ABOUT THE AUTHOR

Bronwen Chisholm was born in Central Pennsylvania, the youngest of four sisters. Though she was not introduced to Jane Austen's work until later in life, she grew up reading the Bronte sisters, *Gone With the Wind*, and other classics as well as watching vintage Hollywood movies. Her love of books and literature could have led to a career as a librarian. Instead, life and love carried her to Virginia where she took a position as a state employee and began raising her family.

As her children grew and became involved in their own interests, Bronwen returned to her love of the written word. No longer content to simply read it, she began writing. In 2015, she released three *Pride and Prejudice* variations, *The Ball at Meryton, Behind the Mask*, and *Mistress Mary and the General. Georgiana Darcy, Matchmaker*, was released in the fall of 2016; *A Beneficial, If Unwilling, Compromise* in the fall of 2017; *Mrs. Collins' Lover* in the late summer of 2019; and *Missing Jane* in the summer of 2020. In 2021, she began releasing her *Defying Propriety Series*.

Her love of writing has led her to several writing groups, including The Virginia Writer's Club, Lake Authors, and James River Writers. She is currently serving as the Vice President of The Riverside Writers and advises the Riverside Young Writers.

Bronwen has plans to explore other genres, but for now, she has a list of Regency romance, specifically Pride and Prejudice variations, to complete. For more information, visit her website at www.bronwenchisholm.com.